MW01629899

WITHDRAWN
FROM LIBRARY

THE
GIRLS
TRIP

ALSO BY ALLY CONDIE

ADULT NOVELS

The Unwedding

YOUNG ADULT AND MIDDLE GRADE NOVELS

Matched

Crossed

Reached

Atlantia

Summerlost

The Last Voyage of Poe Blythe

The Only Girl in Town

PICTURE BOOKS

Here

There

THE GIRLS TRIP

ALLY CONDIE

GRAND CENTRAL

New York Boston

Copyright © 2026 by Allyson Braithwaite Condie

Cover design by Alan Dingman. Cover images by Stocksy and Getty Images. Cover copyright © 2026 by Hachette Book Group, Inc.

Grand Central Publishing
Hachette Book Group
1290 Avenue of the Americas, New York, NY 10104
grandcentralpublishing.com
@grandcentralpub

First Edition: April 2026

Grand Central Publishing is a division of Hachette Book Group, Inc. The Grand Central Publishing name and logo is a registered trademark of Hachette Book Group, Inc.

The publisher is not responsible for websites (or their content) that are not owned by the publisher.

The Hachette Speakers Bureau provides a wide range of authors for speaking events. To find out more, go to hachettespeakersbureau.com or email HachetteSpeakers@hbgusa.com.

Grand Central Publishing books may be purchased in bulk for business, educational, or promotional use. For information, please contact your local bookseller or the Hachette Book Group Special Markets Department at special.markets@hbgusa.com.

Library of Congress Cataloging-in-Publication Data has been applied for.

ISBNs: 9781538773451 (hardcover), 9781538773475 (ebook)

Printed in the United States of America

LSC-C

Printing 1, 2026

for Jodi Reamer

THE
GIRLS
TRIP

Never tell all you know—not even to the person you know best.

—Agatha Christie, *The Secret Adversary*

IT'S NOT EASY TO disappear anymore.

They can track your phone; they can see your history; they can check cameras you didn't know were there; they can send out drones to look for you.

But there are some spots where it's easier to vanish, where nature still rules in certain places or at certain times.

Out in the deserts, below in the oceans, high in the mountains, deep in the canyons.

Not everyone who's gone missing has been found.

Yet.

People can't return after death, but bodies can. They can be trapped under water, crushed against stone, left in a high place with only birds to pick and see.

But sometimes
bit by bit
or as a flood
the water lifts, lowers
the stone nudges
the animals scream and
the bodies
make their way out.

BEFORE

"IS THIS THING ON?" Ash asks, her face popping up on-screen.

"It's always on, Ash," Carolina says patiently.

"Hi, Ash," Hope says from the screen. The stunning backdrop behind her—blue pool, bright sky, waving palm trees—isn't fake. It's her home in Santa Monica.

"Hope!" Ash says. "You came! I thought you said you might not be able to make it!" Her brown eyes widen in delight and she scoots closer to her computer. She's forgotten to take off her work apron, the sturdy blue canvas one that ties around her neck. Summer freckles scatter across her nose, and there is a dab of sunscreen near her jawline that hasn't been rubbed in all the way.

"I'm here," Hope confirms. "It was my turn to choose the book, so I figured I'd better show up." She's makeup-free, her long brown hair in a topknot, and even though they've all been friends for almost two years now, the other two still can't *quite* believe that they are friends with *Hope Hanover*. Hope's a rich and famous actress who is also still one of them—three friends who met under unlikely circumstances and who now text and talk constantly and get together once a month online for their book club.

"I couldn't put it down," Carolina rakes a hand through her chin-length dark hair. "I read it in a day and a half."

"What about you, Ash?" Hope asks, though Ash always likes the book, because Ash finds the good in everything.

Ash bites her lip. "I didn't read it." The other two gasp, because Ash *always* reads the book.

"This month has been bananas," Ash says.

"What's been going on?" Hope asks. "I know wedding season is coming up, but is it more than that?" Ash runs her own flower business, which has become more consuming and successful than she'd ever anticipated. She tells the others all the time that it's gotten out of hand.

"Basically," Ash says. "It's not interesting. Let's talk about the book. Don't worry about spoiling it for me. And I can't wait to hear the latest in *your* lives."

Carolina's giant black Lab, Howie, has popped up into the frame and stares at them all cheerfully, wagging his tail. She leans down to scratch him behind the ears. "The twist was great. I didn't see it coming."

"Did you guess the murderer?" Hope asks.

"I didn't!" Caro says, and Ash and Hope sit back in surprise. Caro *always* guesses the murderer.

"Seriously, say whatever you want about the book," Ash says. "I won't listen. Even if I do, I'll forget. My brain is mush lately."

"We can talk more about the book later, when you've read it," Hope says. "I have to admit that I have something else I want to discuss with you guys."

"This has to be a record." Caro feigns a look at her watch. "We didn't even spend five minutes on the book."

"What I have to say has to *do* with books." Hope's voice holds an earnest, hopeful note. Behind her, a single white cloud has edged its way into the blue sky. "And the woman who brought us all together."

"*Agatha*," they say in unison. Two years ago, during the pandemic, an independent bookstore in San Francisco held a virtual book club for one of Agatha Christie's novels (*A Murder Is Announced*). Somehow, of all the people across the country during that time with nothing to do, Ash, Caro, and Hope were the only three who showed up.

It was early days of online events during the outbreak, so perhaps it was that other people weren't yet used to virtual meetups. Each of the three women had wanted to leave but hadn't been able to bring themselves to do it, thinking it would be too rude to the host, a kind and frazzled bookseller. And then, ten minutes in, when the host had vanished (her screen going inexplicably dark midsentence), Ash, Caro, and Hope had somehow remained connected. They'd sat in stunned silence for a moment before starting to laugh. A warm and funny conversation about Agatha Christie and life and the disaster that was the pandemic ensued. At the end of the call, the three of them had decided to reread Christie's *The Murder of Roger Ackroyd* and discuss it the next month. They'd exchanged phone numbers, and during the month they texted about the book and their lives, and and and…

…here they are.

For the first couple of meetings, Hope hadn't appeared live on-screen. Instead, she'd used a photo that showed her with her back turned and her hair a different color. And she'd continued to go by the fake name she'd entered for the meeting (Grace Hartwell—she always used virtue names when she didn't want to reveal her true one). Carolina and Ash had both felt (but hadn't said out loud) that Hope's voice seemed somewhat familiar, though neither of them could place *where* they might have heard it before. It wasn't until later that Hope had revealed her identity. Ash and Caro had both tried to keep their cool, with varying degrees of success.

"Remember," Hope says now, "how when Agatha Christie's husband told her he was leaving her for his secretary, Agatha disappeared for eleven days, and no one could figure out where she was? Remember how even Scotland Yard couldn't find her?"

"Of course we do," Carolina says. "We talk about it literally all the time."

"And about how nice it would be to disappear from our lives for a minute," Ash says dreamily.

"Because work is stressful," Carolina says.

"And the people in our lives can be a lot," Ash says.

"I love how she got bad news and got the hell out of there." Hope's tone is longing. "Can you imagine *anyone*—let alone anyone *famous*—being able to do that in this day and age?"

"Oh, Hope," Ash says. "I bet *you* want to get away."

"I do." Hope leans forward, her gorgeous green eyes wide. Ash and Caro lean in, too. Hope Hanover can pull in whoever she wants, whenever she wants. It's to her credit that she doesn't wield this power as often as she could. "And that's what I want to talk to both of you about. I think it's time we met in person."

"*Yes,*" Ash and Caro answer in unison, because the three of them have been saying this for ages now.

"I mean for real," Hope says. "Let's do it this time. My movie got canceled. I have three months with no filming."

"Your movie got canceled?" Ash asks. "Are you okay? Is that okay?"

"Honestly, it's amazing." Hope folds her arms and sits back, a beatific expression on her face. "I said yes to it because it's total Oscar bait, but it would have been so grim. I would have had to walk through endless mud wearing a period costume. Maybe while having my actual period. And everyone knows the guy they cast as a lead is an absolute narcissist."

"Really?" Ash is momentarily diverted. "Aidan Stone? I thought he was a nice guy."

"Oh no," Hope says. "Total jerk."

But even Ash doesn't linger long on Aidan Stone, because a thrill is running through her at the thought of the three of them finally meeting in person. *This might really happen.* If Hope, who is actually famous, can come, then what excuses do the rest of them really have?

"I am so, so serious about this," Hope says. "I'll pay."

"We're not going to let you do that," says Carolina.

"Absolutely not," Ash agrees.

But Hope's still going. "And another thing. I think we *should* disappear."

Ash and Carolina look at her, waiting.

"Like Agatha did," Hope says. "We won't tell anyone where we're going. We'll just *go*."

"Hope," Ash says, in a tone of great severity. "Have you become embroiled in a scandal? Is that what this is about? Are you trying to lie low while something blows over?"

"No scandal." Hope smiles at them. "Can you imagine it, though?"

"Being in a scandal?" Ash says wistfully. "I mean, maybe."

"Not that." And now it's Hope's turn to sound wistful. "Disappearing from our lives for a while?"

"I can't." Ash is rueful.

"None of us can," Caro says, but there's something in her voice that sounds like she's opening the door to the possibility.

There's a silence. *Could they?*

"Every single one of us deserves a break," Hope says. "We've all had the world pulled out from under us the past few years."

This is inarguable. There was the pandemic, of course. The way things have been going in the world, in general, and for them, specifically. Ash is juggling her business and her family. Caro has been swamped at work for years. Hope is an actress in her thirties in the most ageist career in the world.

And these are only the things they've told each other about.

"We won't *completely* disappear," Hope says. "We'll tell our people—families, work, whatever—that we're going on a trip. But we don't have to tell them *where* we're going. We clear our calendars and get the hell out."

"Do we tell them where we were when we get back?" Caro asks.

"If we want," Hope says. "I don't see why not."

"If we do it," Ash asks tentatively, "when would we go?"

"How about next week?" Hope asks.

Ash blinks. Caro folds her arms across her chest.

"We can't—" Ash begins.

"Let's try," Hope says. "Maybe doing this kind of last-minute is how we actually get it done. Every time we've tried to plan something in advance, it's always fallen through." She's right. The first time, Ash's youngest daughter was rushed to the hospital for an appendectomy the day before they were set to meet up in LA. Another time, Hope had to cancel at the last minute because of work. A third time, Caro had to go and take care of her father, who's been struggling with Alzheimer's.

"We might as well *discuss* it," Ash says, almost in a whisper.

"Might as well," Caro agrees.

Later, they can't remember who or what tipped the balance. They sorted it all out, thought about the ways they *could*, hypothetically, move heaven and earth, and they realized that they could manage a few days in June. They would walk away. They would vanish.

Later, the ones who were left asked the same thing over and over again—*who decided?*

All of us, they had to agree.

It was all of us.

DAY ONE
Tuesday

On the chalkboard outside the Sonnet resort main office

MOVIE ....
Butch Cassidy and the Sundance Kid, 1969, PG, directed by
George Roy Hill

FILM FACT ....
Much of the movie was filmed near Eden National Park, where
the outlaw Butch Cassidy once lived and operated. Although
infamous for his criminal career, he never killed anyone and was
considered a Western hero by the locals.

1

PAGE

THE KIND OF RICH people I hate the most are the ones who say they *aren't* rich.

Oh really? I want to ask them. *Do you have enough food for the whole week sitting in your cupboard all the time? Do you pay your utilities without even thinking about it? Do you have more than one pair of shoes? Did you lift the sleeve of that $70 sweatshirt in the gift shop to check the price tag and* not *rule it out immediately? Then you have more money than most people. More money than me, that's for damn sure.*

Sometimes it's hard for me to make eye contact with the guests when I'm giving them the *Welcome to Sonnet* spiel, the one where I talk up the amenities of the resort and the natural beauty of the nearby national park. I tell them about our restaurant, our food truck, the gourmet s'more kits on offer, the gift shop, the drive-in movie theater where you can sit in vintage cars eating popcorn and watching classic movies after a long day of hiking. You know, like all the other *un*-rich people in the world.

Yes, yes, they say as they nod, *we've seen pictures online, the drive-in is so charming, we are so delighted to be here, oh, that's wonderful that you have a farm-to-table menu, we expect nothing less, even though we also want authenticity (but not the* wrong *type of authenticity). Oh really, sometimes the hot water runs out during the busy times of day? Um, okay. No, no, that's quite all right, yes, yes. We* do *understand we are right at the edge of a national park. But the thread count on the sheets? Could you tell us about that? Wonderful. Oh, we're* very *outdoorsy, can't wait to get out on those hikes / go canyoneering / see the stars / bathe in nature.*

You should see their faces when I tell them there's a wood-burning stove in each of their tents and that that's what they'll need to use if they get cold at night. At first, they wear expressions of total shock, because they didn't think glamping would be *quite* that close to actual camping and they didn't read the website description all the way through. Or, if they did, they thought the wood-burning stoves were for charm, not the primary source of heat.

Most guests rally, though, and pretend like they know how to light a fire. This cracks me up and pisses me off at the same time. I watch them leave for their tents, knowing we'll get front desk calls later. The guests will say that their stoves "don't work." They'll never admit that it's for sure and one hundred percent user error. One of the staff will take care of it. If it's my shift, it might be me. I'm great at lighting fires. I've been doing it all my life.

It only really gets to me if they don't say thanks or don't bother keeping their personal lives out of the way for the few minutes it takes me to get the fire going. I don't need to hear your argument or how much you love each other or how horny you are right now. I'm a person. You don't have to talk to me the whole time, but don't act like I'm not here when I am.

I also hate it when they refer to the park as *Edens* National Park. I've been corrected by guests when I say it right. I have to grit my teeth when I respond. *Actually,* I say, *there's no* s.

Really? they ask. *Are you sure?*

Oh, I'm sure.

And now and then they like to point out that I'm spelling my name "wrong." "Did they forget to put the *i* on your nametag?" they'll ask. Or, "What an unusual spelling!" That second one's more subtle, but the subtext is still crystal clear: *We are smarter than you. We know more than you do. We can tell you the* right *way to spell your name.*

Anyway. Rich people.

I have my eye on that group of women right from the moment they duck inside the main tent. You don't *have* to duck—the ceilings are high and the door is tall and wide—but people seem to have that tendency with tents, even when they're enormous and multi-peaked, like this one. The main tent houses a restaurant, a reception area, a gift-and-snack shop, restrooms, and a sporting-goods outfitter. One of the women puts her hand up to touch the side of the tent, which is also something a lot of people do. From a distance, it looks smooth, like ceramic or porcelain, maybe, but up close you can tell that it's made of extremely sturdy fabric. The floors are weathered wood, and we have electricity and running water. Of course. And Wi-Fi.

There are a few reasons why the three women catch my eye.

First, they have the right gear and they brought their own, which means at least one of them knows what they're doing.

Second, they seem so *happy*. Like, actually, genuinely happy and delighted to be with each other. They're laughing and talking like they're getting away with or from something. "Should we sign our real names in the guest log?" the one with the long blond braid asks.

"No," says the one with the orange Patagonia baseball cap. "That defeats the whole purpose."

"Wait," says the most serious-looking one. She glances at me. "Do we actually have to sign in here?"

"No," I say. "You don't." The leather-bound guest log is largely for show, so people feel like they're having an authentic wilderness-adjacent experience. They can ooh and aah over how far other guests have come to be here. Sometimes they take pictures of their own signatures to post on social media.

They all seem pleased with my answer. "Let's not sign, then," Patagonia Hat says.

I think about reminding them that they *should* sign the logs at the trailheads when they hike, but that info's on the park website and what they do in Eden isn't my responsibility.

The last reason that I have my eye on that group, the biggest reason, is that the one in the hat is famous. An actress. She's friendly, super low-key. That's what makes the other guests milling around miss who she is. They might glance over and think she's pretty and that she looks a tiny bit familiar, but the fact that she's not trying to hide makes it seem impossible that she could be who they think she is. Plus, this resort isn't Amangiri or anything. We're fancy, but no Kardashians or Biebers have ever stayed here. Can you imagine one of them having to light their own fires?

But I still know right away who she is, even though her credit card and driver's license have a different name than the one she's famous for.

Well hello, I think. *So* you're *my ticket out of here.*

2

CARO

"IS THIS HOW YOU pictured it?" Caro asks the other two. Her voice is almost reverential.

"Yes," Ash says. "No."

Caro's heart is full. The three of them are standing on a plateau, red dirt at their feet, an enormous evening-blue sky above. Earlier they were talking and laughing, breathless and giddy to be together in person, in the flesh, but now they've quieted.

The landscape stretches out before them like a living thing, like *many* living things. The colors and the view shift, according to the weather and the light. The mesas turn red, pink, purple, orange, white. The sky changes—it can be vast, calm, empty, swept with clouds. It's blue, gray, black as obsidian, spotted with diamond-bright stars. Sage, rabbit brush, cactus, and ephedra grow green, gray, silver. Only those who didn't know the desert could ever call it barren. It's ripe with life, particular with geography both large-scale and minute. The others are staring in wonder.

Caro grew up less than an hour away from here, in the desert town of St. John. Although she now lives several hours away, she visits home often. It always comes back to her quickly: the desert, the way it feels. How dry the air is here, how beautiful the bones.

"What about all of *us*?" Hope turns away from the view to smile at the other two. She's wearing a faded orange hat and sunglasses that offer the right amount of concealment without being obvious. Ash smiles back, her freckled nose wrinkling, looking younger than the mom of three teenage girls has any right to look. *What do* they *see when they look at me?* Caro wonders.

"Gorgeous," Ash says, with the sincerity Caro has come to know so well, even at a distance, even through a screen. "You're both so gorgeous. I love you two so much!" She throws her arms around Caro and Hope, herding them into a group hug. "I cannot *believe* this is happening!"

"Thanks for suggesting that we come here, Caro," Hope says as they draw apart. She pulls off her sunglasses and Caro is faced with the full effect of her Hope Hanover green eyes. "It's perfect."

"I don't know that I can take the credit," Caro says. "It was your idea to come to southern Utah."

"But you found this resort," Hope reminds her.

"It's so beautiful out here, I can't believe it's real," Ash says. "It's so different from Oregon."

"Film directors love this part of the country," Hope says. "It's cheap to shoot here, and the landscape is ridiculous." She takes a deep breath, and everyone else follows suit, Caro included. It's a pleasure to inhale the clean air of this place, the smells of pines and sage and rivers carving their way through rock. Hope glances at Caro. "I'm not telling you anything you don't know, I'm sure."

"Hollywood does like to film Westerns here," Caro agrees. "And use Utah as Mars or Generic Desert Planet."

"I get that," Ash says. "It's so…otherworldly."

"But it's *our* world." Hope's voice is warm, and so is her arm around Caro's shoulders. "How lucky are we?"

3

HOPE

THEY MAKE THEIR WAY toward the food truck, passing fire-pits and groups gathering to play horseshoes and Ping-Pong in the resort's super-chill and ultra-hip recreation area. The drive-in movie theater stops them momentarily in their tracks. It's *adorable*—a big screen set up in front of rows of cherry-red and cotton-candy-pink and powder-blue '57 Chevys and vintage Mustangs. A staff member is handing out red-and-white-striped bags of popcorn.

"Should we?" Ash asks, catching Hope's eye. "I mean, it's Robert Redford and Paul Newman. In their prime." The two men race across the screen on horseback, practically gilded with 1960s sunset light.

"Another night," Hope says. "I promise. Tonight, we have to get ready for the hike." To kick off their trip, they're hiking through a famous slot canyon called the Underground. They'll start early the next morning and camp in two different places in the canyon before hiking out. The Underground is gorgeous—a pristine turquoise creek running through high red rock walls, green trees growing, impossibly, here and there. It's in the backcountry, with no cell phone coverage. They will truly be unreachable.

Hope can't wait to get started.

"And I'm *starving*," Caro says. Caro is always starving. It's one of Hope's favorite things about her. When they're online, Caro is forever snacking on something or wandering off to the kitchen and returning with a plate of food. She never sits entirely still, either, and almost every time she shows up on-screen, she's either in her scrubs, fresh off a shift at work, or still wearing athletic clothes after having some outdoorsy adventure with her husband, Dan.

The food truck is painted pink, mint green, and white, clearly intended as a pastelized riff on the National Parks logo. Hope saw it on the website when Caro sent along the link. The other two had balked at the price of the resort Hope had originally chosen and refused to let her foot the bill. So they'd had to find somewhere else that would work. Hope swears she's not a diva, but when you're in any way famous, you've got to be conscious of certain things, like privacy and security.

She has to admit that she loves that Ash and Caro wouldn't let her pay their way. It's sweet. So many of Hope's other friends aren't even putting up the most desultory of protests anymore. But what Hope's book club friends don't know yet is that she's taking care of their costs anyway.

It's the least Hope can do, given what she's got planned.

The food truck is a perfect spot for staging photos or reels to post on social media, if you're interested in that sort of thing, which Hope is not, not for this trip anyway. Lights glow overhead, and families and groups gather at the tables. Delicious smells waft from the truck and mingle with the clean-scented desert air. They've all been taking deep breaths since they arrived, and Ash draws in another one next to Hope.

"I swear my lungs have been saying *thank you* ever since we got here," Hope says, thinking of the smog in LA that everything—even the light—has to filter through.

A twentysomething kid with dark hair cut into one of those ironic haircuts that make people look like confused roosters is taking orders at the food truck. His name tag reads Gareth, which is a name Hope has never been completely sure how to pronounce. Underneath his name it says *Las Vegas*. Hope likes those name tags—it's fun to know where people are from, plus it always reminds her of Disneyland, a place she's inordinately fond of.

"Any questions about the menu?" Gareth asks. They're all craning their necks, taking in the options.

"What's your favorite?" Caro asks.

"The nachos are *insane*," Gareth says. "Ty's the best cook. He makes it all fresh. There's guacamole, salsa, shredded pork…"

The cook waves at them. He's broad-shouldered and wearing a baseball cap that almost brushes the ceiling because he's so tall. Hope begins to crush on him immediately. Why not? She and her most recent boyfriend, the actor Colin Edgware, broke up four months ago, largely because Colin was always exactly like you'd imagine a Colin Edgware would be, and she's been feeling like she might be ready for another foray into romance. A guy named Ty who can cook might be the perfect antidote to a Colin who can only method act.

"What about the shakes?" Ash asks. "Are they also amazing?"

"They are," Ty calls out. He has, Hope decides, a voice that matches his looks. Pleasing. "Burgers, too. And the cheese fries."

"Seriously, don't hold back," Caro says. "It's all MREs and smushed sandwiches and granola bars and fruit for the next two days."

Since Caro's the most local of the three, she's figured out all the logistics for their hike into the Underground. She sent Hope and Ash links to all the gear they needed to get—the right socks and boots, hiking backpacks, dry bags to go *inside* of the backpacks, moleskin for any blisters that might crop up, nature-safe sunscreen; the list was endless.

"That's true," Hope says. "All the food you told us to buy looks kind of like if birdseed and organic Play-Doh had a baby."

"It'll keep you nice and satiated," Caro says. "And regular."

"Oh great," Hope says, laughing.

Ash is plying Gareth with more questions. "We saw that you guys were playing *Butch Cassidy and the Sundance Kid* tonight. What else are you showing this weekend?"

"I'm not sure," Gareth says. "But they'll be posted on the chalkboard in the reception area and on our website each morning." He puffs out his chest and his voice rises, as if he's leading a tour instead of standing inside a food truck. "Every movie we show at Sonnet has been filmed nearby."

"Were any of them filmed *in* the park?" Hope asks.

Gareth shakes his head. "Commercial filming isn't allowed in Edens National Park," he says. Caro, who the others know cannot *bear* to hear the park's name mispronounced with the additional *s*, mutters something under her breath and Hope has to stifle her laughter. "But," Gareth continues, still using his tour guide voice, "movies have been filmed in many of its surrounding areas."

"So cool," Ash says brightly. She reaches for one of the postcards sitting in a small tray on the ledge of the food truck. They're winsomely designed, colorful. Some are photos of the resort itself—the drive-in theater, the food truck, the main tent lit up at night with the plateau as backdrop. Others bear famous wilderness quotes, or iconic Eden National Park landmarks—a certain spot in the Underground, the astonishing monolith and precarious path of Seraph's Perch, an aerial shot of the red road winding through the park. They're all marked with the Sonnet logo. "How much are these?"

"They're complimentary," Gareth says. "We have them in the gift shop, too. And if you drop them off at reception, we'll stamp and mail them for you free of charge."

"That's great marketing." Hope loves it when a place is on top of its game. Each of the women take several cards from the tray. "No mailing them until the last day," Hope reminds her friends in a low voice, and they nod.

"What name should I put on the order?" Gareth asks Hope.

"Chastity Bentley," Hope says, and Caro snickers outright. Hope always uses a virtue name when she doesn't want to give out her real one, and this is the one she's selected for this trip. Neither Ash nor Caro can keep a straight face when she uses it.

Gareth hands Hope a metal stand affixed with a card bearing their number, *26*. She turns around to take it over to one of the picnic tables and almost runs into two men standing behind her.

"Whoops," Hope says, "sorry."

"No worries," says one. They're around the same age as the women, and they look enough alike—trucker caps, similar builds—that Hope thinks they might be brothers.

"Hey," the shorter of the two says, "you look a lot like…"

Without a word, as if they've coordinated it beforehand somehow, Ash and Caro move.

"I have a spot in mind already." Ash links arms with Hope and begins pulling her toward one of the tables. "And I had the *best* idea for tomorrow…"

"I heard the nachos are the way to go," Caro says to the men with authority. She's so striking—her dark hair, her tanned skin, her long, long legs and no-nonsense, straightforward way of speaking—that they're distracted and Hope is away, tucked in at a table off by itself under a tree with Ash.

"Oh my word," Hope says when Caro joins them. "You guys are better than any security detail. How did you know how to do that?"

"Instinct." Caro's running her hand through her hair, a gesture Hope has seen her do many times online. The sunset light illuminates Caro's lovely face, the gentle crow's feet developing around her eyes. She's the middle of the three women in age—they stairstep two years apart, like sisters. Ash is thirty-eight, Caro is thirty-six, Hope is thirty-four. Ancient, in Hollywood years. *But young enough that if I died it would still be referred to as a "tragedy,"* Hope thinks. There would probably be a cover story or two. *I might be remembered longer that way, on net.*

"I learned it from watching *The Bodyguard*." Ash starts humming "I Will Always Love You," which makes Hope laugh.

"We've got you." Caro gives Hope's shoulder a playful nudge. Hope's surprised by the contact—not many people feel like they can be so informal with her these days. Plus, it feels so natural, like they've been friends forever—but they haven't.

She has to keep reminding herself of that.

"You should get to have your dinner in peace," Ash says as Gareth arrives with their nachos and salads and shakes.

They're in a gorgeous place eating delicious food. They are the youngest they will ever be. *Eat it all,* Hope wants to tell her friends. *Drink in everything with your wide-open eyes before the sun goes down.*

In the dimming light, she feels herself relax. The darker it gets, the less likely she is to be recognized.

Even by the people who think they know her.

Even by herself.

4

ASH

"THE TENTS DON'T LOCK," Ash tells her husband, Wade, on the phone.

"That doesn't seem very safe," he says.

"I know." Of course, Ash is aware that the walls are canvas. So anyone could get in at any time, really. But do they have to make it so *easy*? Couldn't they put a padlock or something on the door to make everyone feel better?

"It seems strange that Hope would pick a place that's so lax on security," Wade says. "Isn't that dangerous for her?"

"She researched the resort before we came here," Ash says. "There's a twenty-four-hour security patrol. They say they've never had a problem."

"Of course that's what they're going to tell you," Wade says. There's a rustling sound, and she can picture him changing out of his work shirt and into a T-shirt, maybe the ancient one from their alma mater that makes his blue eyes seem very, very bright. Ash loves his eyes, and she loves his rolling, deep voice. She's always been a sucker for someone who sounds like they could sing baritone in a choir. So what if Wade is going kind of bald. She's going to have prematurely aging skin from her job even though she's always wearing a straw hat and applying copious sunscreen.

The point is to grow old *together*. To know all the different incarnations of one person over and across decades.

"Hope's actually staying in one of the Airstream trailers," Ash says. "Which *does* lock and has its own bathroom." Hope is famous. She couldn't allow herself to be swayed by the romantic feel of the tents the way Ash and Caro had been, and even though the community showers are fancy (subway tiles and brass fixtures and individual wooden chambers you can lock, plus the same thick towels and high-end toiletries that are in the tents), it's ridiculous to think of Hope Hanover not having a private shower.

"Okay, then," Wade says. "So you *had* a better option, and you chose not to take it?"

Ash feels a sting of embarrassment. He has a point. "I guess I didn't fully think through the security aspect," she says. "It seemed fun to be in a tent. They have skylights, so you can see the stars." The interior is fancy—pillowy beds, cute little woodstoves, planked floors, leather butterfly chairs. It's romantic, even. "I wish you were with me."

Wade laughs. "*Do* you, Ash?" There's that edge to his voice, the one that's been creeping in more and more over the past few years. "You haven't even told me exactly where you are."

"I'm not supposed to be calling you at all," Ash says, feeling defensive. "I wasn't supposed to tell you anything about where we're staying." Wade *knew* this was part of the trip. That the disappearing was the whole point. She'd been sure he'd say no to the idea, but instead he'd told her to go. At the time, he hadn't seemed angry. He hadn't seemed anything. She'd wondered if she should dig deeper, make sure it was really okay, but she hadn't wanted him to take it back.

Ash still can't believe she's here, glamping with a celebrity when she should be home with her girls and her husband and her business. She can't believe she's here in any aspect of her life. If you'd told her seventeen years ago when she got married, at the ripe old age of twenty-one, that she and Wade would be talking to each other like this, so jaded and matter-of-fact;

that she'd own a full-on *flower* business, of all things; that somehow she'd be lumped in with a kind of trad wife lifestyle that she doesn't actually live or believe in—she hates cooking, she doesn't know how to knit, she runs straight to Eddie at the tailor's if any of the stupid dresses that she wears in her videos need hemming—young Ash would have laughed in your face. None of it would have made sense to her. (The term *trad wife* hadn't even been coined when they got married! Everyone was wearing flannels and band T-shirts, not peasant skirts and hair bows!) If she'd been able to tell her younger self how things had turned out, maybe that younger Ash wouldn't have made the same mistakes.

Her job was *supposed* to be a hobby. She started it when her girls were small and they still had acres of debt from Wade going to dental school. The house they'd bought had been a run-down farmhouse near the edge of Portland, and they'd been charmed by it because the neighborhood had a small-town feel (they'd both grown up in small towns before they met in college), an old barn, and a flower garden that was the previous owner's pride and joy. Ash had had no intention of keeping it up, but then somewhere along the line she'd hated to let it die. Reading about flowers while she nursed her babies and rocked them to sleep and waited for Wade to get home was soothing. All the varieties! Their histories! Their names! The colors! It was something she could do with her girls from her very own house. And so, Three Sisters Flowers was born, and somehow, after a few years, it took off. Now Three Sisters ships nationwide, and she's had to source from other farms. She wrote a coffee table book that's selling very well.

Ash does wonder if anyone even reads the book or if it merely sits in their living rooms, looking pretty. But so what if that's all it does? The photographer they hired was brilliant. The cover is gorgeous. Her girls thought it was cool, which isn't always how they feel about Ash's work. The older two die of mortification if they have friends over and Ash comes in the house still wearing her straw hat or with her sunscreen not rubbed in all the way.

Ash didn't include the girls in the book much, not their faces anyway.

She wants to protect their privacy, never sell them out. So in the book there are glimpses of their hands now and then, and their cottage-door-green Hunter boots, and a couple of photos of them turned away, the light streaming through their hair.

Ash's daughters are objectively beautiful. She gave birth to Maggie, the oldest, two days after graduating from college. Now they're sixteen, four-teen, and ten, and she loves them way too much.

Ash knows it seems ridiculous to other people to have had three children when she was so young. At the time, it made sense to have her family all at once. She's still not sorry, because if she hadn't done it this way, she wouldn't have *them*. Not these *exact* girls. Her Maggie, her Kit, her Claire. They all have Ash's wild, golden-brown hair and Wade's bright blue eyes. But they all have very different faces, varying combinations of Wade and Ash, that startle people when they turn around, because they expected the sisters to look the same.

"How's everything there?" Ash asks. "How are the girls?" It's always been hard to leave her children. Now that they've paid off all of Wade's student debt and saved up some money and his practice is taking off, she's been wondering, *Is it worth it to keep doing all this?*

Ash does love the charity, Second Bloom, that she's been able to run in tandem with the flower business. She takes leftover bouquets and arrange-ments from events to nursing homes and hospice centers and women's shelters in the Portland area. It's a tiny thing, but it makes her so damn happy to do it.

"They're fine," Wade says. "They're used to you being gone."

Hey, Ash wants to say. *If you add up the hours of my business trips, I'm still gone less than you are for your job*, but they've had this argument before and none of her reasoning ever seems to hold any water with Wade. "Thanks again for covering for me," she tells him now. "I really appreciate this."

"It's what I do." The edge is gone from his voice now and he sounds tired. She gets it. She's tired, too. "You really can't tell me where you're staying?"

"I can't," Ash says. "And after tonight, I won't be able to call you for the rest of the trip."

"Right," he says. "I remember." He pauses, and a door creaks in the background of the call. It's their back door; Ash knows that sound. She pictures Wade standing on the back porch, looking out over the patio area—flagstones, a few scattered Adirondack chairs, the firepit—to the flower gardens beyond. Is he going to miss Ash while she's gone? Is he missing her now? She misses him. Sometimes she feels like she's been missing him for years.

"I need to go," Ash says. "I shouldn't have even made this call." But she hopes the others are making them, too. Checking in again with the people they love one more time before they vanish for these few days. Maybe Hope is secretly on the phone with her agent, Raye, or her publicist, or one of her very cool friends. Maybe Caro's talking to *her* husband, Dan.

"Okay," Wade says.

He and Ash both wait, as if daring each other to say *I love you*. When did saying it first become so vulnerable? They've been married for seventeen years. It should roll off the tongue.

Ash's eyes fill with tears. He knows. She's been trying to keep it from him, but he knows.

Of course he does.

"I love you," Ash says.

But he's gone.

5

HOPE

"WELCOME," HOPE SAYS.

Their faces are devilish in the firelight, the shadows bringing out the angles, the lines of their cheekbones. She holds up a skewered marshmallow to salute the others. "Ready to disappear?"

Ash sits down on the low-slung Adirondack chair next to her. They've gathered at the firepit nearest Hope's Airstream. Despite the fact that it's June, the desert air has a bite at night. Over their T-shirts, they're all wearing bright orange hoodies emblazoned with the Sonnet logo that Hope insisted on buying for each of them. Their legs are still mostly bare, shorts and Tevas. If Hope squints hard enough, they could be ten years younger, ten years of life undone and unlived.

"Let's do it." Ash reaches for one of the s'mores kits that they picked up at the resort's general store. Caro is already squishing a perfectly golden-brown marshmallow between two graham crackers. It's camping food, but it's *artisan* camping food, befitting the atmosphere of the resort— puffy, nearly square homemade marshmallows, graham crackers with an almost-shortbread heft to them, chocolate squares so thick and rich that Hope doesn't even have to lift them very close to her face to smell their decadence.

"Okay," Hope says. "Let's go over the rules. Everyone turned off their location when they left home today, right?"

"Right," Caro says, and Ash nods. Her head is tucked down as she focuses on her skewer in the fire.

"Great." Hope reaches behind her chair. "And now, we *really* go dark." She brings out a metal lockbox and sets her phone inside before handing the box to Caro. Caro puts her phone inside, too, and passes the box to Ash. They've agreed to this—they won't be using their phones for the duration of the trip, even after they get out of the Underground. Hope's going to lock them away so no one's tempted. But Ash hesitates for a second before she places hers inside.

"I'll put the box in my Airstream and lock it up," Hope says. "Is that still cool with everyone?"

"It feels scary, to be honest," Caro says, threading another marshmallow onto her skewer. "But I know I need this. I've been tethered to phones and pagers since medical school." A shower of sparks spits up from the fire. "But what about pictures? I do want to be able to take some photos of all of this. Of us."

"I've got you." Hope reaches into the duffel bag at her feet and pulls out three disposable cameras. "We can put these in our dry bags when we go through the water."

Ash grins. "Oh my gosh, *this* takes me back. I think we had those cameras at my wedding."

"For the guests to take their own pictures, right?" Caro asks. "Dan and I did that, too. Were most of the photos totally unusable?"

"Yes," Ash says, cracking up. "Wade's little cousin got hold of one and she was short so we ended up with a whole roll of shots of people's crotches."

"That's fantastic," Hope says. "Did you sit around identifying who was who?"

"We threw them out," Ash says. "It was too much information." She tucks the camera into her hoodie pocket. "And I brought my fancy camera for any super-high-quality photos that we might want."

"Perfect," Caro says. "Dan's hoping we'll get some great shots. He loves this hike, but we haven't done it in years."

"Do you really think you can go without talking to Dan during this trip?" Ash asks.

"Yeah," Caro says, but she has that starry-eyed look in her eyes that often happens when she mentions her husband. Hope thinks it's sweet. Dan is an emergency room nurse, and he's tall and lanky, like Caro, with wavy brown hair. They seem perfectly matched, always taking Howie on walks or kayaking or hiking or working on remodeling their cute old house in Salt Lake City piece by piece.

"Okay." Ash puts the phone in the lockbox and hands it to Hope, who closes the lid and turns the key before Ash can change her mind.

"There we go," Hope says. "I don't know any of your passcodes. And I promise not to open this again until we're ready to go home."

"Did you get the burner phone?" Ash asks.

Hope nods, pulling it from her pocket.

"This is so hardcore." Ash looks thrilled.

"It's a good thing we trust you, Hope," Caro says drily.

"Too Draconian?" Hope asks. "I'm sorry. I really wanted to have an excuse to buy a burner phone."

"No, it's great," Caro says. "It makes sense." They've talked about all of this already, trying to figure out the best way to get away for a few days without being *totally* unreachable.

"I've added the emergency contacts you each gave me." Hope holds out the burner phone to Caro. "I've already texted them to let them know the number. This is what I said."

Caro sets down her skewer for a moment and wipes the stickiness from the marshmallow on her shorts before taking the phone to read what Hope sent.

Got here safe! Heading off the grid now. Back in contact on
Sunday. Text this number if there's an emergency. Thanks
for letting us disappear for a few days. xx

"We'll check it once a day to see if anything comes in," Hope says as Caro passes the burner phone to Ash so she can double-check her contact's number. "Except for when we're on the hike. There's no coverage in the Underground, so I'll leave the burner in the lockbox while we're there."

"This feels so weird." Ash is jiggling her leg up and down. "My girls still can't believe I'm doing this."

"It's probably good for them," Hope says with mock severity. "Let them miss you."

"Can I say," Ash says, glancing down at the burner phone and then back up at Hope, "that it's a privilege to be on a vacation where someone else is taking care of all the details? I feel so parented. So *pampered*. Thank you."

Hope feels pleased. She *has* put a lot of thought and work into this. "Of course."

"It's my pleasure," Caro says. "I can't wait to get you guys out there into the Underground. You're going to love it."

"I'm worried that I haven't trained enough for this," Ash says. "I don't want to be the weak link."

"*Please*," Hope says. "You're in great shape. You're always outside working. You're going to be fine."

"My dad always says that the best way to train for hiking the Underground is to get two bowling balls and then bang them on either side of your ankles," Caro says, laughing. "Because so much of the hike is in the river and the rocks and cobble are always clunking against your ankles. You both brought your hiking boots, right?"

They nod.

"Great," Hope says. "Okay. We've taken care of the phones. Everyone has their gear for the Underground. That brings us to the next item of business. Ash?"

"Right." Ash reaches into the small crossbody bag slung over the back of her chair and pulls out three tiny notebooks and a package of pens. "We're each going to write down what we're disappearing from on a piece of paper. And then we're going to burn them."

Hope smiles to herself. This ceremony was Ash's idea, and it feels very true to her nature. Ash is the one who remembers everyone's birthdays, who made the group spreadsheet for the trip, whose floral arrangements are famous for being wild and singular but also have a well-considered, nearly invisible structure to them. Hope takes a paper and pen and looks down. Should she be honest? She should. She reminds herself, *No one's going to read this.*

It's still hard to write.

Hope scrawls a single word on the paper and folds it up. She catches Caro's dark, pooled eyes across the fire. Hope smiles at Caro, and Caro smiles back. Here they are at last, no miles or screens or physical distance between them. Another shower of sparks rises upward, and Hope looks at Ash. Her brow is furrowed, as if she can't think of a single thing she'd get rid of from her perfect, messy life.

But Hope knows better.

Everyone has something.

"I'll go first." Hope lowers her voice, and they both lean in to hear her. She holds her paper over the fire but doesn't drop it. "So, there's something I haven't told you guys."

"Uh-oh," Caro says. "Spill."

Ash looks uneasy. Hope understands. How well *do* they know her, after all? And yet they were willing to hand over their phones to her. Their lives, to some extent, if she's being dramatic.

"I told you all that my movie got canceled." Hope hears a rare hesitant note in her own voice. Although in many ways she's sort of the default head of the group, she's also the youngest. Right now, she feels it. "But that wasn't actually the truth."

A log on the fire cracks and settles. No one flinches. Ash and Caro are intent on Hope, on what she's saying. Somewhere in the distance, an animal— a dog? a coyote?—howls.

"They actually fired me," Hope says. "They decided to recast the role after the first day of filming."

"Oh, Hope." Ash reaches over and puts her hand on Hope's arm. "I'm so sorry."

"I blame the World War I lighting." Hope manages a laugh. "I think they got me into full makeup on the set and decided I looked haggard and terrifying and ancient instead of young and beautiful and sympathetic."

"You *are* young and beautiful," Ash says fiercely.

"And sympathetic," Caro adds.

"But not young and beautiful and sympathetic *enough*," Hope says. "Anyway. I was feeling really shitty, and I figured that with all my new-found spare time I could make sure I read the book for book club this month, that at least I could manage *that* and not let you guys down—"

"You never let us down," Ash interjects, and Caro nods.

"—and then I remembered how we all met at that Agatha Christie book club, and how Agatha was actually *alive* in World War I, and she was, like, this awesome volunteer during the war, and how before her husband became a piece of garbage he was a fancy military pilot and she was head over heels for him, and I felt for *her* all over again."

Hope laughs, a ragged breath, holding her folded-up square of paper over the fire. "So. I'm leaving behind work. I know, I know. Not the most earth-shattering thing I could choose. But I really am. All the expectations. All the things I haven't done. All the wanting to eat something at a party and not having a single bite because a potential director might be watching, and you don't want them to think you might get too big. All the chemical peels and preventative Botox and hoping it's enough and not too much. All the roles I didn't get and the ones I still want. It's all going up in flames." She drops her paper into the fire, and it catches fast, the edges blackening to the middle, the whole thing turning into ash.

There is a brief, crackling silence.

"I'm burning work, too." Caro tosses her paper into the fire. "I'm not copying you, Hope. I'd written that down before you said anything."

"But your job actually *matters*." Hope knows she can't keep the bitterness from her voice. "You're a *doctor*." Caro doesn't seem to know how to answer that, but thankfully Ash throws her paper into the fire as well.

"Let's make it a hat trick," Ash says. "Because I wrote down work, too." She ducks her head. "And...I also wrote down my family. I know that sounds terrible. It's only for the next few days."

"It doesn't sound terrible," Hope says. Ash has been a mom for sixteen years, and she runs a small business that keeps taking off in unexpected ways. Of course she needs a break.

"Sorry," Ash says. "I don't know why I'm crying."

"Cry all you want," Hope says. "That's what this trip is for."

"And screaming," Caro says, and they look at her, surprised.

"Yes," Hope says. "Absolutely for screaming." She prods the tiny ashes that are left from her paper with her skewer, the fire blackening the last of the marshmallow clinging to the stick. *What would it be like to* actually *scream?* she wonders. *Not as a character, but as* myself? *What if I screamed right now?*

"I made you both something." Ash digs into her pockets and pulls out three beaded bracelets. They catch and glint in the firelight and at first, as she and Caro each take one, Hope can't tell what colors the beads are. She can tell what the beads with letters on them spell out, however: EDEN.

"Ash, they're beautiful," Caro says. "Thank you."

"The beads are each of our favorite colors," Ash says. "And I thought, I'll make us all another one for every place we go together. So: Eden to start." She's eager now, as if she's willing these future trips, this continued friendship, into being.

Hope's heart twists almost painfully. *Who says we're going to go anywhere else together? Nothing lasts. Things fall apart. Everything is a risk.* Pushing away her own thoughts, she pulls the bracelet onto her wrist. "Perfect," she says. "Let's make a deal. We don't take them off for the rest of the trip."

"Sounds good." Ash's voice is flooded with what sounds like relief, and Hope feels it wash over her, too.

"Deal," Caro says.

"Okay," Hope says. "We made it. We're all here." She looks up at the stars. Even with the light from the campfire, they are profound, numberless. She lifts her skewer into the air. "To us."

"To us," Caro and Ash echo in perfect unison. They follow suit, skewers hoisted high, bracelets glinting.

And as Hope catches their eyes across the fire, she thinks, *It's happening. We're really going to do this.*

6

BEFORE

It's their third book group meeting, and they each worry that this might be too good to be true. How did they stumble into this bright pocket of possibility and friendship in the middle of the pandemic, which has felt both utterly dehumanizing and deeply personal?

Hope doesn't turn on her camera. She leaves up the old picture of herself that she's had as her avatar for ages. It was from a trip to New Zealand with a boyfriend she had once. He was basic. The trip was not. She's facing away from the camera, so all you see is her hat and her coat and her Lululemon tights and her hiking boots and her hair, which is in a ponytail. She could be anyone who ever hiked a mountain and had their significant other take a picture of them with their back turned. Her butt does look great, though.

Ash is the first to pop up, and Hope lets her in. "Hi," Ash says, smiling nervously into the camera. Seconds later, Caro appears, fresh-faced, her hair pulled back into a kind of sprig, her even, unruffled personality setting both the visible Ash and the invisible Hope at ease.

"It's so good to see you guys," Hope says. "I'm sorry that my camera isn't working again." Can they hear the lie in her voice? She really wants them to like *her*, to get to know her as herself. It has been years since she's had this chance.

"No worries," Ash says easily. "We're all still figuring this out. I had a meeting today where I muted myself by accident."

The last time they met, they told one another about their jobs. Hope told them she was a "storyteller." Ash and Caro were too polite to drill down on a job that sounded vague enough to seem synonymous with unemployment. Between that and Hope's profile picture, they might be thinking she's some kind of itinerant poet. Or maybe they think she's one of those trust fund girls who travel for a living, eating and praying and loving in their expensive leggings and various winsome hats. For her part, Hope is intrigued by both of them: Ash, who spends every day tending flowers and daughters, and Caro, who works in a hospital, who sees life and death and specializes in putting people in a place that is somewhere in between.

"To confirm, Caro's on East Coast time and the rest of us are on West Coast time?" Hope asks.

"I'm actually on Mountain time," Caro says. "I live in Salt Lake City."

"What?!?" Hope is delighted. "I love Utah! It's so beautiful there. I've visited a few times."

"I grew up in the southern part of the state," Caro says. "But I came to the University of Utah for medical school and liked Salt Lake so much I never left."

"Ash, do you ski?" Hope asks. "Maybe we should plan a trip to Utah."

"I don't, actually," Ash says. "But for you ladies, I'd be willing to learn."

"And Caro can fix us up if we fall and injure ourselves," Hope says.

"I'm an anesthesiologist, not an orthopedic surgeon," Caro says drily.

"We should get together someday," Hope says. "In real life. Don't you agree?"

Yes. They do.

Wednesday

On the chalkboard outside the Sonnet resort main office

MOVIE
Mission: Impossible II, 2000, PG-13, directed by John Woo

FILM FACT
Like Paul Newman before him, Tom Cruise is known for doing many of his own stunts—including the famous rock-climbing sequence (shot in Utah at Dead Horse Point).

7

CARO

THERE ISN'T A CLOUD in the sky or in the forecast. It's an early, pearly blue above, the kind that often deepens to brilliant azure as the day goes on. They're standing at the top of a cliff, getting ready to descend into the slot canyon of the Underground.

Caro smiles to herself as she hooks the rope through the anchor bolt screwed into the stone. She's been looking forward to this part of the trip. For the past few years, hiking the Underground has required a permit, which you have to enter an online lottery to get. Caro hasn't been lucky enough to be chosen since the permit system started. But Hope got one somehow. *Hope Hanover magic*, Caro and Ash call it behind her back, and sometimes to her face.

Caro wants, needs, physically *aches* to get away. She's seen patients die before—it's an occupational hazard, being an anesthesiologist—but the most recent loss has sent her reeling. It was a woman about her own age who died in childbirth from a uterine rupture. Caro had known her by sight. They lived in the same neighborhood, the cozy area called Sugar House with its bungalows and pocket yards. "Oh, hello," they'd said to each other in the operating room, the way they'd said it to one another in passing on the sidewalks. Caro had learned that the woman's name was Esther Nelson. Her husband was called Owen, and he'd been excited and nervous. It was their first baby. Caro had administered the epidural and was still in the room, as per procedure, when everything went to hell. They had saved the baby—a relief, a wonder—but Esther had hemorrhaged to death despite everyone's best efforts. There were no words for how fast it happened, how bloody it was, how bewildered and shocked the husband had looked, how quickly all color and life had drained from Esther's body, how alone the baby had looked even as it was surrounded by a team to whisk it away to the NICU. It's been six weeks and Caro still hasn't returned to work. She knows she needs to get back on the horse, back to the job.

She doesn't know if she can.

Caro glances at the others. "Who wants to go first?" The sight of Ash and Hope makes her want to laugh—her wonderful friends, together in the flesh for the first time, wearing candy-colored canyoneering helmets with chin straps that make all three of them—even Hope—look like befuddled Easter eggs.

"Don't laugh," Hope says severely. "We have to be safe. Looking like M&M's is a small price to pay."

"I was thinking we're giving Toad from Super Mario," Ash says, which makes both Hope and Caro laugh out loud.

"Hope, you've been rappelling before, right?" Caro asks. "Want to show us how it's done?"

"Sure," Hope says. "It's been a minute, but I'll do my best."

"Since *Downfall*?" Ash asks.

"Yes, actually," Hope says. By now, they're largely accustomed to how much Ash knows about Hope's career and movies and celebrities in general, but Hope sounds impressed. "That's a deep cut," she says. "That was one of my earlier movies."

"Filmed in Colorado," Ash says.

"Right again," Hope agrees.

"I think it's so badass that you do all your own stunts," Ash says.

"Hardly." Hope presses her soles into the sandstone wall and leans back to go over. Caro grips the rope to belay her down. "I'm no Tom Cruise. I only do the fun stuff that doesn't require, you know, almost dying." As if belying her words, Hope drops backward into the canyon. Her steps along the wall are quick and smooth. Confident. Caro's impressed.

After Hope's down, Caro belays Ash (who, despite having never done this before, is steady and sure-footed, a natural) and then comes down herself. *Nice*, Caro thinks as she secures the rope to the outside of her pack, where it'll be handy the next time they need it. *This hike should be a dream. The parts we can control, at least.* She looks up at the sky again. It's still a perfect, pale morning blue. From here on out, their view of what's going on in the heavens will be limited to the glimpses they can catch above the canyon walls.

"Wow," Ash is saying. "I didn't expect there to be so many plants. It's like hanging gardens everywhere you look." She's turning around on the sandy bank of the creek that they'll follow through the slot canyon, staring up at the ferns, moss, and wildflowers growing from shallow alcoves in the walls, where they've found purchase and soil in spite of everything.

"Are they spring-fed?" Ash asks.

"Yup," Caro says. Ash knows her plants, even in a different climate. "The water seeps from the walls."

"They're so beautiful." Ash pulls her good camera out of her dry bag. "I'll be fast, I swear. I don't want to hold us up." Hope's still walking farther down the canyon. She hasn't noticed yet that they've stopped.

"No worries," Caro says. She pauses while Ash snaps a few quick pictures, and then they fall into step together as they hurry to catch up with Hope.

"We'll need to keep an eye out for flash floods as the day goes on," Caro says when they reach her. "Even though everything looks good now, we won't be able to see the whole sky again until we come out of the Underground near the end of the hike."

"Got it," Hope says. "We'll be vigilant." They all glance up at the slice of blue sky visible above them. In the few moments since Caro last looked, it's changed color, deepening toward the azure it will become at midday if the weather stays clear.

"The thing about flash floods," Caro says, "is that they can happen even if the weather seems fine where you are. It can rain up on a plateau miles away, and then the water runs off into the canyons and gets bigger and bigger and faster and faster as it feeds to the creek."

"We're really in the wilderness now." Ash sounds elated and nervous.

"Even if we had our cell phones, there's no reception in the canyon." Caro looks at Hope. "Otherwise I wouldn't have agreed to put them in the lockbox for the hike. It would be handy to have a signal if we run into trouble."

"We'll be very careful," Hope says.

"Holy crap." Ash pulls up short. They've come to one of the iconic spots of the Underground, where the rock walls belly out in the subway-tunnel-shaped formations that give the hike its name. Caro understands the disbelief in Ash's voice, even though Caro sent them all a picture of this exact spot when they were planning the trip. It's so beautiful, it's hard to believe it's real, that it exists outside of screensavers and posters.

The sandstone surfaces are a variety of hues: red, burnished gold, sooty black, and almost white. The hanging gardens of bright-green moss and plants cling to the stone. The creek gathers in pools colored pristine shades of turquoise, deep green, and purest blue, like jewels set in a sandstone crown miles long and millennia old. The smallest pools are iced over at the edges, frosty white tendrils branching out over aqua water.

They pause, listening to the creek as it gathers in the pools and runs on through the canyon. Caro feels like she can sense what the others are feeling. *We could let go and be part of all of this. Let the moss grow over our sandstone bones, the water move in our veins, the light fill our hearts and the furthest corners of our minds, until we are erased.*

It's always such a pleasure to see people experience this place for the first time. And though she's been here before, the hike is always different in some way. It's like that saying about never being able to step in the same river twice. You could come to the Underground every day and it would never be the same. The water would be higher or lower, the temperature cooler or warmer, this tree would be in bud, that creature would have come through before you, leaving prints, and on and on and on. Like how kids are always changing, how you're not the same person each day of your life. It's like nesting dolls, or sandstone layers, or snow on red rock. Everything and nothing. Timeless and gone in a moment.

"It's almost *too* beautiful," Ash says softly. "I can't take it in."

Hope nods in agreement. "It's like, *Go home, eyes, you're drunk.*"

That makes Caro laugh.

Ash takes out her camera again. "I know, I know," she says. "A picture can't do it justice. But I can't help myself."

"Me either," Hope says, snapping away with her disposable.

Caro can't help it—right now, she wishes Dan were here. Dan, with his boundless enthusiasm and his wide brown eyes. (He always jokes that he's all one color—brown eyes, brown hair, brown skin that tans even deeper the minute he steps outside.) She loves Dan. She loves hiking with him. She loves doing everything with him.

So why hasn't she told him about Hope?

She hasn't *lied* to him—Dan knows she has book club friends named Hope and Ash and that Caro's on this trip with them. He's waved to them both as he's walked past her screen during their meetings; he's laughed out loud as she's read him texts they've sent. But he doesn't know that Hope is Hope *Hanover.* Caro feels bad about that, but Dan tells people things. He can't help himself. He is zero percent malicious about it and always feels terrible later. Caro wouldn't mind *him* knowing, but he'd let it slip. Not telling him feels like protecting Hope. And Hope trusts Caro. They all trust each other, which is why they're here, doing this.

When Ash and Hope finish taking photos, they all carry on along down the creek. The canyon swells out and then narrows in around them. They're moving at a good pace, but Caro can tell that her friends are taking it all in by the *ooh*s and *aah*s she hears.

This is one of her favorite parts of the Underground—the miles where the hike follows the creek bed exactly, and the water-smoothed rocks roll and crash against your ankles as you make your way through the creek, which can be anywhere from ankle deep to hip high to over your head, depending on where you are and how rainy it's been.

Back when she was growing up, before permits were required, she and her father had hiked this canyon every summer. Some summers, her dad would hike the Underground several times. With Caro, with his friends, with local church youth groups he was asked to lead because of his experience. He and Caro's mom had hiked it together often, before she died. (Caro was always sad the three of them had never done it together—she'd been too young before her mom passed away.) But she'd gotten to bring Dan here about eight years ago, when they were first dating. Caro smiles, remembering that trip—her and her father exchanging glances as they'd come around each turn, knowing what waited for Dan ahead, looking forward to his reactions.

Henry, Caro's dad, always knew what to pack for any wilderness excursion. His hiking gear was decidedly utilitarian rather than stylish. Caro had teased him mercilessly about it—the khaki shorts, the button-up Patagonia shirt older than she was, the too-tall socks sticking out of his hiking boots—and about his knobby knees. Her father's hair had gone prematurely white in his late thirties, and he wore thick-rimmed black glasses that brought to mind his celebrity doppelgänger, Steve Martin.

Whenever she went anywhere with her father, people called out to him. "Dr. Stewart!" He'd been a family practitioner in town for decades, the hometown boy who went away to college and med school and returned to practice and serve in his community. Before the dementia began to take hold, he'd been known for his memory. "Now *she* gave me a scare when she was three," he'd say, pointing to a tween walking through the grocery store, a pack of Oreos tucked under her arm, her ponytail bobbing with every step. "Bailey Hammond. The youngest of Amy and Devon Hammond's kids. She came in with a fever of 107, and I ran across the parking lot from my office to the hospital with her in my arms." He was also constantly bumping into current or former students. Henry had taught an Introduction to Anatomy course at the small university in St. John for years, though his adjunct pay was pennies compared to what he made as a doctor. He'd loved meeting the students; he'd loved writing their letters of recommendation to help them get into medical school; he'd loved it when they'd emailed him to let him know where they were and what they were doing now. He'd loved his life, and now it had become so much smaller.

As she catches up with her friends, Caro hears other voices echoing up through the canyon. "Oh, yeah," Ash says. "Other people. I'd almost forgotten anyone else existed."

"Right?" Caro says.

Before long they begin catching glimpses of the group ahead of them. They look to be college-age kids, about five in number. Caro loves this about hiking, the way you come upon other groups and pass them, or they pass you, never to be seen again, or you do a sort of back and forth for the duration of the hike. It's like at Disneyland where you come to know people because of being in the lines. *Ah, there's that family with the toddler and the surprisingly helpful preteen. They've made it through eight Go-Gurts now and counting. Oh look, the young couple that was arguing is hugging again, the guy wrapping his arms around the woman from behind, both of them laughing, their Mickey Mouse ears no longer looking ironic instead of sweet.*

"You guys ready to swim?" Caro asks her friends.

They've come to the biggest pool yet, and it looks deep as well as long. The frost's crystalline patterns are beautiful up close. Caro can smell the water. She can feel the scoop and sway of the stone.

"Absolutely." Hope takes one of the bracelets from her wrist and uses it to pull her hair up into a topknot.

"Can't wait," Ash says drily, but she's smiling.

"Great," Caro says. "I'll go in first. It'll be chilly, you guys. Hope, do you mind bringing up the rear?"

"No problem."

Caro laughs at the others' reactions as they enter the water (Ash shrieks,

Hope swears). The water is take-your-breath-away cold, and Caro shivers, feeling her body absorb the shock of it even through her wetsuit.

"We all good?" she calls back.

"So good," Ash yells, and Caro grins, because she knows what Ash's likely experiencing. Once you're actually in the water, you feel *great*. You feel *beyond* alive. Caro is trembling and shaky and new and strong, like a baby deer or some other animal that has only recently come into the world.

They hold their packs over their heads and make their way carefully through the pool, trying not to slip on the stones beneath or crash into any of the large boulders submerged in the water. In spots, the creek is so deep that it comes up to Caro's armpits, but they don't have to actually *swim*.

Once they're all out of the water, they realize that they've nearly caught up with the group ahead of them. As they get closer, Caro can see that they've come to a steep drop, the first place that they'll have to make a descent while *in* the canyon. The water cascades over a rocky outcropping. The college kids have a rope, but it's not long enough for the rappel, and they're stuck. She groans inwardly. Like her dad, she hates it when people come into wild places unprepared.

Hope glances at her watch and then at Caro. They need to keep moving if they're going to stay on schedule.

"I'll get you guys down first," Caro says to her friends. "Then I'll help them out and catch up." She can't leave them stranded. Plus, the rope the kids have should be long enough for the rest of the drops. This first one is the biggest.

"They don't have helmets," Ash says. Though the creek is shallower than it's been in other places, it's particularly slippery here. Slick, green-black algae clings to the sandstone and grows in tangled strands patterned like shallow waves.

"Most groups actually don't," Caro says. "It's not required. Only suggested." She pats Ash on her helmeted head. "I'm abundance-of-cautioning for this trip."

"I appreciate that," Ash says.

The group of kids look up as the three women come closer. There are five in total, two guys and three girls, and Caro can tell that at least some of them are thinking about jumping into the water instead of rappelling down. "Hey," Caro says. "We've got a rope. Mind if I belay my friends down first, and then you guys can use it, too, if you'd like?"

One of the guys is walking along the edge. "I'm going to jump!" he calls out, confirming Caro's hunch.

"Can we do that?" a girl with brown hair asks Caro.

"In theory, you can, but I wouldn't recommend it," Caro says. "Rappelling is the safer route. The depth of the pools varies drastically, and you don't know how deep it is." She swings her pack around to the front and begins readying her climbing rope. There's a bolt in the rock that they can use, right where she remembered. *Perfect.*

"It's spring, though, right?" the other guy asks. "So we should be good. Lots of water."

"A few years ago, someone died jumping here." Caro can tell that the guys are feeling stupid for not having brought a long enough rope, so she hopes they'll swallow their pride and use hers. She's trying to be extremely cool and nonchalant so that they won't see her as a challenge to their manhood or their youth and they'll accept her help. "Ash, you ready to clip in?"

"Yup." As their eyes meet before Ash steps back down over the edge, Caro sees that Ash gets it, that she knows exactly what Caro's doing. A few moments pass in silence as the others watch Ash go over. "I'm down!" she calls out, and Caro brings the rope back up so that Hope can clip in.

"That actually looks pretty fun," the brown-haired girl says. She's trying to convince the others, Caro can tell. The boys are edging closer along the rock.

"Oh, it is," Hope says. Hope's orange hat is pulled low and no one in the group gives her a second glance. Once Caro and Hope have checked that Hope's clipped in properly, down she goes.

"She made it," one of the guys reports, looking over the edge.

"I'm down!" Hope shouts.

"Head on out," Caro calls. "I'll catch up with you."

"How will *you* get down if you help all of us?" the brown-haired girl asks.

"I've done this enough that I can belay myself," Caro says.

"Did someone really die here?" asks a redheaded girl with a glint in her eye. "Or are you making that up to freak us out?"

"I didn't make it up," Caro says.

"This exact spot?" the first guy asks.

"No, farther down," Caro says. "They jumped instead of using a rope." She gestures to their gear. "And yours should be fine for the rest of the descents. It's only this one where it won't be long enough."

"I don't believe you," the red-haired girl says. "About someone dying."

"You don't believe anything, Roz," the brown-haired girl says. She looks at Caro. "If it's okay, I'll go down on your rope. Sorry. I know we're slowing you up."

"Not a big deal," Caro says.

While the two guys and the redheaded girl discuss what they want to do, Caro belays the other two girls down. They're cautious but not skittish, and she's pleased when they reach the bottom safely and when the guys swallow their pride and let her help them, too. The red-haired girl goes last. As she clips in, she says to Caro, "You were trying to scare us, right? About the person who died?"

"No," Caro says. "My dad's a doctor. He was hiking the canyon that day. He tried to help her, but she was dead before he got there."

"Oh no," says the girl, her eyes serious now, and she goes down maddeningly slowly, inch by inch. But none of the others tease her, and Caro's glad. After she's finished, Caro lets herself down and pulls her rope through, securing it to her backpack. The kids thank her profusely, all pride gone now, and they settle on the rocks to eat lunch, offering Caro one of their Red Bulls, which she laughs and refuses because caffeine always makes her feel jangled up.

As she hurries to catch up with her friends, Caro is alone in the canyon, an unusual feeling. *The wilderness has a million secrets*, Henry used to tell her. She's always believed him. It's easy to feel small and lost out here because you are, because you are nothing.

"Hey!" she hears Hope calling from ahead. "Caro! We found another spot from the pictures you sent."

As she catches up with the other two, Caro draws in her breath at the sight of a familiar, famous alcove. A log, smoothed out by water and bleached bone-white by sun, is propped up against the side of the canyon. It had fallen—or been brought by the creek—decades ago, and, despite flash floods and nature in general, it's been here as long as people have been hiking and photographing the Underground. One end of the log is positioned against the canyon wall, the other slanted down into a pristine pool. A tumble of large stones nearby makes it a perfect stopping point.

It intrigues Caro how one added element—a log, a scraggly tree, a human body standing near something—gives a scene perspective.

Hope shrugs her pack from her back. "How about we eat lunch here?"

"Perfect," Ash says.

Caro sits down on one of the rocks near the log. They've eschewed the fancy boxed meals you can buy at Sonnet. Instead, they're eating lunches that she and Ash made for everyone this morning from groceries they'd picked up on their way to the resort. Ash had sliced their sandwiches into triangles and cut up apples and pears into skinny slices, the way her kids liked them best. Caro had brought chocolate chip cookies she'd baked the day before.

"What did you put *in* this?" Hope asks, holding up her sandwich to the light. "It tastes like heaven."

"It's always like that with food you eat outside, isn't it," Ash says. She's making her way through her second sandwich with gusto.

"Thanks a ton, you guys," Hope says.

"No problem." Caro takes another bite of her sandwich. The peanut butter sticks to the roof of her mouth the way it did when she was a kid. The sensation is not unpleasant.

"What kind of a tree do you think it was?" Hope asks, pointing to the log.

"I'd guess some kind of pine," Caro says. "It's too big to be an aspen and the wood isn't as fibrous as a cottonwood."

"Aspens are the skinny white ones with the leaves that turn gold, right?" Hope asks.

"Yeah," Caro says. "Oh, that reminds me. Did you guys know that Pando's near here?"

"Panda bear what?" Hope asks.

"The world's largest living organism," Caro says. "Have either of you seen it?"

Everyone shakes their heads.

"I've heard of it," Ash says. "But I've never gone."

"It's pretty wonderful." Caro leans forward, her sandwich dangling forgotten from one hand as she gestures with the other. "It's a single aspen tree that spreads for a hundred and six acres. There are lots of stems—trees—but it's all one root organism."

"Wow," Hope says. "How long has it been around?"

"They don't know for sure," Caro says, "but they're estimating that it started at the end of the last ice age."

"*That's* a while."

"We should see it while we're here," Ash says, and they all go quiet. "If we have time," she amends.

"We should," Hope agrees, and Caro's shoulders relax.

The three of them chew in companionable silence. Being in a canyon, Caro thinks, is like being inside a seashell. The pink and red curves of the walls, the way sound seems to cup itself around you. There's a vastness in the sound of the canyon, too, the sense of spaces as wide and expansive as the ocean.

They hear echoes from farther up the canyon, people coming down. The college kids must be catching up with them.

"Aw," Hope says. "It was nice having this place to ourselves."

"I'm surprised we had it as long as we did." Ash balls up the bag from her sandwich and puts it into her pack.

When the other group comes around the corner, Hope stands up and holds out her disposable camera. "Hey," she says. "Would you guys mind taking a picture of us?"

"No problem," says the red-haired girl, taking the camera. *Roz*, Caro remembers. *That's her name.*

Caro and Ash exchange glances. This feels daring, like Hope is challenging someone to recognize her. Does she really think they're going to look right at her and *not* know who she is?

"Okay," Roz says, once the three women have assembled themselves next to the log. She lifts the camera and pushes the button. It clicks. "Let me get another," she says, "in case." She lifts the camera again, presses the button, frowns. "I'm supposed to hear a click, right? Last time I heard a click."

"She doesn't know to wind it," Ash says under her breath, and they dissolve into laughter. Roz looks upset, and Caro hurries to help her. "Don't feel bad. We're just old," she says, which seems to mollify Roz. She shows Roz how to wind the camera and comes back to join her friends in their pose. They're tucked in tight together, arms around shoulders and waists, canyon walls behind them, feet in the water.

"Thanks again," Hope says when they've finished. "No problem," Roz says, and away the kids go, quick and sure-footed, still confident. Caro hopes they'll be safe. They're past the biggest descent, they have a rope, she did this canyon herself long before she was their age, but that's the thing about this place. They could jump in somewhere else, a spot that looks deep and safe, and get hurt instead. They could fall, it could flood, loose rock could tumble down from above...

Life is so fragile and impossible and stubborn and common that it takes Caro's breath away.

"They're not your responsibility," Hope reminds Caro, catching her eye. "You've helped them as much as you can."

8

PAGE

"WHERE'VE YOU BEEN?" CARMEL asks as I walk into the staff kitchen. It's the brief afternoon pause right after two, when the rush of guests checking out or eating lunch has ebbed and the day's new guests haven't yet reached full mass.

"It's my day off." I open the fridge and take out a leftover sandwich wrapped in brown waxed paper. Carmel is the head chef at Bristlecone, the resort's restaurant, and she and Ty, the food truck cook, bring leftovers in here for us to eat so they don't go to waste. They're both at least a decade older than most of the staff. They, and Sonnet's manager, Colby, take care of us in a sort of non-coordinated, completely unofficial way—with the food, with checking in on us, stuff like that. At the end of every summer, Carmel gathers all the staff together and takes a picture because, as she says, *We'll never have exactly the same group again.*

"Lucky you." Skye's sitting at one of the tables. As usual, there's a hint of snark in her tone. As usual, I ignore it. There's nothing lucky about having a day off. We all have them once a week. Skye's one of those girls from LA who decided to work here for the summer because they believe they're outdoorsy and cool. Eventually they learn they're not actually as outdoorsy as they thought; they've just had parents rich enough to buy them all the gear and experiences they want.

It can be a rude awakening.

Still, Skye is having a good summer, even though she hates the bunk tents the staff sleep in (she's not into "communal living"). She's amassing more and more followers every day on LikeMe. On *her* days off she packs designer dresses in her backpack, hikes to different picturesque locations in the park, and takes pictures to post on social media. Malcolm, one of the other employees—the one who's sitting with her now and who has dirty-blond hair and gentle, deerlike brown eyes—goes with her whenever he can. They're together. They're the two hottest people here, so it's inevitable, although for a minute at the beginning of the season Skye was crushing on Ty (even though he's way too old for her) and Mal seemed pretty into me.

This is my third summer working at Sonnet. I've been here ever since I graduated from high school, and I'm one of the few employees who stay on year-round. It's a good place, much better than the wedding venue where I used to work with my grandma. Colby, our manager, trusts me. We started in our different positions at around the same time. He'd been to a fancy Ivy League university back East and majored in hotel management (I didn't even know you could major in that). He ran a couple of hotels in the Pacific Northwest before taking the job at Sonnet, and he'd never even been to Eden before. He always says I saved his life that first summer.

In theory, Colby and I should not have that much in common. He's at least ten years older than I am, he's grown up in places with lots of water and money, he's charismatic and genuine, while I'm quiet and hide all the time. But for whatever reason, we clicked right away. So when he told me he needed to be gone for a while to handle a personal matter and asked if I thought I could take care of things here, I said yes. Of course. He already lets me do some of the things that are technically the manager's job, so I've had experience with nearly everything he needs me to do.

I like the round-robin style of working at Sonnet. The staff takes turns manning the reception desk, the gift shop, the food truck, and waiting tables at Bristlecone. I don't wait tables, though, since I'm not twenty-one and can't serve alcohol.

We also don't cook. Ty and his backup cook handle the food truck, and Carmel and her line cooks handle Bristlecone. They are the most experienced of the staff, with prior catering and restaurant experience. They live year-round in Spring Creek, the closest town, since Bristlecone and the food truck don't close in the off-season. (Off-season tourists still want a fancy place to eat, and the food truck travels around to festivals or events in towns near here.)

We also don't help with housekeeping, unless it's to light the fires or bring over fresh linens and towels on one of the golf carts. There was a theft a few years ago, so the housekeeping staff are well vetted. They're locals who come in and take summer jobs. The people around here don't make much money, so you often see them picking up extra work during the summer—housekeeping (usually women) or working for the city keeping up the parks and the cemetery (usually men).

It's awkward and depressing as hell whenever I run into my old biology teacher Mrs. Phillips at the resort, but we've both settled on pretending that we don't know each other from before. We act like we only know each other from now. "Hi," she says. "Hi," I say back, colleagues now, and we step around each other and on we go.

"What have you been up to today, anyway?" Carmel sits down at the table across from me.

"Not much," I say. "Went for a drive." I lift my sandwich, hold it in Carmel's direction as if to toast her. "This is great. Thank you."

"No problem," she says. "Your car still running okay?"

My car, a hand-me-down from my sister, is a red Chevy Blazer so old that it has a CD player inside. It's a long-standing joke among some of the staff, but not Carmel. She knows how it is to stretch something out years longer than expected, to be grateful every day that you don't have to face that particular expense yet. When the Blazer broke down last summer, she referred me to her brother, a mechanic who gave me a discount.

"It is," I say.

"Where'd you drive?" Skye asks, nosy, and because it's her, I shrug and say, "Around," without giving any specifics. She's trying to suss out even more places for LikeMe; she knows I have places I don't tell her about. She doesn't understand the finding of things, the wandering and coming upon them, or having someone show you because they *want* to share them with you, not because you expect them for the asking.

Often on my days off I like to take this long drive called the Devil's Backbone. It's an old road that winds up and over a nearby mountain to another small town called Story, and it's terrifying. The road is only wide enough for a single vehicle, and in lots of places the drops on either side are sheer and absolute. When I get to Story, I head to the grill and get lunch to go, which I eat outside on one of the picnic benches on the lawn. It's my one splurge—the lunch, and the gas it takes for the drive. Then I drive back along the Backbone to Sonnet. I like driving. I like the dusty old smell of the Blazer and rolling down the windows to let the clean air in.

But today I went into Spring Creek to get a few things I needed. On my return, a few miles before the turnoff to the resort, I took a right up another road to the top of the Underground trailhead. The parking lot gravel crunched under my feet as I walked over to the trail register, looking at the names written down for today. As I scanned them, I thought, *There's no way, there's no way...*

They did it. They wrote their real names, including Hope Hanover. *Why?*

I stood there, shaking my head, not sure if I was impressed or appalled by the way they'd put it out there, the names, how they announced that they were going into the canyon. Anyone who wants to come looking will know where to find them.

I pulled out my phone and took a picture of the log. Of course, I already knew from listening in on them the night before that they were planning on hiking the Underground today. But it was nice to have confirmation.

It's hard *not* to eavesdrop when you're staff. The guests sit around outside the firepits and talk loudly. The outdoor air on their skin and the drinks in their hands make them free and easy with what they say. If you *do* happen to get noticed, you always have a good excuse as a member of staff. You're checking to make sure they don't need anything; you want to let them know about yoga or a hike or a mindfulness gathering in the morning; the cook told you that tomorrow there will be this special or that; what do they think of the stars?

They love them, always. They *love* the stars, even if they haven't bothered to look up at them until you ask what they think.

If anyone had noticed me last night, I could have given plenty of reasons for being there. But I didn't need to.

No one saw me.

Skye elbows Malcolm, and he leans across the table toward me. "Hey, Page," Mal says. "Speaking of days off." He's handsome, and he's funny and nice and smart, which means it's easy to feel nothing for him now that it's clear he's into Skye. I think it's easier to shut down when you can forget that people are real. When you can turn them into a character in a movie, someone you're never actually going to know, only watch.

"Why do you all have this thing for Page?" Skye asked Mal once, when they were in our tent and I was in my upper bunk and she forgot to check to see if anyone else was there before they started making out. "Is it the hair?"

"The hair?" Mal asked. "What do you mean? Her hair's always in a ponytail. Or a braid."

"Exactly," said Skye. "She's very granola. People can be into that." She snorted with laughter. "*Wait.* Do you think she's a *sister wife*? One of those fundamentalists? Don't they always wear their hair in braids?"

"A what?" Mal asked.

That was when I chose to roll over in my bunk. They froze, and then they left, Skye pissed yet again about the lack of privacy. In her real life she's a guest at places like Sonnet.

"What?" I ask Mal now. Behind him, the door swings open and Ty and his backup cook, Evan, come inside. They wave to us, and Ty grabs a sandwich from the fridge and stands in front of the bulletin board with all of the staff pictures to eat. *Avoiding Skye*, I think. Evan takes his food and leaves, probably for the staff tent. I'm not the only one around here who likes privacy. But right now, with Colby gone and other things on my mind, I have to stay in the mix. Skye heads out, too, leaving Mal to do whatever dirty work she wants done without her.

"Someone was saying there's a ghost town around here," Mal says. "We want to go tomorrow." He holds out his phone. "But it's not showing up on my Google Maps."

He's asking about Afton, I realize. The small, abandoned ghost town with the brief, complicated history that no one's lived in for decades. Skye's tag-teamed Mal in, since she knows I won't tell her. I can picture how they'll experience the town, Skye and Mal, laughing and walking down the street holding hands, making fun of it, talking about how hot and dusty and boring it is, *but ooh, wait*, Skye will say, this *works*, and she'll take off her backpack and find the gauzy white dress she packed inside, and as the sun is starting to come down, she'll slip into one of the abandoned buildings and change, Mal watching, the hem of her dress trailing across the dusty floor, and she'll stand in front of the house, backlit by the sun, leaving nothing to the imagination.

"Sorry," I say. "You can't go there. No one can."

"Why not?" Mal asks.

"They had a sewage line rupture a few years ago," I lie. I need to think of something that will keep Skye away. The chain across the road and the NO TRESPASSING: CLOSED TO VISITORS sign won't do the trick. "No one's lived there in forever, so they didn't bother repairing it. Now it's turned into kind of a biohazard. They've had the road blocked off for years." That last part, at least, is true.

"Oh, okay, thanks," Mal says, nodding, his smile a white flash against his tanned skin. "Good to know."

"No problem," I tell him.

I don't feel one bit guilty for stretching the truth.

You'd better have a good reason if you want to walk among the ghosts.

9

HOPE

"I HAVEN'T BEEN THIS naked in public in a long time," Ash says.

"I can't believe we're *choosing* to be in this water," Hope says.

When they reached their first campsite, they'd dumped everything in a pile, oohing and aahing over the beauty of the place. None of the campers for the other two sites have arrived yet, and—almost without discussion—Hope, Ash, and Caro stripped down to their sports bras and underwear and headed for one of the natural pools scooped out along the creek bed. All three women are sweaty and salty and tired, and the perfect blue-green of the water is irresistible, even though it's turned out to be very, very cold in spite of the pools being in the sun.

The red-rock canyon walls loom above them. A steep and tiny slot canyon on the west feeds down into the larger main canyon of the Underground, benches of dirt and sandstone rising up against the walls. A few trees and bushes cling to the benches and, in some places, to the canyon walls. Hope glances over at their campsite, which is one of three marked sites on a sandbar on the eastern side of the Underground, each identified by small wooden posts with metal numbers affixed to them. Hope loves the utilitarian, bare-bones feel of the way things are marked in national parks—no artifice, only utility—splintered, weathered gray posts that have been battered through the seasons, numbers that mark the spot, nothing more or less. Their campsite number is her lucky number, six.

She hopes it means that nothing will go wrong. That everything is going to proceed according to plan. *How are the others feeling?* she wonders. *Are they nervous?*

"How long are we going to stay in here?" Caro asks, teeth chattering.

"I think they say you're supposed to stay in eight minutes to get the full benefit," Ash tells them. "But I'm not sure of the water temperature here. This may not count as a true cold plunge."

"I can't believe you haven't ever done this before, Caro," Hope says. "It feels like it would be right in your wheelhouse. And aren't you a swimmer?" She's shivering now, too, and the conversation is helping her keep her mind off the way the cold seems to be going straight to her heart.

"A runner," Caro says.

"I mean, I know *that*." Hope kicks her feet around in the pool to try to generate some warmth. "But I always thought you were a swimmer, too."

"I'm decent," Caro says. "Not amazing."

"It's going to feel really good in a few seconds," Ash says encouragingly. "I swear."

"You seriously do this year-round?" Hope asks. "*Outside?* I mean, everyone in Hollywood is very into contrast therapy, but it's always indoors. You can get right into a sauna after."

"It's what gets me through the gray season in Portland." Ash has slid in deeper than the rest of them, right up to her chin, her long hair topknotted like Hope's.

"Keep talking," Caro says through gritted teeth. Her face is so grim and she's so uncharacteristically *not into* this very outdoorsy thing that Hope starts laughing again. "I'm sorry, Caro," she says. "It's your own fault for not having any body fat."

"You should talk," says Ash.

"No," Caro says. "We're not doing that. All of our bodies are amazing, the end."

"You're right," Hope says. She tries dipping herself lower into the water. As she shifts, she slips, going all the way under before she comes back up, spluttering, to a seated position. The others are giggling at her and she makes a face at them, but she's laughing, too. For a moment, she forgets everything.

And then it all comes back.

"Dang it," Ash says. Hope follows her gaze to where three hikers have emerged from the upper part of the Underground onto the sandbar. "I don't want to get out in front of them."

"Be real quiet and maybe they won't notice us," Hope says, but then the hikers start checking the campsite markers, and when they get to 7, they begin shrugging off their packs and looking around. "Great," she says. "Looks like they're camping here tonight."

"And all our clothes are still over there," Ash says, gazing forlornly at campsite 6.

"They see our stuff, but they don't see us." Caro snorts. "Look at them." The hikers, three men, are pointing at the pile of backpacks and gear at campsite 6, looking around, then up, as if whoever has left the packs has managed to scale the walls or disappear into the sky.

"Ugh," Hope says. "Two of those guys look like the ones we saw at the food truck last night. Remember?" She turns to Ash. "They're probably named Brad and Chad?"

"*Quiet,*" Caro whispers, because Ash and Hope are getting the giggles again. "I don't want them to see us yet."

"Or ever," Hope says. The sun goes behind a cloud, and the canyon darkens. *It's too cold*, Hope thinks.

"Don't worry," Ash says. "One of us will go get the clothes eventually, and it won't be you, Hope. We'll bring them to you."

Hope loves that they feel protective of her. She worries, though, that it won't last. Inevitably it's hard to keep female friendships in her line of work, and she gets it, she really does. The attention vortex that she is, that she attracts—it's consuming. What people don't understand is that *she* feels the double-edged-swordedness of it, too, that she's grateful for the opportunity and the privilege and the money, and she also hates it so much, hates that she is always the center of attention, required to perform in some way, never allowed to simply *be*.

Except with these women.

Hope has a sudden urge to protect this moment, their privacy, for as long as she can. It won't last. She knows what happens next, and what *has* to happen after that. But she can make this moment last as long as possible. *"Get down,"* she whispers to the others, and she lowers herself so that only her eyes and nose and mouth and the top of her head are above water.

Caro follows suit.

"You guys look like alligators," Ash says, grinning. "Or crocodiles. Which are the ones with eyes on top of their heads?"

Caro is trying not to laugh, too. Hope cracks up, and the men turn but don't see them. Yet.

"Duck," Hope orders, and they all go under, and while they're down in the water the sun comes out again. Hope feels it, and she opens her eyes. She has never opened her eyes in water this cold, not even when she was filming *The Deep*. The water is clean but silt floats through it, and looking across she sees that neither Ash nor Caro have opened their eyes; they are still screwed tight shut, which is probably the smarter move—who knows what Hope is getting in her eyes right now, is that a bug floating past, is she going to *watch a bug* as it swims *into her own eye?!?*—and then a shadow crosses above.

The others open their eyes, too, and Hope sees that they all know: *We've been found.*

10

CARO

"HOLY CRAP," ONE OF the men says. "What are *you* doing here?!?"

He's tall and tan, with dark eyes and a shaved head. He wasn't with the other two at the food truck the night before. And he looks entirely different from the last time Caro saw him, which had to be what? Fifteen years ago? Still. She knows him instantly.

"*Caro?*" he says. "Caro Stewart?"

"Oh my gosh," she says. "Spencer Clayton."

Out of the corner of her eye, she sees Hope raise her eyebrows. *There's no need*, Caro wants to tell her. *Spencer's cute, but we haven't seen each other in years, and even then we were friends. With occasional benefits.*

"How long has it been?" Spencer's standing a respectful distance away but still, perhaps, too close, given that she's in her bra and underwear and would prefer to have this reunion fully dressed. "Ten years? Fifteen?"

"That's exactly what I was thinking," she says with a laugh. "What are you doing here?"

"Same as you," he says. "Hiking." He gestures to the two men who have now caught up to him. They've got their trucker hats on again. One of them has a tattoo of what appears to be a date on his forearm. "This is my friend Kevin," Spencer says, gesturing to the non-tattooed guy, "and his brother, Tony."

"Nice to meet you guys," Caro says. "Or, rather, see you again." In answer to Spencer's quizzical look, she explains, "We ran into each other at the food truck last night." She darts a quick glance over at Hope, who has turned her back to the group. Ash has already moved to partially block her from view. "Um, I'd love to talk more, but it's actually freezing in here and we need to go get our clothes. Could you guys—" She pauses, not sure what to ask. But Spencer was a nice guy when she knew him in high school and when they hung out and made out the summer after her freshman year when she was home for college.

And it appears he's still a nice guy now. "Oh yeah, yeah," Spencer says. "Of course. We wanted to hike farther down anyway and see what's in store for us tomorrow before we settle in here for the evening." Kevin and Tony's expressions indicate that this is news to them, but Spencer gives Caro a cheerful wave. "See you later!" he says over his shoulder. "Let's catch up! It's been too long."

"Sounds good," Caro says.

—

"That was nice of your friend to get the guys out of here so we could get dressed." Ash glances over at the men's campsite. "We're the only ones without a tent. Do you still think that's fine?"

They're dressed and have warmed up, their wet hair drying into tendrils in the desert air. The men have returned and are setting up their tents at site 7.

On Caro's advice, the women decided *not* to bring tents—less to pack in and out of the canyon, the forecast was good, and they all felt like sleeping under the stars. They knew that there would be other people camping near them, but perhaps they hadn't realized exactly how that would feel. Although flimsy fabric walls don't offer any real protection, it would offer some privacy. "I'm sorry," Caro says. "Maybe we *should* have brought them. We'd be less out in the open. They're kind of cumbersome. I know we wanted to keep this as streamlined as possible."

"Oh, for sure we made the right call," Hope says. "I *love* sleeping in the open air all bundled up in my sleeping bag." Her cheeks are pink and her eyes bright. "Like, with only my nose out. I *want* my nose to be cold."

"Same," Caro says.

The men have finished putting up their tents. They glance over at the women. Tony removes his baseball cap and ruffles his hair. It stands up in sweaty spikes, visible even from a distance.

"I think they want us to cheer or something," Hope says. "They're looking at us."

"We're looking at them," Caro points out.

"I bet they send your boyfriend over to talk to us," Hope says, and Caro rolls her eyes.

"I'm married," she reminds Hope. "Remember Dan? You love Dan."

"I do love Dan," Hope agrees. "I'm feeling kind of middle school right now. It might be the matching hoodies."

They are bundled up in their Sonnet sweatshirts, sitting with their backs against a giant log washed up on the sandbar, eating the food they packed in, which is, as they were joking last night at the food truck, gerbilesque.

"Incoming," Ash says. "Hope was right. It's happening. Caro, that guy you know is headed our way."

"What's his name again?" Hope asks.

"Spencer," Caro says. They all watch as he makes his way over to them, walking across the sandbar with a cheery confidence Caro remembers.

"I've been sent as an emissary," he says when he reaches them. He's so *likable*, which Caro has to admit has always been her type. She was into the golden retriever boyfriend long before the term existed. "We're wondering if you ladies might want to come over and have a drink and play cards with us."

"That depends," Caro says. "Tell me more about these guys you're with?"

"Kevin and Tony Jameson," Spencer says. "They're both a few years older than us. Kevin actually married one of my sisters."

"Oh," Caro says. "One of the triplets?" Then she starts laughing, remembering. "Hey," she says to her friends, "you'll never believe this. His sisters are named Hillary, Chelsea, and Monica."

"Seriously?" Ash asks.

"Yeah," Spencer says. "My poor parents. They named the triplets back in 1996. They had no idea what was coming for them."

"The poor *triplets*," Ash says. "Walking around with those names."

"Good thing your name isn't Bill," Hope says. She'd pulled on a beanie when they got dressed and, between that and the lowering light, it seems that she feels comfortable enough to enter the chat without worrying about being recognized.

"It actually *is*," Spencer says seriously. "Spencer is the name I had to adopt when everyone in high school started making fun of us."

Hope doesn't buy it for a second. "Nice try, but I can tell you're kidding." There's a touch of flirtation in her tone and Caro feels an irrational twinge of—jealousy? She smiles to herself at the ridiculousness of it.

"We wouldn't keep you long," Spencer says. "I have enough sisters to know that you don't mess with a girls trip."

"You're kind of infantilizing us by calling it a girls trip," Ash says matter-of-factly. Her hair streams wild and loose behind her, and she looks like one of her daughters—the middle one, Caro thinks.

"Sorry," Spencer says. "That's what my sisters always call the trips they go on. I didn't mean—"

"We forgive you," Hope says. "Right, Ash?"

"Yeah." Ash gives him a wry grin. "But don't do it again."

"So is that a yes?" Spencer says. "Or a no?"

"What are you drinking?" Ash asks.

"What are you playing?" Caro asks.

"Beer," Spencer says. "And poker."

"Sure," Hope says. "We'll be over in a minute."

Caro and Ash turn to look at her in astonishment. Hope is leaning back on her elbows against the log, her smile wide.

"Great." Spencer sounds surprised. "Come on over whenever you want."

"Will do," Hope says. "Thanks for the invitation."

"You *want* to hang out with them?" Ash asks Hope after he's left.

"I think it might be useful," Hope says. "Don't you?"

"And why are you talking like that?" Ash asks.

But Caro already knows what Hope is doing. She's affected a southern Utah accent like the one the guys have (and like Caro herself sometimes has, if she's honest, especially when she's been back in St. John for a few days). Dan teases her about it.

"I'm disguising myself," Hope says. "I'm talking like a local."

"You're *good*," Ash says. "You sound exactly like them."

Caro feels like she's being mocked, though she knows it's a smart move, if they're going to hang out with the guys. Hope Hanover doesn't wear dirty hiking pants and a beanie and no makeup and talk like she went to St. John High. She might get away with being someone else.

"Last night at the food truck—" Ash begins.

"I wasn't ready then," Hope says. "But I'm ready now." She squares her shoulders and looks at Caro. "You didn't tell Spencer we were coming on this hike, right?"

"*No.*" Caro's shocked. "I haven't seen him in years. I haven't *thought* about him in years."

"That doesn't mean he hasn't been thinking about you." Before Caro can protest, Hope carries on. "Are you with me?" She looks at Caro, then at Ash.

"Yes," Ash says.

"Yes," Caro agrees.

"Okay," Hope says. "Off we go, then. To the lions' den."

11

ASH

FIRES AREN'T ALLOWED IN the Underground, so the men have set up two camping lanterns and dragged over pieces of driftwood to sit on. Ash misses the flicker of a campfire—that always seems to make things cozier. *Here we go*, she thinks. *We're really doing this.*

"Want one?" The guy named Kevin holds up a six-pack of beer. Ash wonders how much they brought, why you'd choose to pack in that unnecessary weight. But the men are all in good shape, so it probably didn't affect them that much. "No thanks," she says, holding up her water bottle. "I'm good."

Hope takes a can. Caro declines. Spencer, Ash notices, also isn't drinking. "So, poker," Hope says, rubbing her hands together. Ash hears a wicked note in Hope's voice. "I should warn you guys, I'm pretty good. What are we playing for? Cash?"

"Sorry to disappoint you." Spencer gestures to a few cans of Pringles. "We're using those as chips."

"Very literal," Hope says. "I like it."

"One of us gets too mean when we're playing for money." Kevin's tone is dry but he doesn't seem to be completely joking. *Who?* Ash wonders. It seems unlikely he'd be sending himself up, and Spencer appears to be a decent human being. So, Tony?

"I'll deal." Tony starts handing out the cards, dropping them onto a striped camp blanket that they've spread out between the lanterns. Ash hasn't played poker since college. She is going to be very, very rusty.

Tony's sleeve slides up and she sees the tattoo again. "What do the numbers of your tattoo mean?" she asks, and then she wishes she hadn't. It's his business, not hers. She always does this—talks too much when she's feeling nervous.

"A date that's important to me," Tony says. "My daughter's birthday."

And even though that's a sweet answer, Ash still feels uneasy about Tony. She's not sure what the difference is between him and his brother, Kevin, who is striking fewer chords of wariness with her. Spencer is by far the most likable of the group, and he's cute and smart. He'd have to be, though, if he'd ever dated Caro.

Ash has always prided herself on being a good judge of character. Lately, though, that's taken a hit. There was the employee she hired who quit within a week and went to work for another florist, who started copying Ash's arrangements. There's the shift in Wade lately, to someone she doesn't completely know.

And lately, Ash feels like she doesn't entirely trust *herself*.

So what does that say? About her, or her ability to judge character? And when did the self-loathing begin? She feels like it's always been lying dormant in her, ready to rear its head when she's feeling unsafe, like middle school and high school, until she can get it to retreat and lie down again. So why has it been back the last couple of years?

"Done," Tony says, putting down the cards. "Let's play."

Ash takes a look at her hand. It's not great; she remembers that much at least. Which is fine. She doesn't care if she wins. Also, she hates Pringles. She gets why Hope wanted to do this, but she still wishes it were the three of them hanging out at their campsite. She wishes Spencer hadn't come over with the invitation. She wishes Caro didn't know him. This makes everything so much more complicated.

"Did you go to high school in St. John?" Tony asks Hope. "You seem familiar."

"No," Hope says. "Juniper City." It's a town near here, Ash knows. But she doesn't know much more than that. Does Hope? And of course Hope wouldn't want to reveal her real identity, but why wouldn't she choose something closer to her actual life?

Hope's still talking like the guys, with a kind of southern Utah accent. Ash finds this fascinating. She knows Hope is a great actress, but she's never seen her invent a part on the spot.

As they take their turns and the sky darkens by degrees, Ash doesn't think Hope's drinking much of her beer—she's pretending with that, too. And it turns out that Hope is good at poker, which shouldn't surprise Ash. But none of them have cards that can beat Tony's. He pulls the pile of Pringles toward him across the camp blanket.

"Don't break the money," Spencer says, joking.

Tony pops a chip into his mouth. "I thought you said you were good," he tells Hope, giving the words a weight that suggests he's trying to make a double entendre. *Ugh.*

"Oh, I'm good," Hope says. Her hair has dried almost as wavy as Ash's, which is a surprise. Ash didn't know they shared that because Hope is always so tidy. Her fingernails, Ash notices as Hope gathers the cards and shuffles them, are clean but short, not a hint of polish, and there's no trace of the eyelash extensions Hope usually wears. "But my cards were bad."

"I've heard *that* one before." Tony still sounds leery. Ash glances over at Caro and wants to laugh. Caro has *no* poker face. She's looking at Tony with an expression that can only be described as unveiled disgust.

"I have an idea." Hope reaches over, takes one of Tony's chips and pops it in her mouth. "Let's make this next round more interesting."

Don't say it don't say it, Ash thinks, but of course Tony does.

"Strip poker?" he asks.

"Even better," Hope says. "*Secret* poker."

"Which is?" Tony asks.

"The person who wins gets to ask anyone in the group one question," Hope says. "And they have to answer it. Honestly."

And now Ash specifically does *not* look at Caro. Because what on earth is happening? Did Caro know this was coming? Ash isn't going to reveal any real secrets in front of these men. But she doesn't want to let on that she's as surprised as the guys. Hope must have a reason for what she's doing.

"Why don't we play truth or dare?" Tony asks.

"Because that's boring," Hope says. "Because we've all done that a million times before." She grins and takes another chip. Tony reaches out to stop her but she's too quick. "And because if *I* win, I promise I'll ask *you* a question."

"You think I might *want* to tell you my secrets?" Tony asks.

"I do," she says.

Ash thinks, *Hope's so good at this*. And is she leaning even further into her southern Utah accent?

"Okay," Tony says. "It's a deal."

"Do you have any more beer?" Hope asks, and Tony nods. "Go grab some," he tells Kevin.

"Do it yourself," Kevin says.

"I'll go." Spencer stands up. "Is it in your tent?"

Tony springs to his feet. "Never mind," he says. "I'll get it."

Kevin stands, too. All three of them end up heading for the tents.

"Interesting," Hope says. "Why did they all feel the need to go? And what do you think Tony has in his tent that he didn't want the others to see?" She snickers.

"What the hell, Hope?" Caro says. "Why would you suggest *secret* poker?" She wrinkles her nose. "Is that even a thing?"

"It is now," Hope says. "And I suggested it because we might find out more about them. Obviously."

"They're not going to tell us anything *real*," Caro says. "Not like this."

"Sometimes what people don't tell you, or how they lie, is just as good," Hope says. "And I promise that none of us will get picked."

"How?" Caro asks.

"Because I'm not going to let any of them win," Hope says.

The men are already heading back in their direction, Tony swinging another six-pack of beer at his side.

"Okay," he says, handing Hope the cans and sitting down in a spot closer to her than before. "Let's go."

Hope takes a can, cracks it open, and hands the pack back to Tony. "Kevin deals this time," she says. "Let's see if you can win if you're not the dealer."

"Fine," Tony says. Kevin shuffles the cards with a practiced hand and deals them in. Ash checks her cards. *I hope I don't have to ask a question or tell a secret*, she thinks. She wants no part of this game, but she's in too deep now.

Ash feels a thread of tension looping and tightening around the group as the game progresses, as if an invisible rope is pulling them in. The sky above hints as to what time of day it is—right now, they're sliding past sunset. "So which high school did you go to in Juniper City?" Tony asks Hope. "Juniper High or Canyon View?"

"Juniper High," Hope says smoothly.

"Nice." Tony crumples a can in his hand and tosses it to the side. Spencer surreptitiously reaches for it and puts it in the trash bag. *Is he too much of a Boy Scout to be real?* Ash wonders. And her heart is beating quickly. *Is Tony onto Hope?*

Caro's mouth has tightened.

"Where did *you* go to high school?" Hope asks. "Red Mountain or St. John High? Are you a Panther or a Rattlesnake?"

Nice, Ash thinks, surprised. Hope really does know her stuff. *So when was she going to let* us *in on this role she'd been planning?*

"A panther," Tony says, grinning at Hope. "So, our high schools are rivals. Think we can overcome that?"

"Time will tell," Hope says, with the perfect amount of slight flirtatiousness and obvious dignity that doesn't piss Tony off—there's no clear rejection—but also doesn't compromise who she is. Hope's so good at this, but Ash hates that she has to do it. That any of them have to deal with guys like this.

Why do the other two put up with him? Ash wonders. They both seem much nicer than Tony. Kevin's his brother, so he's stuck for life, she supposes. But what about Spencer?

"I think," Caro says, putting down her hand, "that I'm going to win now." The others crane their necks to see her cards. "Can anyone beat a straight flush?"

They cannot.

"*Oooh*," Hope says. "You get to ask someone a question. Make it good."

"Okay," Caro says. "Let's see. Spencer." She glances over at her old friend, who spreads out his hands and shrugs as if to say, *Go easy on me.* "What's something I don't know about you from when we were teenagers?"

"Um," he says. "Let me think." He snaps his fingers. "Okay," he says. "I've got it. I stole a CD from the Sound Shop when I was in ninth grade."

Caro is laughing. "Which CD?" she asks. "Was it Fall Out Boy? Weezer?"

Spencer's laughing, too, but Tony's shaking his head. "Come on, man," he says. "Say something that counts."

"It counts," Spencer says. "It's a crime, and I've never told a soul until now."

"That's some weak-ass shit," Tony says. "Say something real." Why is he baiting Spencer? Ash can't quite put her finger on the dynamic between the three.

"Tony," Kevin says.

"It's fine." Spencer's voice is tight. He looks Tony right in the eye, as if daring him to say that he's weak again. Ash is surprised that Spencer is taking the bait, that he's letting Tony get to him. But she also understands. Patterns play out even when you're grown. She's felt herself doing it when she's home with her family, slipping into the role of youngest sibling without wanting to in the least. It can happen with longtime friends, too. Spencer clears his throat. "Caro, when we hung out that summer after your freshman year in college, I was in love with you."

"*There* we go." Tony sits back in satisfaction.

"Oh," Caro says. "Spencer. I didn't know. I thought we were—"

"Really good friends with really good benefits," Spencer says. "I know. I didn't want to mess that up. Don't worry. I'm not anymore. I'm glad you're happy and married and all of that. Seriously." He sounds like he means it. When he grins at Caro, she grins back, and for a second Ash swears she can see the younger versions of them.

"Thanks," Caro says. "It's kind of nice to know, to be honest."

"No problem," Spencer says. "It's kind of nice to say, to be honest."

"Well, *that* was adorable." Hope gathers the cards. "Another round?"

"Absolutely," Tony says.

This time, Hope wins. She looks directly at Tony. "I pick you."

Tony folds his arms.

"Okay." Hope taps her cards against her lips, thinking. Tony watches her with an intensity that makes Ash sit up straight. "What's the thing you want the most in the world?"

Tony leans back and cracks his knuckles. "That's easy," he says. "Money."

"Nope." Hope tone is languid, dangerous. "We're not going to let you get away with that. Not after you put Spencer through the wringer."

Tony shrugs. "It's the truth," he says. "And I *have* money. But who doesn't want more of it?"

"What does money *mean* to you, though?" Hope presses. "Being able to travel? Owning a house? Providing for your family?"

Tony laughs. "I'm already doing all of that," he says. "And that's even with my income cut in half thanks to my shitshow of a divorce."

"Then why do you need more?" Hope presses.

"You can't have too much," Tony says. "Like, you can't be too famous, right?" He holds Hope's gaze for a second, or tries to. This whole time, she hasn't taken off her beanie. This whole time, no one, including Ash and Caro, has been able to *really* see her face.

"I still don't buy it," Hope says.

"You don't have to," Tony says. "Let's go again."

But Hope stands up, stretches into a yawn that she doesn't try to pretend isn't at least partially feigned—the exaggerated nonchalance of it, the way she rises on her tiptoes, how she plays up the length of the inhale and the exhale that follows.

"No." Hope drops her arms and turns away, a smile in her voice. "I think we're done."

12

BEFORE

"WHAT'S THE WORST PART about being famous?" Ash asks Hope. It's a warm summer night in all three places (they've each bragged about their weather, shown the others via their cameras how absolutely gorgeous it is in Santa Monica, Salt Lake City, Portland). Since Hope recently revealed who she *really* is, Ash and Caro are asking her all the questions that have been on their minds in the month since they last met.

They've been chatting for hours. Hope was supposed to go to a party, and she decided to miss it so that she could keep talking to them. This thrills Caro and Ash (Hope Hanover would rather be with them than at a party in LA!). Both Ash and Caro are alone. Wade and the girls are visiting his parents so she can get some work done, because it's wedding season, the absolute worst, and Caro's Dan is on a bikepacking trip with his friends. At some point, Hope said, "Wouldn't it be great if we could keep talking until we fell asleep, like a sleepover, like we did when we were teenagers with our friends?" and they've decided to do exactly that.

Ash is already fighting for her life. They've taken their phones to bed with them, and Ash began to droop the minute she sat down against her headboard, pillows at her back. (Caro and Hope were intrigued to see that Ash has an extremely modern-looking bedroom, not the sort of bohemian flowery vibe they had expected.) "We didn't think this through," Ash says, laughing. She's loopy from the wine she and Hope have been drinking—a white wine from Hope's new line that she sent to Ash and Caro. "We're all going to fall asleep, but then our phones will stay on all night."

"That's fine," Caro says. "What does it matter. Let our batteries die."

"What *are* you drinking, anyway, Caro?" Hope asks. "It looks like antifreeze."

Caro doesn't drink, plus right now she's training for a triathlon. She lifts her glass, which is full of a pale green liquid. "Lime Cucumber Gatorade," she says. "The nectar of the gods."

"Really?" Hope sounds skeptical.

Caro laughs. "When we meet in person, I'll buy you some."

"Famous," Ash reminds them sleepily. "What's the worst part?"

"I think it's exactly what you think it would be," Hope says reflectively. "Losing your privacy. People feeling like you belong to them."

"Have you ever had a stalker?" Caro wants to know.

"I've had a few," Hope says.

"Oh my word." Ash is instantly awake. "You've had *stalkers*? As in, *multiple*? Hope, what can we do?"

"You've reported them, I assume," Caro says.

"Of course," Hope says. "But they do tend to crop up." She shrugs. "It's part of the job, but it also shouldn't be, you know?"

"You say the word, and we will *find* them," Ash says, vehement and wide-eyed. "We will *fight* them. We will take care of it for you."

"I appreciate that very much, Ash," Hope says, smiling. "Now, should we do one last toast before we lose you completely?"

"I'm fine," Ash insists. "I'm *awake*." She opens her eyes wide to prove it and the other two laugh.

"You're sleep-drunk," Hope says.

"I'm *not* drunk," Ash insists. Her eyes are already half-closed again.

"I know," Hope says. "I mean, you're so tired, it's like you're drunk. You work so damn hard, Ash." Love and concern and amusement mingle in her voice. "Thank you for staying up so late to hang out."

"Anytime," Ash says.

Caro raises her empty Gatorade glass. "What should we toast to?"

"Friendship?" Ash says, then cringes, because it sounds so basic, so cheesy. But—

"Perfect," Hope says. "What could be better?"

"To friendship," Caro says.

"And to Agatha Christie," Ash says. "For bringing us together. And, actually, to wine." She lifts her empty glass.

"And to Gatorade," Caro says.

"Now we're getting carried away," Hope says.

We are, they each think. *And it's so nice.*

Hope goes to open a window. Caro gets up to close one. They return. Ash sinks down into her pillows. They keep talking, voices slowing, softening, until, eventually, they fall asleep. Ash is first, Caro second. Hope is last, but not by much. She is not alone for long.

DAY THREE

Thursday

On the chalkboard outside the Sonnet resort main office

MOVIE ....

Indiana Jones and the Last Crusade, 1989, PG-13, directed by Steven Spielberg

FILM FACT...

Keep an eye on the opening sequence! It begins with a shot of a rock formation in Utah that lines up perfectly with the Paramount Pictures logo.

13

PAGE

TELL ME YOU HAVE money without saying a single word.

Buy not one, but *three* $70 sweatshirts without batting an eye.

Pay for yourself—and your friends—to keep the tents, the Airstreams, wherever each person is staying, for two nights in the middle of your stay because it's convenient, even when you've gone off to camp in the Underground and aren't at the resort.

I walk almost silently along the path to where she's staying. The smell of sage is strong and clean. My old running shoes are so worn-in that I can feel the stones underneath my feet.

I'm not going to go full Goldilocks and sleep in anyone's bed, but there are things you can do and things you can learn while the guests are away. If you're careful.

I'm *very* careful.

I glance over my shoulder but there's no one about. Not a soul stirring.

I take a deep breath and lift my hand to the door. I don't love doing this, but I don't hate it either. It is what it is. When you grow up without having any money or power, you take it where you can.

And early morning, right now, is the best time for sneaking in.

I'm not talking when the light is up. I'm talking before that. The time when most of the world thinks it's still the end of the last day, but the animals and I know—it's not anymore.

It's the beginning of a new one.

14

HOPE

THEY'RE UP BEFORE THE men, and they pack quietly and hike out early. It feels like they're getting away with something, sneaking off without saying goodbye. No one says much until they've put some distance between themselves and the men.

"So what do you think?" Caro asks, pulling a granola bar from her pack without missing a beat. She's leading out, her long-legged stride setting the pace. "Did we learn anything last night?"

"Unclear," Ash says.

"I think we did," Hope says. She's a bit out of breath and hoping that the other two don't notice. "Whether any of it's useful, who knows."

"I learned that you can imitate my accent." Caro is always so nonplussed, so stoic and chill about life, but Hope detects an edge of hurt in her voice.

"I wasn't imitating you," Hope says. "I was imitating them."

Caro doesn't respond. Hope can't see the expression on her face. Is Caro offended?

"It was interesting to see you make up a character on the spot." Ash is either oblivious or trying to change the subject. "And you gave those guys your Chastity Bentley name."

"Yeah," Hope says. "I thought I'd keep things consistent." The morning air is cool. She has goose bumps, even though she's wearing a fleece, unlike the other two women, who are getting by with only long-sleeved shirts.

"Makes total sense," Ash says. "We'll have to remember to call you that around them if we see them again."

"I hope we don't," Caro says. "See them again. Except Spencer, of course."

"What did you think of his revelation, Caro?" Ash jogs a few steps to catch up with Caro. "Be honest. Did you sort of know?"

"No," Caro says. "I really didn't."

"I don't like Tony." Ash's brow is furrowed. "Do you think he's dangerous?"

"Potentially," Caro says reflectively. "He definitely has a temper."

"I'm beginning to wonder if we really thought this whole thing through," Ash says.

They all fall silent. And Hope gets it. Even though she's the one who had the idea, there are moments when her confidence that they'll be able to pull it off flags. She's careful to keep those moments from Ash and Caro, though.

"Do you think we'll have campsites near each other again?" Ash asks Caro.

"We'll have to see." Caro glances up, checking the sky. Hope follows suit. Still blue. "I didn't talk to any of them about it."

"We're at campsite twenty-one tonight, right?" Ash asks. "And there are two other sites near us?"

"Right," Caro says. She reaches into her pocket and pulls out a bag of dried fruit. She holds it out to the other two, and they each take a few. They're dried apricots, Hope's favorite. "But let's try not to worry about the guys for now. Let's enjoy the hike. Okay?"

"Okay." Ash crouches down to look at a flower growing in the red dirt. It's cream-colored, three petaled. She shucks her backpack from her shoulders and rummages around for her camera. "Sorry," she says. "I know I'm holding us up."

"Not a problem," Caro says. "We're making good time."

When Ash has taken a picture she likes, she stashes the camera back in her pack and they carry on. The creek is wider and deeper here, and the hiking sticks prove useful.

"So what are your other favorite things about this area?" Ash asks Caro. Then she taps Hope gently on the arm with one of her hiking sticks. "Or maybe I should ask *you*," she says. "Since you're from here and all that. A real local."

"Good thing I knew my high school mascots." Hope researched every aspect of this trip meticulously. If she was going to bring the others into this canyon to disappear with her, she was going to make sure she didn't phone anything in. The stakes are too high. "Of course, Caro's the *real* expert," she says. "I'm the impostor."

"There's a drive called the Devil's Backbone that I love." Caro's voice has loosened, and Hope's relieved. "My dad and I used to do it every fall." She stabs her stick into the creek to maneuver around an algae-slicked boulder. Hope is starting to understand Caro's dad's bowling balls comment—the rocks and cobble under the water *do* knock against your ankles, even with hiking boots, and you can only go so fast in some places in the creek. Still, there's something unfaltering about the way Caro hikes, even when she inevitably slips on a rock or has to adjust to the terrain. Hope watches the muscles move in Caro's back as they walk. "It's this road with sheer drops to either side," Caro is saying. "You can see forever. Into Eden, and into another national park near Lake Powell. There's only room for one car at a time on most of it."

"Is it as terrifying as it sounds?"

"Worse," Caro says. "My dad's old Chevy Blazer had a manual transmission. He taught me to drive it when I turned sixteen, and when he thought I was ready he made me take it on the Devil's Backbone. He said if I could drive stick shift on that road, I could drive anywhere."

"How many times do you think you've driven it since?"

"Who knows," Caro says. She tucks the empty fruit package into her pocket. "At the end of the Devil's Backbone there's this small town with a really great grill. We always stopped there to eat."

"Do you and your dad still do that?" Ash asks.

"Not recently," Caro says. "Maybe I should try." She exhales. "The truth is, he's kind of unpredictable. He might love it. He might hate it. He might not even know where he is and think I'm a stranger kidnapping him and taking him someplace he's never been before."

"That's so hard," Ash says. "I'm sorry, Caro."

"Me too," Hope says.

A cacophony of noise is echoing its way up to them from farther down the canyon. The voices are high, birdlike, excited. *Teenagers*, Hope thinks, and as soon as they round the bend, she sees them: A gaggle of kids in brightly colored clothes with wild hair and skinny limbs packing up gear on one of the natural sandbars. They've clearly been camped there for the night and are getting ready to leave.

"Sorry about all this," says a woman in a T-shirt that says LEAVE NO TRACE as Hope, Ash, and Caro come within range. "We're getting a slow start this morning."

"Looks like fun," Ash says. A few teenagers shriek with glee as one of their tents disintegrates into a pile of poles and nylon.

"That's one word for it," the woman says. A harried-looking man lets out a piercing whistle. The teenagers cover their ears and turn in his direction. "Sorry about that, too."

"No worries," Caro says. "Good luck."

"Thanks."

The teens wave at the women as they pass the campsite, and several of them call out, "Good morning!" Ash, Caro, and Hope call and wave back.

"Everyone in southern Utah is so friendly," Ash says. "Has it always been this way?"

"I think so." Caro's glancing back at the group with fondness in her eyes. "Remember being that age?"

"I was never that age," Ash says. Then she grins. "Kidding," she says. "I'm still that age."

"I think we all are in some way," Caro says.

Hope doesn't know if she agrees. She doesn't know how old she feels. Her industry will screw you up in that regard in every single way. Other people always picking at her body, commenting on it, saying whether they'd want to sleep with it or not, wanting it to look like this, dressing it like that.

And all the procedures. She hasn't done nearly as much as most—if she starts to look like everyone else, she won't look like anyone. She's smart enough to know that, and she's lucky that she grew up with parents who emphasized exercise because you loved it, not because it could make you thin. But in adulthood she's had to exercise to look a *specific* way, to have a certain shape, and sometimes that shape changes for different roles. She's always being plucked and highlighted and trimmed and tanned and untanned and freckled and de-freckled, whatever the role requires. There are the steam rooms and saunas and workouts and injections and lasers and facials, and yes, she can see how it might sound amazing, but it leaves her with the feeling that her body is a thing meant to be maintained, not enjoyed. There was the freezing of her eggs before she turned thirty. She did three rounds, and it was no joke. But Hope's nothing if not prepared, and what if she actually met the right person too late?

Well.

Hope shivers as she looks at the EDEN bracelet on her wrist. She wonders which of the favorite colors—pink, orange, purple—is supposed to be hers.

Her friends don't know her as well as they think they do.

Hope *wants* people to know her. But she can't ever seem to let them in. Or tell them the full truth. She's gotten so very, very good at acting the parts. Who is she, for example, right now? This very second?

She doesn't know. And if she doesn't know, then—

No one does.

15

CARO

CARO CAN'T SLEEP.

Spencer, Tony, and Kevin are camping near them again tonight, but the two groups aren't alone anymore. A fit older couple who look to be in their mid to late sixties have the campsite between Spencer's group and Caro's. The couple (Ed and Jean, from New Mexico) were friendly but have kept to themselves other than initial introductions and hellos. Which is perfect, Caro thinks. Something seems to have eased up with the arrival of Ed and Jean. They all exchanged pleasantries, but no one offered to hang out again tonight. Which is good, because Caro has enough on her mind. Too much.

Caro's tried and tried, but she keeps going back to what happened at the hospital six weeks ago. Her brain won't let up. Won't leave it alone. It's like when her dog Howie has a hot spot on his leg—an inflamed, infected place he can't seem to stop worrying at, making it worse and worse.

Although how could this be worse?

It could be, she reminds herself. *The baby could have died as well.* She's seen the baby in the neighborhood, worn by her dad in a front carrier on their walks. The father often has a protective hand on the baby's head when Caro sees him. His shoulders are hunched. It seems to her there is a heaviness in his steps. He and the baby are so clearly alone. Once, she saw him in their neighborhood grocery store and they made eye contact. He was holding a basket that held a single loaf of bread. Somehow Caro registered this before they turned away from each other. At the time, she'd felt grateful that they'd both had the same reaction. And that he wasn't going to blame her somehow, that he didn't yell at her or take what happened out on her. (In no way has anyone during the ensuing wrongful death suit insinuated that she, the anesthesiologist, did anything wrong in the delivery.) Still, she had asked for some time off.

"I understand," her supervisor had said. She was—is—one of the only people who knows everything that Caro's going through, that it's not only the loss of the patient and caring for her dad that's taking a toll. "Take a leave. We'll always want you back, whenever you're ready."

Caro's beginning to think she will never be ready. She can feel that baby's head against her hand.

Careful not to wake the others, she climbs out of her sleeping bag and onto the sandbar. The sound of the water masks any noise she makes. Caro wants a look at the stars dotting the thin, midnight-blue ribbon of night sky above her. She casts a nervous look over at the men's tents, but they've quieted for the night. She glances at her watch. It's a few minutes past eleven p.m.

Another step and her foot hits water. The sandbar is not as large as she remembered. She switches on her flashlight and catches her breath in alarm.

The river. Something is happening.

The water is swelling around her ankles. It has begun to *move*, the current intensifying by the moment. It was pristine and clear before but has now gone muddy. Caro watches for a moment, transfixed. The river is rising before her eyes, like when she looks up and sees clouds moving so quickly that she can track their progress across the sky.

It's a flash flood.

"*HELP!*" Caro shouts, running back toward her friends, stumbling on the sandbar. She figures it's the word most likely to wake people, to get them moving. "*HELP!*"

Sure enough, she sees Ash or Hope sitting up in her sleeping bag. On her way to them she keeps yelling, she shakes the tent that she thinks is Spencer's, she cuts back over and shakes Ed and Jean's tent on her way to Ash and Hope. "Flash flood's coming," she hollers. *"Get out!"* In the light from her flashlight she sees that someone at their site is now standing, shouting back at her. "What's wrong?" Ash calls out.

"Flash flood!" Caro shrieks. "We have to get up high!" *There is no time no time no time*, she can feel it in her bones. She grabs the pack with the climbing gear. *"Now!"*

"Did you warn the others?" Ash already has her shoes on.

"I tried!"

They glance over. Ed has come out of the tent, and someone's emerging from the men's campsite, too.

"Shit," Ash says. "Where's Hope?"

"Oh no," Caro says, because Ash is right, Hope's not here, and then she sees her, illuminated in the flash of someone else's headlamp, making her way over the already swollen river from the men's camp to theirs.

What the hell? Caro wonders for a split second, but there is no time for this.

"Okay," she says. "Ash. Turn your headlamp on. Hope, you too. Look at the river." They do, all three of them swinging their lights to the water.

It's swallowing the sandbar.

Caro points at where the river is still narrowest, and at the bench up higher. "Okay," she says, a tremor in her voice. "We're going to cross the river, and then we're going to climb."

"Do we have time?" Ash asks, but Caro has made the call; she has to, she is the one who knows this place. "Try to cross if you can!" she shouts. Can Ed and Jean or Spencer and his friends hear her across the rising roar of the river?

Ash is turning back to make sure. Caro seizes her by the arm. "We have to *go*," she says. *"Now.* I'll go first. We're going to hold hands."

They do what she tells them. "Do *not* let go," Caro says, but is that even the right advice? Will they drag each other under? She plunges into the water. The cobble underneath is uneven and they all struggle to stay upright. The water is up to their thighs. Caro glances back, sees the men gathering things, the couple trying to pack up their tent.

"Leave it all!" she screams. *"There's no time!"*

Two of the men plunge into the water, trying to cross, too. She sees their figures, she can't tell which is which, but then she notices that Spencer has stayed behind the other men. He's trying to get Ed and Jean to come with them. Caro is sick. The water has gone from thigh-high to waist-high in a matter of seconds.

This is bad.

"Get out of the creek as fast as you can," she says, her voice tight. Hope catches her eye in the briefest of glances. The walls are sheer. If they don't get to the bench in time...

A deep, sturdy, steady, *whoosh* from up the canyon.

It's coming for us.

"Up now," Caro shouts, and, crashing into each other, stumbling, clinging hands, they push for the side of the canyon.

Something bumps Caro's leg from behind, almost taking her down. The water is filled with small debris—pine needles, pine cones, small plants—and large logs and branches. An enormous branch grazes Caro's leg before she can move in time, and it tears a gash along her thigh. After an initial sharp burst of pain she feels nothing.

Caro doesn't look to see what's happening on the other side of the river with the men, with Ed and Jean. *Are those screams she hears farther down the canyon?* Caro's heart sinks. *No.* She has to be imagining things. There is no way she can hear anything that far away above the rush of the water and of the blood in her ears and the shouts of those around her. *The college students, the ones who needed help with the rope. They made it out, right? The high school kids they passed in the canyon—they're going to be fine, aren't they?*

"Up!" she screams. *"Now now now!"*

Caro grabs at any small indentation she can find in the rocks. Her fingernails break as she pulls her weight up, but she makes it to the rocky ledge and lies on her stomach, reaching down. She grabs Hope, pulls her up on the bench. Hope reaches down to help Caro haul Ash up; they're all three out of the water, safe for a very short moment.

"Oh my god," Hope says.

"We should keep climbing, right?" Ash asks. They're all breathing hard and fast. Caro looks down at the gash in her thigh and the blood streaming from it. No time to deal with that now. *"Yes,"* she says. "As high as we can get before—"

The rest of what she says is drowned out by a roar.

"Oh my god," Hope says again.

"Keep climbing," Caro calls out, her voice a ragged tear of fear. *"Go."*

But it is impossible not to look.

The river bellows from the canyon, swollen and fast, carrying pieces of trees and debris like the flotsam of a shipwreck. The water seems *alive*, bearing down on anything in its path with terrible, devastating purpose. Something bobs along in the current that is not a piece of nature—a waterlogged sail, something inside of it. It is there and then gone, but not before Caro thinks, *A tent*.

"Can you see Spencer anywhere?" Ash asks. "The guys? Ed and Jean?"

"They might have gotten to higher ground," Caro says. "Like we have to do. *Now*."

There's another bench higher up along the cliff wall, but it is a scramble along the thinnest of rocky ridges, where knotty juniper trees tethered into dirt over the sandstone hold the ground in place, slippery and loose. Caro grabs on to anything she can reach: sagebrush, bushes prickled with thorns. Her hands are cut through and bleeding. It is rock climbing with no rocks, bouldering with no boulders, the river roaring, rising.

"Shit," Ash says as the ground beneath her gives way, and she slips, crashing into Caro, knocking her off-kilter. For several terrifying, breath-gone seconds Caro slides, slides, slides, until a scraggly juniper arrests her fall, slamming into her ribs. She clings to the trunk with both hands.

"Caro!" Ash calls out. *"Caro!"*

It wasn't Ash's fault, of course, no one can predict exactly where the terrain is loose, but Caro can't reply. She has to hold on. She glances up and sees that Ash is pulling the extra climbing rope from her pack. She loops it around another small, wiry tree and climbs down to help. When Ash reaches Caro, Caro wraps her hands around Ash's, which are also bloody and torn. There are tears in Caro's eyes. It was so brave of Ash to do this, but it's not going to work.

"I don't know that it can hold both of us," she says, nodding to the tree. "I'm going to let go. You climb up."

Ash looks at Caro, a question in her eyes.

"I'll be fine," Caro says.

And then—

she lets go.

16

ASH

CARO LET GO OF the rope. She's falling.

She's scrabbling with her arms and legs, trying to catch herself, but she's sliding; she can't find any purchase. Caro's tumbling, almost to the bench, and if the bench doesn't catch her—

Ash realizes that she is screaming.

Hope grabs on to Caro, slowing her fall, and the two of them tumble, they slide, they hit the lower bench—

and Caro stops, caught by the lip at the edge—

but Hope

oh, God, Hope

is gone.

DAY FOUR

Friday

On the chalkboard outside the Sonnet resort main office

MOVIE ....

Gravity, 2013, PG-13, directed by Alfonso Cuarón

FILM FACT ....

The final scene of this Academy Award–winning movie was filmed near Sonnet. It is the only scene in the film that did not require a green screen.

17

CARO

THE AIR IS FULL of the smells of earth and stone, of mud and broken trees, of things torn up and changed forever. It is light enough that Caro can now make out Ash's eyes, the pallor of her skin. It's cold, but the rain has stopped. The sky—at least, the part of it that Caro can see—is lightening.

We made it through the night.

The two of us, anyway.

Caro thinks with a deep, gut-wrenching ache of Hope. Of Spencer, his friends, of Ed and Jean. The college students. The high school kids and their leaders. Of whoever else might have been in the canyon.

But mostly of Hope.

Caro and Ash had huddled together on a small ledge of rock. Water came down from the plateau there, too, but it didn't take them. All night long they heard it sluicing around them as it descended from the plateau; they heard the roar of the river below. Caro doesn't think either she or Ash slept. For a time, they called for Hope, they tried to talk, to figure out how they're going to get out when morning came, and then they quieted down and held on.

And all the time, Caro also thought of Dan.

She might make it back to him.

I've been greedy to want so much. I've been weak to let things get me down. I should only want Dan and the life I already have. That should be enough. That is enough. Let me get back to it. Please. Please.

Is she praying? Caro lets out a breath that it feels like she's been holding in all night, but her chest is still tight.

The college kids down the canyon, the tent they saw go by, the cheerful teens and their leaders, the guys on the other side of the river, especially Spencer, Ed and Jean—Hope again—

Stop.

It doesn't do any good to fall apart.

Caro meets Ash's eyes and she knows they are both thinking the same thing. *Hope is gone. What now?*

As the sky lightens by degrees, Caro sees that they're surrounded by the debris from the plateau and the tiny ravines that thread to the canyon, and she also sees a place where a pile of something has been deposited: rocks and earth and a splintered small tree, and who knows what else. She notices a spot where the bench of earth they're huddled on has come away farther down, and she bites her lip. A few feet more, and they might have gone over, too.

"Hey," Ash says. "Do you hear that?"

Caro does. Her heart skips a beat. "I think someone's coming."

"Who do you think it is?" Ash asks, and Caro chooses the best possible answer, the one she wants the most. "A SAR team," she says. "Search and rescue." It could also be other hikers, but the calls she hears don't sound like people in distress.

"HELP!" Ash's voice is loud and ragged. It echoes around the sandstone walls.

"Let's both yell on three," Caro says, because if they combine their voices, there's more of a chance, isn't there? "One, two...*HELP!!*"

But she's the only one who screams this time. She looks over at Ash, who is staring at the tangle of debris.

"There's something here." Ash's voice is shaky.

"What is it?" Caro asks, a tiny flare of exasperation rising up in her because what could be more important than getting rescued?

"I think," Ash says, her voice very small, "it's someone."

At first the words don't register, but then, horribly, they do. Caro's gut sinks. She thinks of Hope, though how would Hope have gotten here from where she was, and then she realizes it might be someone else, someone trapped up high in the flood? Someone who fell?

Ash has made the discovery, but it's Caro who moves closer, of course; Caro is a doctor, and she will know what Ash has found. And now she sees it, too. A jangle of what she took to be branches that could be bones, splinter-white and pink-mudded, held together by what used to be…clothes? Caro sees a strip of blue-plaid fabric. And there, in a swirl of debris behind it, a patch of bright yellow plastic. *A dry bag*, she thinks. Another hiker, but not a recent one.

"Okay," Caro says. "It's okay. This is older. It must have washed out from one of the side canyons or crevices above us."

"It's *okay*?" Ash is incredulous. "It's not okay! Hope is lost, we're stuck in a canyon, and so what if it's been around for a while? This is…this is—"

Ash can't seem to bring herself to say it. She wraps her bright-orange-sweatshirted arms around herself.

"A body," Caro says gently. "It's a body."

18

SOMETHING IS STIRRING. MY *bones? my soul?—begin to gather themselves and coalesce.*

How long have I been here?

I don't know.

Will I wake up?

Yes.

I think I will.

19

PAGE

"THEY'VE GOT SOMEONE."

A radio crackles near me, and I push closer to try to hear more. The air is electric with snapping, charged urgency. The search and rescue team, with their bright yellow jackets and orange helmets, their cables and carabiners and gurneys, is on the ground.

"How many?" someone asks. Everyone—the SAR team, the EMTs who have come in to assist at the rescue site—are like tightly coiled springs, ready for action.

The people who are trained for this are here. They're going to do what they can, but it won't be enough for some.

There's no way everyone survived the Underground last night.

"Two women, one man," the SAR leader calls out to the EMTs. "A possible spinal injury. That's all I know."

The parking lot at the end of the Underground has been turned into a triage site. A bright red SAR operations tent takes up part of the lot, where the SAR team leader, a woman with a radio, is coordinating the rescue efforts. I've made my way through the barriers, acting like I belong here, to find out what I can before they inevitably kick me out. Eden National Park ambulances and ranger trucks fill most of the lot. On the plateau near us, helicopters churn into the air to get visuals on the canyon.

101

Rangers stand sentry at the parking lot, turning people away. I made it just in time.

Thunder cracks the heavens.

There's another storm on the way. From this vantage point, I can see the livid, still-weighted sky north of us, the gray-blue slant of heavy rain coming down on the plateau that might shear its way toward us, causing another flood.

The window to get people out of the canyon is closing.

Unlike in the Underground, the scope of the sky up here is infinite, the world laid bare and to waste beneath the heavens. The air smells the way it did last night, like electricity, and in the distance jagged bolts of lightning zigzag down.

"They're coming in!" one of the EMTs calls out, and everyone swarms into motion, readying their equipment, running toward the figures in bright yellow making their way up the slope, carrying gurneys between them. I catch my breath.

"We've got three, all alive," one of the SAR team shouts, and then the group is upon us, heading for one of the ambulances, carrying three figures on their rescue gurneys. "Holy shit," someone says, "they're in *bags*," and it's true, all three people are in plastic bags and are strapped to their gurneys with heavy black straps. "That's okay," someone near me says. "That's to stabilize them," and then I see someone shoving through the crowd toward a gurney. The ambulance is already wailing its siren, preparing to move. I follow in the person's wake. I *have* to see who they've found.

The SAR team hands off a gurney to a group of EMTs. When the SAR team turns away, I see that their faces are haggard, their eyes bright, adrenaline racing through them in a way that they're trained to manage. There's not a lot of work harder than this—technical climbing into a canyon to retrieve someone, making sure you don't accidentally kill yourself or one of your teammates on the rescue mission. Time is a factor, terrain a factor, weather a factor—

"Hey," I say, surprised. "Joe?" We went to high school together.

"Page," says the man nearest me. Lightning snakes the sky behind him. "You have someone missing?"

"Sonnet does," I say. "Eight people."

"Damn," he says, but someone's already calling to him. He has to go.

"Good luck," I say, and he nods, already breaking into a jog. Lightning darts down again. If I stay the hell out of the way and keep my head down, maybe I can learn more. I glance back at the barrier where the rangers are trying to manage the crowd. It's increased even in the last couple of minutes. There are families, frantic, who started driving the minute they heard about the flood, locals who have come to help but haven't been given tasks yet. There are rubberneckers, and yes—there it is—a local news truck. They're behind. The situation in the canyon is already all over social media.

Someone grabs my arm. I turn, and it's one of the people they brought out from the canyon, his face battered and bruised, eyes bloodshot, holding on to me for all he's worth from his stretcher. The EMTs carrying it pull up short, turning to look at me.

The man holding my sleeve is a twentysomething guy I don't recognize, not one of our guests, and he is staring at me in absolute panic. "Gone," he says. "They're all *gone*."

"Get back!" one of the EMTs says, pushing my arm from the man's grip, but not before I see that his pupils are dilated and his face battered. From what? Did he fall? Did the flood in the canyon do this to him, or was it something and someone else?

"Wait," the man says, pointing. "Can she come with me?"

I turn around. Look behind me.

He's talking to me.

"Are you his wife?" an EMT asks me. "Sister?"

"No," I say.

"Family member of any kind?"

I shake my head, my eyes still locked on the man's. Why did he pick me? Do I remind him of someone he knows? Is it just because I'm here?

"Then you have to stay behind," the EMT says. The ambulance doors are open, waiting.

"It's okay," I tell the guy, holding his gaze as they lift him inside, as I get elbowed away. "You'll be okay."

This is a lie. He will not ever be fully okay again.

"We've got more coming in!" someone shouts. Radios crackle to life, and in the distance, another helicopter is chopping our way.

The rescue team lifts the man smoothly into the ambulance. I'm briefly confronted with the back of the vehicle. It's emblazoned with a blue-and-black symbol of the park, the words SEARCH AND RESCUE, and a red cross. They close the doors.

"Hey!" someone shouts behind me. "You!"

I break into a run. I'm almost out of time.

20

CARO

THEY SPILL OUT OF the helicopter, surrounded by the SAR team, who are helping Caro along. Thanks to the gash on her leg, she's moving slower than Ash. "Our friend is missing," Caro's telling everyone, anyone who will listen. "She's still in the canyon." She knows they've radioed it in; she and Ash talked about Hope and the men and Ed and Jean, the college students and the high school kids, for the entire helicopter ride. The SAR team has promised they're relaying the information. But it feels like she and Ash have to keep talking about Hope until they actually see her back, in front of them, safe and sound.

Caro knows how unlikely this is. She saw the fall. Hope probably drowned in the river or broke on the rocks below. But until they have proof of her death, Caro is going to assume that Hope is alive.

"She's injured," one of the SAR team tells the EMT who's ready to help Caro to the ambulance, but Caro waves it off. "I'm a doctor," she says. "It's largely superficial." Once onboard the helicopter, she'd used their equipment to disinfect and wrap her leg. As she climbs inside the ambulance, Caro takes one last glance back at the body she and Ash found in the debris, now zipped up into one of the SAR team's bags.

What was her name? How long had she been in the canyon?

Because Caro's pretty sure it's a woman.

She could tell from the way they handled the body and from her own knowledge and experience that those weather-worn bones would be both light as driftwood and heavier than you'd think. Caro's no forensic pathologist, but she gave Ash her best guesses about the body as they waited to be rescued. *I think whoever it is must have fallen, a long time ago.* The skull had been cracked…

Hope.

Once Caro's inside the ambulance, the EMTs begin to close the doors. As they do, Caro catches a glimpse of one of the young women who works at the resort. She's running toward their ambulance, someone shouting at and chasing after her. "Wait," Caro says. She stops the door before it can shut entirely, and one of the EMTs mutters at her. She's annoyed at herself on their behalf—she's being the absolute *worst* patient. "Page?" she asks, hoping she has the right name, and the girl nods. "Our friend is missing, in the Underground," Caro says. "She disappeared. We saw her fall in the canyon."

"There's a group of guys who were staying at Sonnet who were in the Underground, too," Ash says, appearing over Caro's shoulder. "Have you heard anything about them?"

Page shakes her head.

"We have to *go*," the EMT says, attempting to pull the doors closed. The driver turns on the siren, and Page shouts, trying to be heard. "Wait," she calls out. "*Wait.* I heard they brought in a body with you?"

Caro nods.

"Who is it?" Page asks.

"We don't know," Caro begins, but before she can add, *It's not recent, it's okay*, the EMT has pulled the doors shut, Page's face vanishing behind them.

Caro submits to the vitals check, the examination of her leg and its dressing. She asks, "Are we going to the regional hospital?" After the EMT nods, she tips her head back and closes her eyes, but not to rest. *Who does she still know at the St. John Regional Hospital from when her dad worked there?* And does she know anyone in search and rescue anywhere? How can she help Hope?

This wasn't how they were supposed to disappear.

"I'm fine," Ash keeps saying, over and over, to the EMT checking on her. She's sitting on the bench across from Caro, and Caro feels a surge of love and relief that Ash is okay. The EMTs hand them both the fuzzy hospital socks Caro is so familiar with from work. She's been in many an operating room where the patients are wearing those blue and yellow slippers with their white plastic tread. Before long, the EMTs have finished with their vital checks and have determined that they are, by and large, in good shape. Caro will definitely need stitches in her leg; Ash might need sutures on her face; they both have bruising.

"We've got to call our families," Ash says, her long blond hair wild. Nearly all of it has escaped from its braid. "We have to let them know we're okay."

But, Caro realizes—and she wonders if Ash does, too—*our families* aren't *worried*. If they've followed Hope's rules, their families don't know they're anywhere *near* this disaster.

"They'll help you get in touch with them at the hospital," says one of the EMTs, a weathered woman who looks to be in her fifties with short gray hair. "Don't worry one bit."

"What about the people missing?" Ash asks. "We have a friend—" Her voice breaks.

"You can ask about them at the hospital, too," the woman says. "Hopefully they've already been rescued, or they'll be there soon." Her voice is even, and she pats Ash's knee. "You two are lucky. You're going to be fine."

Fine, fine, fine. The word echoes in Caro's exhausted brain. It makes her think of the fine, slender bones in the canyon, of the empty eye sockets looking back at her. She feels as if something began stirring the moment they came near the bones, as if there's the slightest presence haunting her now.

Which means she's exhausted. Caro doesn't believe in ghosts.

But still, the question hovers over her.

Who did we find?

21

BEFORE

ASH IS PRETTY SURE that her husband thinks she's having an affair.

It's golden hour, and she's out in her office in the flower barn. She's hoping that Wade won't get it into his mind to come out and see what she's up to. (Why would he? She often works late, and he hasn't come out to the barn in ages. She's being paranoid.) She made dinner, fed everyone, and cleaned up. The girls are out with friends. Wade is watching a basketball game on TV.

The flower barn is a converted carriage house down the driveway from the main house. When Ash had had the idea to resurrect the gardens and sell flowers as a side business, Wade had wanted to help her, was proud of her fledgling idea. He spent his spare hours doing thankless tasks like hauling the old frames and tools that couldn't be salvaged to the dump, helping her build a greenhouse, going over flower options with her, and sanding and painting the splintery wood of the barn. They'd spent hours out here together working, chatting or in companionable silence, the baby monitor propped up on a metal stool so they could listen to the girls. They'd eaten meals out here. Made love on the old sofa they'd brought out to the barn. One memorable night they'd fallen asleep there, Ash tucked up against his chest, both so exhausted that neither of them had moved all night long. They'd only been awakened when baby Claire's loud *squawk* of indignation crackled through the baby monitor.

Ash opens the camera on her phone so she can get a sneak peek at what she'll look like on the call. She's left the curtains open so that the soft evening light can stream in. She does not look as tired as she feels, thank goodness. Her heart lifts, which feels so wonderful it scares her.

Ash is pretty sure that she needs this more than the other two.

It's her fifth conversation with Hope and Caro, and she's been looking forward to it since the moment the last one ended. When she gets their texts between book club meetings, she wants to drop everything. Sometimes she does, turning her back on a tableful of flowers or an Excel spreadsheet or her own children to read what Caro or Hope have said. Sometimes, she laughs out loud.

She's in love, that's for certain. Or infatuation. And she knows it can't last, but she's damned if she's not going to get everything she possibly can out of it while it does.

Because, really. How long can this actually go on? How long is she going to be in a book club—how long is she going to be *friends*—with these extraordinary women? Carolina, who is an outright doctor and who is so cool, calm, and collected she makes Ash feel that way, too? Like she responds to Caro, sees a way to be that she might dare to try on? Caro, who is effortlessly lovely and loved, her doting husband always wandering through the background of her screen, who is such a good person that she helps people every day *for her job?* Ash does some nice things, it's true, like making up the leftover flowers into bouquets for women's shelters and old folks' homes, but her business itself is very much for gain. Sometimes she feels like all she thinks about is profit margins and seedlings and color palettes for LikeMe wedding season posts.

And, of course, there is the huge revelation that happened along the way: Their sparkling, winsome, wicked, hilarious, wise friend is actually *Hope Hanover*, the movie star.

Ash has kept Caro's and Hope's existence from Wade and the girls.

Well, that's not exactly true. They know she's in a virtual book club, but they don't ask questions about it. Mostly they want to know what's for dinner or when she'll be done with work or if she knows where the car keys are or if she can make up a bouquet for one of the hygienists at the practice who recently lost their mother...

Ash wants this time. This time with her friends each month. Is that too much to ask?

Yes, she knows. *It is.* She already has her flowers, after all. That's what everyone says. "I love the way you've made this happen for yourself," a woman interviewing Ash told her admiringly. "I love that Wade lets you do this," his mother always says when the subject of Three Sisters Flowers comes up. "It's such a lovely hobby." *This "lovely hobby" paid off Wade's student loans!* Ash wants to scream. *It makes our lives possible as much as his job does!* When she'd been interviewed for a local magazine, they'd put her on the cover with her arms folded and her head tipped to the side, standing in front of a table full of flowers and wearing a patterned apron. FLOWER CHILD, the headline ran, OR BOSS BABE? Ash still finds herself cringing at the thought of it.

The girls, of course, do not think she is a boss babe. They think she is their mom, and that's great with Ash because that's what she is. She does, however, wish now and then that they thought she was a *tiny* bit cool for doing what she's done.

Would the girls even think *Hope* was cool? Or would they think that she wasn't relevant? She's not an influencer, at least not the way they seem to admire, and she's not in her twenties.

Ash looks at her computer. It's time. And within seconds there they are, on-screen. Caro, her lean, intelligent face and kind eyes. Hope, grinning away. That devilish tilt to one side of her mouth when she smiles is so appealing it makes Ash's heart hurt. For a minute, there's a flicker, as if another screen is about to pop up, but it's gone before Ash can blink.

Ash is trying to figure out where Hope is today from her background— is she in her California home in Santa Monica, a gorgeous old Spanish revival that, yes, Ash googled after catching glimpses of it in the background of their calls? Or is she somewhere else? Could she be *on location*?

"Wow," Hope says, at the same moment that Caro says, *"Ohhh,"* in a reverent tone that Ash hasn't heard her use before. It takes Ash a minute to realize that they're both staring at her—not her, actually, but *her* background, what's behind her. Ash turns to take it in. The light is streaming gold through the window and perfectly illuminating the rows of Nicholas dahlias she'd cut earlier.

"Is that the flower barn?" Caro asks.

"It is." Ash's heart leaps.

"It is absolutely dreamy," Hope says.

"You must be so proud," Caro says, at the same time Hope says, "You must be exhausted."

"*Thank* you," Ash says, because that is the truth of it, plain and simple. She *is* proud of what she's made. She *is* exhausted. "I love it, and at the same time I want to set it all on fire." The moment the words are out of her mouth she wishes them back, but she's shocked to see that her friends are nodding vigorously. "Amen," Hope says, and Caro says, "Ditto."

For the first time in years, Ash is seen. And more than that—she's *understood.*

22

BEFORE

Hi!

Its Page.

I thought that I should rite you a letter. How are you? How is colege?

My school is bad not good because Brad Wilton is still mean and most of the boys are mean to most of the girls but Brad Wilton is espeshuly mean to me. Gram says that is becusase he likes me but shes wrong. He is the kind of mean that is only mean.

I miss you. I wish you didn't leave. Everyone goes. First mom and dad. Now you but I know colege is good and I would like to go someday too. I wish there were a colege in Spring Creek.

I love you. Please rite to me. I love you. I miss you.

Page

23

ASH

A SWARM OF GUESTS FILLS the reception area in the main Sonnet tent, but they part like the Red Sea when Ash and Caro enter. Ash brings her hand to the bandages on her face, self-conscious of them and of her dirty clothes. At the hospital she'd washed up and combed her hair with the cheap plastic comb that a nurse brought her, but she knows that she and Caro still look rough. The Lyft driver had looked askance at them when they'd climbed in the car at the hospital, clearly wondering what was going on.

People might not know that we were trapped in the canyon or that our friend is missing, Ash thinks, *but it's obvious we've been through* something. A teenage boy who'd been complaining loudly shuts up and steps back.

"Come with me," Page says before either Ash or Caro can speak. She nods at the other staff who are manning the reception desk: Gareth and a kid whose name tag reads MAL. "I'll be back as soon as I can. Try to get in touch with Colby again."

Page leads them out the back door and into another large white canvas tent. *This must be the staff tent,* Ash thinks, noting the bulletin board with photos and announcements tacked to it, the long counter holding a microwave and coffee maker, the tables dotting the room with chairs surrounding them. One of the tables has playing cards scattered across it, as if the players were interrupted mid-game. Page gestures to two squashy-looking couches facing each other across a low coffee table piled with brochures and magazines. "Please, sit down," she says. "We'd have come to get you from the hospital if you'd called. I'm so sorry." The wild-eyed girl from the rescue site is gone, and she's back to the composed resort employee. Or she's trying to be. There's a worried look about her that tugs at Ash's heart.

"It seemed more efficient to get ourselves here," Ash says. "You must have your hands full."

Caro has no time for small talk. "Have you heard anything about our friend?" She doesn't say Hope's name, real or fake. Once word gets out that Hope Hanover is missing, it's going to be even more of a zoo than it already is. They talked about what to do regarding Hope's identity when they were at the hospital, but so far they haven't been able to figure out the best course of action.

"No," Page says. "I'm sorry. Are you in contact with the police?"

"Yes," Caro says. "We spoke to an officer at the hospital. But if you hear anything, we want to know. In case you find out anything first."

"Of course," Page says, and Ash thinks, *She's a kid. How old is she, twenty?*

"We need the key to our friend's trailer," Ash says. "It's number 18." She feels something kicking in, her boss babe. Or her mama bear. They *have* to figure this out. They *have* to get in touch with their families and they *have* to find Hope. The rest they can deal with later. "We put our phones in there for safekeeping during the hike, since the tents don't lock. We need to get in touch with our families."

"Oh," Page says. "I'm sure you can use our phones to call out. I'm not sure about letting you into someone else's—"

"She came with us," Ash says. "She's *missing*." Her tone brooks no argument. Caro gives Ash a sideways glance. Caro hasn't fully seen this side of her before, Ash knows. She tries to keep it hidden, to make things comfortable for other people, to keep them *liking* her. But right now, she can't help herself.

"Let me try to get in touch with Colby, our manager, again," Page says.

"I don't—" Ash says, but Caro puts a hand on her arm. "Thank you," Caro says, and Ash, until this moment so electrically charged, so tightly wound, sags back briefly in the chair, exhaustion coming over her. She's thinking of her kids, of how she and Hope and Caro never should have come here in the first place; she's thinking of *Hope*, who is who knows where going through who knows what, or, worst-case scenario, not going through anything, because—

Because they've lost her.

Because she's dead, or gone.

24

CARO

CARO CAN'T STAY STILL. While Page holds the phone to her ear and Ash puts her head in her hands, waiting, Caro paces the room, desperate for any distraction. Her gaze lands on a bulletin board, and she walks over to look at it. There are the usual things tacked to the board—announcements, a reminder about the holiday schedule for the Fourth of July, a copy of the notice that is framed in the reception area of the main tent—WE ARE ON PAIUTE AND PUEBLO LANDS—and there, something else. Caro leans closer. A few photographs are tacked to the board. They seem to be pictures of staff doing different things—here in this room celebrating, out on a hike together among orange-red rocks—and then another shot, printed from a computer. It looks like—

A picture of Hope?

Caro leans closer. It looks like Hope, but younger. She can't be sure—

"Caro?" Ash says, and before she can think about what she's doing, Caro swiftly tugs the photo down and sticks it into the pocket of her absolutely filthy hiking pants.

"Have you been able to reach Colby?" she asks Page.

"No," Page says. Ash stands up from the couch and Caro folds her arms, but before either of them can do anything, Page comes to a decision. "Okay," she says. "I'll let you in."

———

"This breaks my heart," Ash says as they stand on the threshold of Hope's trailer. It's furnished much like the tents—striped wool rug, king-sized bed, leather sling chair, small sofa, two end tables, and a kitchenette (sink, microwave, mini fridge). Caro is immediately struck by how tidy Hope is—everything is hung or folded or placed neatly, her luggage zipped up and standing in a corner. Even the dishtowel has been threaded carefully through the chrome hand towel holder affixed to the cabinet.

"Has housekeeping been in here?" Ash asks.

"I don't know, actually," Page says. "I can check."

"What about the police?" Caro asks.

Page seems unsurprised by the question. "Not as far as I know," she says. "But I can check on that, too." She seems to have made up her mind to help them. Caro isn't sure why. Has Page figured out who Hope is? Or is it a general voyeuristic interest about a guest who's missing, that age-old desire to be part of something instead of on the edges?

"Thanks." Ash holds out her hand and says, "I'll take the key." Caro is fascinated by this Ash—the one on the screen and in texts and in person up until the flood was so cheery and funny and breezy. This one is like a heat-guided missile, honed-in and single-purposed. Caro has had only glimpses of her before.

"I can't give you the key," Page says. "In fact, I should probably stay here until you've finished looking around."

"If you don't have time for that," Caro says diplomatically, "we could text you when we're done and you could come back and lock up."

Page considers this. Then her walkie-talkie crackles, Gareth's voice saying, "Page? Where are you? We need you here. I still can't get ahold of Colby—"

That seems to convince her. "Okay," Page says. "Once you find your phones, text me, alright?" She starts off at a jog back to the main tent.

Ash is the first to step into the room.

"Wait," Caro says, a foreign, fatigued uncertainty coming over her. "Do you think we should be going through Hope's things? What if we mess up some kind of—evidence?"

Ash halts. "What kind of evidence would there be?" she asks. "I mean, I get what you're saying, but we both saw what happened, right?" She's right. They *saw* Hope fall. Caro closes her eyes against the memory, but it's there, burned into the back of her eyelids.

Ash crosses the room in a few quick strides, heading for Hope's bed. "Do you think she hid it under the mattress?" She lifts a corner of it.

Caro glances over at Hope's neatly zipped luggage and decides to try there. Across the trailer, Ash has moved the mattress and is rummaging around underneath.

Caro kneels on the rug, her body aching, and rifles through the weekender bag sitting on top of the suitcase. Nothing in there but a jacket of Hope's, the book she was reading (*We Never Liked Him Anyway*, their most recent book club pick), a makeup bag, and a bottle of water.

The minute Caro tips the suitcase on its side, she knows she's found it. There's a heaviness, the feel of shifting, inside. She unzips the case. *There.* A few items of Hope's clothing have been wrapped around a heavy rectangular object. "Ash," she calls out. Feeling invasive, she unwinds Hope's clothes and sure enough, there it is, the lockbox. When Caro lifts it out, she feels the *clunk-clunk* of what has to be their phones inside.

Was it really less than three days ago that they sat by the fire, locking their phones away? Agreeing to disappear?

And now Hope has done it. Completely.

"Oh, thank goodness." Ash sinks to her knees on the rug next to Caro. She reaches for the lockbox and clutches it to her chest. She looks up at Caro, her face worried. "Do you really think we should tell our families where we are? And what's going on?"

"What?" Caro's shocked by the question. Has Ash lost her mind? Wasn't she pushing to get back the phones so they *could* call their families?

Ash rubs the sutures on her cheekbone. Caro resists the urge to tell her to stop. "We know our families are okay," Ash says. "But we've got to look out for Hope."

"So you *don't* want to tell your family that we *almost died*?" Caro raises her eyebrows. "That one of us is missing?"

"I'm worried," Ash says. "It feels like if word gets out about where we are—or, more specifically, that Hope Hanover is missing—I feel like everything will go off the rails." She looks at Caro with wide and urgent eyes. "*Of course* search and rescue and everyone should be out looking for Hope. And they are. But maybe we shouldn't let the *world* know that she's missing, yet. Is that what Hope would want?"

Caro folds her arms, listening. Her stomach growls.

"At least," Ash says, "I don't feel like we should be the ones responsible for getting the word out. I know we trust our families. But if we tell them, who knows who might say something? No one can ever keep a secret. People always have to tell one person, and then *they* tell one person, and it might be one of the people somewhere along one of those conversation lines who lets it out into the world that it's Hope who's gone. And if she's still alive—she *has* to still be alive, then wouldn't she want—" Ash's voice breaks.

Ash has a point. "Okay," Caro says, and Ash sags in relief.

"But *do* you think that's what Hope would want?" Ash asks.

"I'm realizing that I don't know Hope well enough to know what she'd want." Caro is so tired. She wants to make the right decision, but when you're exhausted the way she and Ash are, mistakes happen. "Hope was so set on disappearing in the first place." Caro shakes her head. "Was she afraid of someone we *don't* know about?"

Neither of them is saying out loud what probably happened. What the most likely outcome of that fall would be.

Just then, the box in Ash's hands begins to shake.

25

ASH

"THAT'S TOO LOUD FOR one phone." Caro says what Ash is thinking. "More than one of us is getting a text at the same time." She presses her fingers to her mouth. "What if it's Hope?"

Ash puts the box on the floor and grabs the bottle opener from the minibar. The box vibrates again, juddering across the floor away from her. She snatches it back.

Something primal has ignited in Ash. She feels lean—wolflike— with purpose. Her friend needs her. She uses all her strength to leverage the bottle opener against the thin lip of the lockbox. But her efforts only result in her scratching and gouging the box without gaining any purchase. It's not the fanciest lockbox in the world, but it's doing its job. Ash swears in frustration and the bottle opener slips, almost cutting her palm.

The box goes still.

"Let's try to find the key," Caro says. That *is* the logical first step, but Ash didn't even think of it. She needs to slow down.

Any hesitation about going through Hope's things has vanished. The phones rattling around in the lockbox, the *aliveness* of it, has altered things. Ash takes the weekender and suitcase and Caro goes over the room.

"Nothing," Caro says after a few minutes. She blows a strand of hair away from her face. "I need a shower," she says. "I feel like an animal."

"Same, on both counts," Ash says. She has checked every pocket of every article of clothing, felt around in Hope's shoes, unballed her socks, gone through every nook and cranny of the suitcase and the bag. She thinks about picking up the lockbox, taking it to the Sonnet gathering area, and flinging it against the stones of the patio until it breaks open. But, of course, that might damage the phones inside.

"How late is it?" Ash asks. "Will a locksmith still be open? It takes about an hour to get to St. John, right?" She feels like she has fallen out of time and that nothing adds up. Like it has been years since they were in the canyon and seconds since Hope has slipped through their fingers.

"Spring Creek's closer," Caro says. "We can go there instead."

"We don't have a car here," Ash remembers. "Hope's rental is still at the end of the hike, and your car is still up at the trailhead."

Caro heads for the door. "We'll ask one of the staff to drive us to Spring Creek." She has changed too, Ash realizes. Caro is still focused, sharp. But there's an expression on her face, in her eyes, as if she's here but also listening to or thinking about something else. Is it her dad? Is she worried about him? Is it Spencer?

"Okay," Ash says. "Do you think they can spare anyone?" In the absence of the manager, Page seems to be doing everything. *Are they missing staff members in addition to guests?* Ash hasn't even thought to ask. *Had some of them been in the Underground as well?*

"They don't have a choice," Caro says.

26

CARO

ASH STOPS NEAR THE main firepit. "Caro, it's Spencer."

Caro spins in the direction Ash is pointing. There, coming out of the main tent, is a man who *looks* like Spencer, but is it? The walk is right, the frame tracks. Her body recognizes the truth while her brain is still wary of accepting such good news, and she's running toward him.

"Caro!" he calls out, breaking into a jog, too.

They stop short of embracing each other. Up close, Spencer looks like Caro imagines she does—he's clearly cleaned up some from the events in the canyon, but his face is—well, wrecked. It's not only the bruises, but the haunted-eyed look of someone who has been through something and has not come out on the other side of it.

"*Spencer*," Caro says. *What the hell.* She throws her arms around him. "I'm so glad you're okay."

"Same," he says, hugging her back. They pull apart and hold each other at arm's length. Caro feels the deep relief of being with someone who has known you for a long time. She remembers his face; she doesn't know all the lines, the way she does with Dan, but there's familiarity there, and it's very, *very* welcome.

Spencer glances at Ash, who's caught up to them. "Is everyone else safe?" He looks worried and Caro realizes she's feeling the same thing. If he's alone, does that mean...

"No." Caro's throat aches around the word. "Hope's missing."

"Oh *no*," Spencer says.

"What about your group?"

"Kevin's okay." She can see Spencer's Adam's apple as he swallows. "Tony's missing."

"I'm so sorry," Caro's trying to remember which one's Tony and which one's Kevin. Tony had the tattoo. Right? She had them straight earlier. Her brain is exhausted. "What happened?"

"We couldn't get across the river," Spencer says. "So we climbed up our side of the canyon as far as we could." He closes his eyes, opens them, the memory still only hours old. "What did you do?"

"We made it across the river," Caro says. "We climbed up on the bench. Then Hope fell." She finds she can't say much more around the lump in her throat, the ache in her heart. When she says it like that, when she pictures it again, she knows the score.

"We lost Tony in the river," Spencer says. "I think. It was dark and we couldn't see a thing. We didn't have time to grab our headlamps. At some point I realized he had...disappeared."

"Oh *no*," Caro says.

"I feel so guilty," Spencer says. "Kevin and I were leading out, since we 'knew' the hike and Tony hadn't been down the Underground before—" He breaks into a rough laugh, shakes his head. "As if we knew a damn thing in that situation."

"I know." Caro remembers the way the others looked to her. The way they followed. She did something because doing nothing seemed like the best way to die, but what if she'd found a better way? Been more careful? Would Hope still be with them?

"What about Ed and Jean?" she asks, though she thinks she knows.

"We left them." Spencer's voice is heavy. "There wasn't time..."

Caro puts her hand on his arm. "We did the same."

Spencer exhales. "We were in a bad place in the canyon," he says. "Our campsites were right where a bunch of flooding came down from the plateau, and the river was swelling from the runoff upstream, too."

"Do you know anything about the college kids who were farther down from us?" Ash asks. "And the teenagers?"

"They're all okay," Spencer says, and Caro's knees turn to jelly, she's so relieved. "I heard the SAR team talking. The college kids didn't end up camping the second night. They decided to keep going because they wanted to get back for a party." He laughs without any mirth. "In theory, that should have been an insane decision. But it likely saved their lives."

"Thank heavens," Ash says.

"Thank heavens," Spencer agrees. "And the leaders for that group of younger kids knew a higher spot to climb to in the canyon. They had a hell of a night, but nobody died."

"I'm so glad." Ash has tears in her eyes.

This is enormously good news. In fact, if Caro was ever inclined to use the word *miracle*, this is the time. She straightens up. There are still things they have to get done, no matter how unbelievable this all feels. "We need to talk to our families," she says to Spencer.

"Oh man, you haven't yet?" He looks surprised. "I'd lend you my phone, but it's long gone in the canyon. Did yours get ruined, too?"

"They're in here." Ash holds up the lockbox. A quizzical look crosses Spencer's face, but Caro will explain in the car. Right now they have to get moving. "We lost the key and we need to go into Spring Creek and find a locksmith," she says. "Our cars are up at the trailhead and at the end of the hike, in the opposite direction from Spring Creek, so if we go get one of them we won't have time to make it into town before things close. It's almost five now." Spring Creek is a small town, and while the restaurants and other tourist spots stay open later, the other businesses shut down at five sharp. It's forty-five minutes closer than driving into St. John, and they *have* to get into that box. They have to find Hope. Since they can't be up in the canyon searching, this feels like the next best thing. "Do you have a car here at Sonnet? Or did you use it for the hike?"

"I've got my truck here," Spencer says. "You're welcome to take it. You can drive stick, right?"

Caro and Ash both nod. "I probably shouldn't drive right now," Ash says. "I'm kind of woozy from the pain meds. Nothing bad, but—"

Caro doesn't want to admit it, but she feels the same way. And she doesn't want to take Spencer's truck and leave him alone after what he's been through. "Where's Kevin?" she asks.

"He's at the rescue site," Spencer says. "But I'm not family, so they cleared me out of there."

"Can your truck fit three?" she asks. "Can we all go?"

"Sure," he says.

Right then the phones start jarring around again in the box, and they all jump.

"Shit," Spencer says. "What if that's Hope?"

"I know," Caro says. "Let's go."

27

POSTCARDS WRITTEN AT THE SONNET RESORT

Hi Wade,

Thanks again for taking care of things at home so that I could come on this trip. I've been thinking a lot and

~~I'm sorry~~

~~I wish~~

~~I miss~~

Is there any way we can get back to where we were?

Or somewhere new?

I'd like to try.

xx
Ash

———

Hey Dad,

I was thinking about the Devil's Backbone Drive and how you and I used to go eat at the grill in Story after. I remembered how they *served everything on mismatched china and had fresh rainbow trout on the menu. Do you? Should we try to go there again?*

    I love you.

Caro

————

Dan,

I miss you. I've been thinking about you, us, all of it. I'm sorry I've been wanting more for too long. I know I've almost broken us, and I'm sorry. I'm the luckiest to have you.

Caro

————

Hi there.

I know a postcard might not be the best way to let you know this, but I wanted to say it before I lost my nerve.

    It's time to call the game.

    I'm so grateful for everything you've done and for everything we've been through together.

    But it's time for me to say this, if not out loud, then at least in writing:

    It's over.

Caro

————

Hey,

I know you won't get this. I know I won't send it.

    I know that even if I did it would be too late.

    Love you anyway.

Hope

28

PAGE

I STARTED THE MOVIE EARLIER than usual tonight as a distraction. It's *Gravity*, and Sandra Bullock is washed out on-screen because the sun isn't all the way down. Still, the cars are packed full and so are the bleachers behind them.

It's good for the guests to have things to do.

Everyone knows about the tragedy in the Underground, of course. A few left quietly, handing over their keys and checking out with minimal fuss. Some threw fits and demanded full refunds, even though nothing bad had happened to *them*. I stood at the reception desk and used the lines I've learned from Colby: "Weather and natural disasters are not under our control, and so I can't offer you a full refund or reschedule your stay." I also adapted his tone: polite and firm.

I miss him. I thought I could handle this week. But I didn't know that we'd have all of *this* going down. I miss his cheerfulness, the way his curly blond hair sticks out from under a hat when he wears one. The way he has to go into his office and take a break after he's been public-facing—a term I learned from him—for too long. I'm not in love with Colby. I don't have a crush on him. But if I could pick an older brother, he's the one I'd choose. I wonder when—*if,* my mind says, always thinking of the darkest possibilities—he'll be back.

I understood why he had to leave. But it's been a hell of a time for him to be gone.

I think I'm doing a pretty good job—an astonishingly good job, actually—at keeping my crap together. But the moment Mal comes to relieve me at the reception desk for my break, I feel a spinning inside me, fear and stress and uncertainty darkening the corners of my vision. I pull off my name tag and leave it behind the counter. Once outside, I stop and take a few deep breaths on the path, looking up at the movie screen. The soundtrack—dramatic, epic—sings tinnily from the speakers inside the cars and in the viewing area.

I pull my hair out of its ponytail and unbutton my official Sonnet uniform shirt. I ball it up in my hand. In my tank top, with my hair loose, in the dusky light, I hope I look like any other young guest at the resort. I hope no one will ask me for anything.

The gravel crunches underfoot as I make my way down the path, past kids running in the direction of the movie, a couple having an argument, the food truck, the firepits. Smoke rises, people lean closer to the fire to see how the marshmallows on their skewers are coming along. Humans are gathering to socialize, in spite of or because of the tragedy. Some get lost and die. The rest live, eat, burn, laugh, scream, go quiet.

When I get to my destination, I pause to make sure no one's watching me. This isn't the smartest thing to be doing, especially when the police might already be on their way. But it's quiet. The music is distant. No one's here, not right now.

These aren't my lodgings, but I go inside.

———

When I come back out, the sky has darkened. The screen is visible above the scrubby juniper trees. The movie's clearer since the light has gone. Sandra Bullock has washed up on the sandy shore of Lake Powell, not far from here. It was an unusually wet year when they filmed the movie, and the typically red hills are covered in green. It looks like Hawaii. It's not.

Sandra claws a hand through the mud, kneads it in her fingers. She's gasping for air. She's been gone for so long.

Skye finds me when I'm almost back to the main tent. I'm breathing almost normally, and there are only a couple of buttons left to button on my uniform shirt. "Hey," she says, and I can't quite make out what's in her voice. Curiosity? Triumph? "Where have you been?"

"I still have five minutes left on my break," I say.

"The police are here," Skye says. "They've been looking for you."

I wasn't sure how I'd feel when I heard these words, but the emotion that floods me is *fury*. Not the worst option, given what I still have left to do. I clench my fist, wishing I could grip the anger like Sandra gripped the sand. Hold on to it until I'm ready to let it drip through my fingers. "Okay," I say. Inside, I think, *What took so long?*

29

ASH

THEY'RE GOING TO DIE.

Ash is sure of it.

Caro's driving the truck over a spiny ridge at the literal top of a mountain. And there's the name of the road on a sign, flashing briefly before them as they pass it—DEVIL'S BACKBONE.

Caro's driving like a bat *out* of one. Hell, that is, not out of a backbone. Though the moment she has the thought, Ash imagines a spine—bones like the ones they saw in the canyon—with bats flying out from between the vertebrae, from under the rib cage, shrieking. She shudders.

Caro glances over. "You okay?"

"Eyes on the road!" Ash says. She's in the middle, between Caro in the driver's seat on Ash's left and Spencer to the right. On either side of the road—which is only wide enough for a single vehicle—sheer drops fall below them. There are jags of rock, trees in precarious places, hairpin turns, astonishing almost-sunset views of the valleys and plateaus below them that Ash absolutely cannot appreciate.

They got to Spring Creek too late. Everything was closed. And then, instead of turning back and driving into St. John, they headed this way, into another tiny town called Story where Spencer has a friend who he's sure can pick the lock for them. *It's faster*, he and Caro agreed. *Plus,*

Spencer said, *I know he'll be open. We can get back to Sonnet quicker this way. And how long has it been since you've driven Devil's Backbone?*

Not as long as you'd think, Caro had said, and then she'd asked him if she could drive.

They're saving time, going to Story instead of St. John. But Ash is convinced they've made the wrong choice. She can picture the truck missing a turn, careening over the edge, their broken bodies and the twisted metal coming at last to rest at the bottom of a canyon, the lockbox still intact.

She's gotten so morbid.

"The road isn't like this for much longer," Caro says, glancing over at her again. The truck is old, old enough that there are keys swinging in the ignition, attached to a faded plastic keychain.

"I have a better car at home," Spencer says, noticing Ash's expression. "This is the one I take when I'm going camping or to one of the parks."

"Oh my gosh," Caro says, very briefly diverted. "Do you remember that Suburban you drove in high school? That thing that was twenty years older than *we* are? You could start the ignition with a *popsicle stick*?"

"Of course I remember the Suburban," Spencer says. "Everyone made fun of me for that car."

"Are you kidding?" Caro asks. "I think that car *made* you. Remember how anyone in student government with us would go out to the parking lot and take it whenever they wanted?"

"I caught Corbin Harris and Stacy Holt making out in the back seat once," Spencer says. He seems completely unconcerned with the way Caro is driving, with how close the edges are. Ash's hands are in tight fists, while he rests his elbow on the open window. The breeze coming through is cool.

"Ugh," Caro says. "If I'd known that, I never would have made out with *you* in the back seat of that car."

They both laugh. Ash feels their bodies shake next to her. *How can they laugh when their friends are missing?* she wonders. As if they've had the same thought, Caro and Spencer both seem to tense up. Ahead, the road has narrowed even further and the three of them are silent as they twist again, turn. For a split second, the wheels hit the softer dirt of the nonexistent shoulder, and Ash can't breathe. Then Caro has them back on the road. They're all quiet while she navigates them along this eternal spine at the top of the world.

There. The road straightens, widens.

"Okay," Caro says to Ash. "The worst is over."

And then they fall silent.

Because all three of them know that *that* isn't true.

⁓

Story is a small town with, as far as Ash can tell, two restaurants (one the Devil's Backbone Grill that Caro has mentioned before, the other a diner), three rock/souvenir/gift/convenience shops, a gas station, a dollar store, a hotel that might or might not still be in operation, and the hint of houses marked by cottonwood trees and smaller streets branching off from the highway.

"This one," Spencer says, pointing to the rock shop at the edge of town. The headlights flash on a sign, which is a board painted white and hand-lettered in green: COOPER'S ROCK AND PAWN. The shop itself has a CLOSED sign in the window, but it looks like there are other rooms behind the shop, and there's a light on at the back. "You two can wait here," Spencer says, opening the passenger side door of the truck. "I'll go and get him to open up and we can figure out the box there."

"Sounds good," Ash says, because she suddenly feels safer inside the truck with Caro. Spencer shuts the door, and she reaches out to grip her friend's hand. "What are we doing?" she asks Caro, despair tightening around her.

"The only thing we can." Caro's voice is steady, even.

"We should be looking for *her*, not her phone," Ash says.

"We're not trained for that," Caro says. "We need to stay out of the way." She squeezes Ash's hand.

"We should be talking to the police," Ash says.

"And telling them what?" Caro asks.

It's a good question.

In front of them, the door opens and light spills out from the room behind. It silhouettes the man standing inside the doorway. Spencer is talking to him, gesturing with his hands. Ash bites her lip, watching. She wonders who—or what—else is inside that run-down building, the houses she can't see. Watching them.

Hope, where are you?

And for the first time Ash truly realizes: If they don't find Hope, Ash will be looking for her everywhere she goes, all her life.

30

CARO

CARO HAS ALWAYS LOVED a rock shop. While Ash, Spencer, and Spencer's friend, who appears to go simply by Coop, huddle around the lockbox, she walks up and down the rows of shelves to distract herself. Enormous geodes that look like portals to another world, bins of smaller rocks sorted out by type: quartzes, fluorite, obsidian. Her dad used to bring her here. She always planned to bring her own kids. Caro swallows, hard.

If anything has changed since she was a child, she can't tell. There's the shelf of amethyst, which she's always been drawn to—she likes the richness of the color. Her wedding ring is, in fact, amethyst.

"Are you sure you don't want a more expensive stone?" Dan had asked her.

She was sure.

There are small cards by each of the stones describing their meanings and energetic properties. Caro has no time for such things. She keeps walking, looking at another shelf. She doesn't know what they'll do if they can't get the lockbox open. Coop has it now. He's an old man in suspenders and jeans, his salt-and-pepper hair neatly combed.

Caro pauses. She knows it's ridiculous, but ever since she was a kid, she's been drawn to the animals carved out of calcite and other stone. She runs her fingers over the back of a simple, pleasingly shaped bear, the animal suggested by only a rounded back, a snout, two legs. She picks it up, liking the feel of it in her hand. It's orange, Dan's favorite color. *Honeycomb calcite*, she sees on the card next to it, which looks like it's been typed out on an ancient typewriter. Maybe she will buy it for Dan, though as a rule they don't bring each other souvenirs from their travels. Neither of them likes superfluous stuff and clutter. She keeps walking, letting her eyes soak in the familiar colors.

She's come to the *pawn* part of Cooper's Rock and Pawn. A cabinet holds a few odds and ends—a camera, an old iPhone, several pieces of jewelry. Disconcertingly, a gun, which seems like it should be locked in a more secure place than a glass cabinet. There are two watches, one of which is a gold-plated Timex like the one her dad wears, which, she knows, is worth less than $50.

Caro hears a *click* and a "Got it!" from the other side of the room.

"*Thank* you," Ash is saying, and Coop says, "No problem," and hands her back the box. Caro is at Ash's side as Ash lifts the lid.

Caro's heart skips a beat.

There are only two phones inside.

Caro recognizes hers, and she also recognizes Ash's, with its special translucent case that holds pressed flowers from her farm (phone cases are some of the items Ash sells in her online shop).

"What's wrong?" Spencer asks.

"Anything missing?" asks Coop.

And Caro suddenly trusts no one, nothing. "We're good," she says. "Thank you so much for opening this."

"Not a problem," Coop says. There are lines around his mouth and eyes that make her think of her father. "Happy to help." He smiles, the wrinkles deepening. "You want to buy that?"

"What?" Caro asks, and then she remembers that she's still holding the bear. "Oh, right, I'm sorry—"

He holds up his hand. "Don't worry about it," he says. "Take it." He's already shuffling out from behind the counter, putting whatever small tool he used to open the lockbox back into his pocket. "And tell your dad I said hello. If you want. I know he might not remember me." He starts for the door. "Good to see you again, too, though I'd never have recognized you if Spence hadn't told me your name. Kids tend to grow up."

"Oh." Caro's impressed he remembers her and her father. It's been so long, and she didn't know that she and her dad would have left any impression. *Just another parent and child coming through the shop.* Her heart aches with what will never be again and what will never be. "Thank you," she says. "I'll tell him."

"He was in here last week," Coop says. He's almost to the door, and Caro's there to open it for him. "My dad?" she says, surprised. "Here?"

"Yup." Coop nods in thanks and assent. He walks past Caro and turns to lock the door after the others have exited, too.

"Thank you so much," Ash says when he's finished. Coop waves a hand at them as he heads back toward his apartment, his gait suddenly very much that of an old man. Spencer catches up with him and walks him the rest of the way to his door.

Ash and Caro turn to each other as soon as he's out of earshot.

"Hope's phone and the burner phone," Caro says. "They're both gone."

"Which isn't necessarily bad news," Ash says, a feverish note in her voice. "If Hope took the phones with her, maybe there's a way to contact or track her. Maybe she *is* the one trying to message and call us."

"Why would she take them with her, though?" Caro asks. "She promised us she wouldn't." She looks at her phone. "And the number for the missed calls that have been happening while the phones are in the box say *Unknown.* Not Hope."

"Exactly!" Ash says. "Could that be the burner phone?"

Spencer's heading back toward them. Caro doesn't want him to overhear. "I think it's time to *make* the police talk to us again," she tells Ash quietly. "And I think it's time to contact Raye. Hope's agent."

"I don't have her number," Ash says. "Do you?"

"No," Caro says. "Okay. The police, then."

"But we promised—" Ash begins.

"All bets are off now that she's gone." Caro keeps her tone gentle. "They have to be, Ash. We've waited long enough. I know you want to stick to the plan because we promised we would. But the plan doesn't work anymore."

Ash puts her face in her hands. She says something that Caro can't entirely make out. Then she lifts her head. "You're right. If she *does* have the phones, there's no way to track her in the canyon, right? That was kind of the whole point. So why *would* she take them?"

Caro hesitates. She's had a thought. "Well…" she begins. There *are* other ways to get into the Underground. Tiny slot canyons. But you'd have to be an expert canyoneer to do any of them, and they're illegal, most of them protected now.

Right then her phone begins to vibrate.

Caro jumps so hard she drops her phone on the ground and has to crouch down to get it. When she reads the message on the screen, her head snaps up. Her eyes lock with Ash. She holds up her phone. Wordlessly, Ash does, too.

They both have the same message.

It's me.

31

PAGE

THE POLICE ARE GONE.

I tip my head back in the shower. I feel like I'm suffocating. I want it all *off*—my clothes, the feel of the day, everything that's happened.

The handle to the shower door rattles right as I reach for the soap, and I jump. Before I can say anything, someone calls out, "Sorry! Didn't know this one was taken!" The noise stops, and I put my hand over my heart, reminding myself to calm down. Then I tilt my head back into the shower stream again.

The water swirls pinkish orange from the sand that, no matter what I do, always ends up in my clothes and hair. I rinse my hair under the shower again until the water runs clean.

I don't bother with drying my hair. It's warm enough out. I stop by the food truck and get a burger and shake. My brain is exhausted and I need calories. I drink cup after cup of water at the hydration station near the food truck while I wait for my order to be ready. When it is, the chef, Ty, opens the back door of the truck and delivers the meal to me himself instead of calling out my number. "You okay?" he asks. His Sonnet cap is on backward, and his hair is bleached from the sun.

"Yeah."

But I can tell he's not convinced. "What happened?"

I aim for the perfect amount of concerned but competent. "Nothing," I say, picking up the tray. I'm not going to eat at one of the picnic tables—too public. I need a break. "Except for, you know, the flash flood and the missing guests, and the ones who are still here panicking or needing to be entertained." The music from the movie's credits sings through the trees and along the paths to where we are. The score is supposed to evoke being in space, but the loneliness of it feels right for the desert, too.

"That's a lot to deal with," Ty says. "And Colby's gone. I hear he left you in charge."

Who told him that? As if he can guess my question, Ty says, "It's pretty much common knowledge."

"Oh," I say. "Yeah, he did."

"Not really fair to do that to someone so young," Ty says, and I instantly bristle. I hate it when people say I'm young. They might know my age in years, but they have no idea how old I am on the inside.

"Thanks for this," I say, and I start down the path, the gravel pebbly and distinct under my flip-flops.

"You know when he'll be back?" Ty asks.

I pretend I don't hear him and keep going. I notice that he's added a fruit salad to my order, a rainbow of watermelon and grapes and pineapple and raspberries dusted with tajin, a lime wedge neatly placed on top.

When I come to the opened-up clearing of the theater, I pause. The smells of popcorn and rain-drenched sage hang in the air, and the rows of classic cars spread out in front of me, emptying now that the film is over. I need to think of more things for the guests to do. Maybe we should show movies all day long. People need distractions. Otherwise they panic, or they try and help. I'm never certain which one is more dangerous.

Which car would Hope Hanover pick if she were here? That one, I'm pretty sure, the candy-apple-red Thunderbird near the far end of the first row.

I open the door and climb inside, setting my tray of food down on the seat next to me while I figure out what to do next. *Breathe.* I can't leave Sonnet, I have to see this through, but I like the feeling of being in a car, of at least the *possibility* of motion…

After I finish eating, I lean my head back against the seat and close my eyes. I am exhausted. I welcome it, though, because I don't want to feel everything that is underneath.

A knock on my window. A face looms in front of me. Another. Adrenaline spikes through me until I realize it's two of the guests. Ash and Caro.

Perfect, actually. Exactly who I needed to see.

"Skye told us where to find you," Ash says. "We're wondering if you've heard anything."

"Nothing yet." I'm disconcerted that Skye knew I was here. I climb out of the Thunderbird so that I'm on even footing with the two women. It's late, and Hope Hanover's friends both look absolutely wrecked. Like they're experiencing that horrible combination of needing to sleep and not being able to sleep because they're in the hell of losing someone they care about.

"Have *you* heard anything about your friend yet?" The question is a courtesy, a way to make them feel like they're the ones who would be in the know.

"No," Ash says, but there's a trace of something in her voice that makes me look at her more closely. No one's heard from Hope. I'd know if they had. So why does Ash sound like she might be lying?

"I've been wondering," I say. "Would either of you prefer a room change?"

"I'm sorry?" Caro asks.

"We've had a few people check out," I say, "and with everything that's happened, it seems like you might feel more—secure?—in the Airstreams?" Ash's shoulders drop in what looks to me like relief. She's definitely thought about this. "They lock, and they have private bathrooms, but if you want to stay where you are, I totally get it. The tents are nice." I pause to let them take in the offer. "Or maybe you're planning to end your trip early?" I make a sympathetic face. *They'd better* not *be planning on ending the trip early.*

"No," Caro says instantly. She glances at Ash. "Not me, anyway. I'm not leaving until we find her."

"Me either," Ash says with the same conviction. "Are you serious about this? That would be great if we could move to the Airstreams."

"How much more would it cost?" Caro asks.

"It's complimentary," I say, but that's not *exactly* true. There's always a price, and this one is hidden. "I can put you two next to each other. I can't get you right by your friend's Airstream—it's on the end of the row, and the people on the other side haven't checked out—but you're close. There's no obligation, of course. Again, you're welcome to stay where you are." I'm speaking so formally that it sounds odd to my ears, but they don't seem to notice.

"Awesome." Ash looks like she might cry. "This is *so* kind of you."

"No problem," I say. "Let's go get the keys."

The minute we enter the tent, Skye leaves the gift shop where she was working and joins us at the reception desk. Skye's loving the whole natural-disaster, people-are-missing vibe. I've been keeping an eye on her LikeMe account to make sure she doesn't post anything that could really screw things up. She's acting like *she* almost died in the flash flood, and her followers are eating it up. They don't know that she was sound asleep when it all happened and that she's never been in the Underground. "Do you need me to help with anything?" she asks, practically salivating. Ash and Caro are as close as she can get to the drama.

"I think we're good," Caro says, and I like the way she seems to have taken Skye's measure in a glance. "Thank you, though."

"I can help move your luggage over now, if you want," I tell Ash and Caro quietly. "There's a golf cart parked out back."

"Yes, please." Ash is practically weeping with gratitude. If anyone's going to talk about what happened when *they* talked to the police, I think it's going to be her. I'll drop her off last when I take them over and see what I can find out.

The two women climb onto the golf cart behind me and we set off on the path, the illuminated solar lights guiding our way. None of us say anything. They're tired. Their bodies sway with the turns and jolts of the golf cart.

I keep myself upright. *Don't look down*, I remind myself, when my mind threatens to go where it can't right now. *Stay here. Do what you need to do.*

32

BEFORE

Hey friends.

Sorry for the old-fashionedness of certified mail. But this is the safest way I could think of to communicate.

Plus, this way I know that only you have signed for these packages. I've specified that you'll have to do it with proof of ID: Carolina Stewart and Ashley Paxton. No spouses, no kids, no partners, whatever. No one else.

But you already know that, because you're reading this letter.

I've written it by hand so that you'll know it really is from me.

You'll also see that I've included a new phone.

(Ash, I can practically hear the wheels turning in your head. But no, this isn't an elaborate way to announce that I've been cast in a Mission: Impossible movie.)

I get why you'd think that, though. This whole thing is convoluted and ridiculous, but it's the best I could come up with to let you know about the situation.

I have some bad news.

We have a lurker.

Someone's been watching us this whole time.

You probably have a ton of questions—who is the lurker? How do I know this? What do I mean by "watching us this whole time"?

There are lots of fancy technical terms for it, but the gist of it is that we haven't ever been alone. Not even in that very first meeting, and not in any of the ones since.

Right now, we have to keep texting like normal and acting like normal and meeting online like normal on our regular phones and computers so we can catch them out.

But we can talk and text freely on our new phones. DO NOT tell anyone about them. Keep them somewhere safe. Don't connect them to any other accounts. They each have their own lines that are separate from your phone numbers. I'll foot the bill, of course. Make sure they're never out of your sight or pocket. Don't let anyone else have access.

The expert I've been consulting (more on that when we talk) thinks it's very likely that whoever's watching us can access one of our computers, even from far away. Like I said, they've been watching all of us since we met.

And they may have been watching one of us for much, much longer.

xx,
Hope

Saturday

On the chalkboard outside the Sonnet resort main office

MOVIE ....

Planet of the Apes, 1968, G, directed by Franklin J. Schaffner

FILM FACT ....

During filming, the actors tended to congregate during breaks based on which types of ape costumes they were wearing. The phenomenon was unintentional and surprising to the director— and an intriguing social development, especially considering the themes of the movie.

33

ASH

FEET CRUNCH ON THE gravel outside of Ash's trailer, and morning-pink light streams through the small windows of the Airstream. Whoever is walking doesn't stop. Ash rolls over in her bed and looks at her phone.

It's me.

The text she and Caro both received last night from an unknown number. By mutual agreement, the three of them had gotten rid of their secret phones from Hope once they'd arrived together at Sonnet. Now they only had their "real" ones, the ones their families could reach.

And other people, too.

Who is this? Ash and Caro had agreed to write back.

No response. At least not for Ash.

Are you up? she texts Caro now.

Yes.

Ash: Anything more from the mystery number?

Caro: No.

How'd you sleep?

Ash: Fine. I mean. You know.

Caro: I do.

Ash: The Airstreams feel louder than the tents. I swear I could hear everyone who walked past last night.

Caro: Same.

Ash: Maybe the Airstreams have less insulation.

Caro: That can't be right. Less insulation than a tent?

Ash: I know.

They're avoiding the issue. But not for long.

We need to go to the police now, Caro texts. Ask them if they can figure out who sent the message. Tell them EVERYTHING. Make sure they've connected the dots—that the Hope who is missing is Hope Hanover. If they're any good at their jobs, they should have already figured it out, but we've got to be certain. And we need to call Hope's agent. Do you know the best way to get her number? Did Hope ever give it to you?

Ash feels relieved. She was trying to hold out as long as she could, to follow Hope's instructions, but really, there's no way Hope could have known things would go like *this*. Hope would understand why Ash had to give in, wouldn't she?

Okay, she texts back. You're right.

Let's meet in 20 at the general store/reception area, Caro texts. Is that enough time?

Yes.

Ash pulls on her clothes quickly, stuffing her air-dried hair back into a ponytail. Even though she's clean again, she feels like she's gone somewhat feral, the way she does during the various harvesting seasons when there's just enough time to shower off the dirt from the day, fall asleep, and get back out in the fields again.

She swings open the Airstream door, locks it, and heads outside, walking briskly toward the main tent. Before she gets there, she veers off and heads for the plateau. No one else is out there except a man with a dog on a leash. The man nods to her but keeps walking in the opposite direction. Perfect. She puts in her earbuds and calls Wade.

"Well, hello," he says. His tone surprises her—it's cheerful, how it used to be whenever she'd call.

"Hey," she says, a lump rising in her throat. And an urge rises up within her, impossible to ignore. What if she...talks to him? Tells him exactly what's going on and where she is, both physically and emotionally? *What if?*

"Are all the other ladies breaking the rules and calling, too?" he asks. "You're worse than the girls." He laughs. "Remember how we took their phones away for a single afternoon on that vacation to the coast and they all lost their minds?"

Ash wants to take umbrage, tell him that he doesn't even know the situation (She's in a place where there was a flash flood! People are dead and missing!), but she's too weary, and besides, he's right. And it turns out that even though she told him more than she should, about the tents and the Airstreams and all that, he hasn't figured out where she is. The tightness in her chest eases incrementally. Maybe she didn't betray Hope as badly as she thought she did.

"I do remember that," Ash says. "How *are* the girls? Can I talk to them?" Sometimes it's easier this way, rather than trying to get each of them on their (now) three individual phones.

"Sorry," Wade says. "You'll have to call them directly. I'm not home."

"They're probably not up yet, anyway," she says, realizing she's forgotten the time difference. It's an hour earlier in Oregon. "Are you at Whole Foods?" She can see it all with such familiarity. Her long-limbed, long-haired girls each asleep in their own beds, Wade out buying groceries for the weekend.

"Actually," Wade says, "I'm out of town."

"Wait," Ash says. "What?"

"My mom offered to come watch the girls," he says. "So Derek and I are taking a boys trip."

Ash wrinkles her nose. She *really* doesn't love the term *girls trip* for adult women, but *boys trip* sounds a thousand times worse. Still. That's not the point.

"That's great," she says, and she means it. Derek is Wade's younger brother. She wishes Wade did more with him, and with his guy friends. All he seems to do these days is work, work, work. It's like he can't get out of the habit, even though his practice is thriving and they've been able to pay off all their debt with the money from his job and Three Sisters. "Where'd you guys go?"

Wade laughs. "You think I'm going to tell you, when you're keeping *your* location top secret? All I know is that you're staying in tents."

She could go ahead and start talking—*Babe, I was in a flash flood, I barely survived, my friend is gone and I'm terrified, I love you and the girls so much and my life has become so complicated that I'm not sure I recognize it. You. Us.* But everything has become such a tangle that she doesn't know where to begin.

"Fair," she says. "That's great, though. I hope you guys have so much fun. Tell Derek hi for me."

"I will," he says. "You have fun, too."

Ash feels relieved and surprised. She's annoyed with herself for also feeling unsettled. The plateau stretches out in front of her, and the formations of Eden rise past it, now almost alpenglow-pink in the sunrise.

Farther along the plateau, the dog has frozen in place. Both it and its owner are looking in the opposite direction from Ash, expressions intent. She turns to see what they do: the spot where the resort road joins the larger one. There, three police cars have turned off the main road and are heading up Sonnet's drive. Ash lifts her phone.

Hey, she texts Caro. Looks like we don't have to go to the police.

They're here.

34

CARO

CARO PULLS UP SHORT by the main tent, heart racing. Even though she headed over as soon as she got Ash's message, one of the police cars is already making its way back down the drive, away from the resort. Caro can't tell if there's anyone sitting in the back. Did they bring some-one here? Are they taking someone away? *What's happened?*

Ash appears from around the corner of the tent, tucking her phone into her pocket. "Any news?"

"Not yet," Caro says as a Sonnet golf cart pulls up. The employee with the dark, sticking-up hair—Gareth—is driving, and Spencer's inside. He unfolds his long legs and climbs out. He hasn't shaved yet, and his eyes are shadowed with exhaustion. "*Hey,*" Spencer says when he sees Ash and Caro. "Did they call you in, too?"

"Who?" Ash asks.

"The police," he says. "They want to talk to me."

"Excuse us," Gareth says. "I'm supposed to take Mr. Clayton to speak with them immediately."

"They're with me," Spencer says. He looks at Caro. "If you want to be?"

Caro glances at Ash. The decision is instantaneous. "We do," she says. They need to talk to the police as soon as they can, and learning anything extra can't hurt. Plus, whatever the police are going to talk to Spencer about can't be good if they have to do it in person, and Caro wants to know what it is. For two seconds, she thinks, *Is Spencer a suspect for something?* and then she remembers, *This is Spencer. Spencer Clayton, who I have known forever. There's no way.*

Right?

Gareth seems to decide that this whole situation is above his pay grade and that the police can handle it. "Okay," he says. "Come on."

———

The two officers waiting inside the staff tent are not the ones Caro and Ash met at the hospital yesterday. They introduce themselves as Officer Clark (male, middle-aged, fit, thinning brown hair) and Officer Flanigan (female, bleached blond, extremely tan, and very no-nonsense).

"We need to speak with Mr. Clayton," Officer Clark says. His voice is sober.

"Is it about Tony?" Spencer rushes on before Officer Clark can answer. "I'd like Caro to be here while we talk. She and I have known each other since high school." He glances at Ash. "It's fine if Ash stays, too." It's clear he doesn't want to be alone for whatever this is. He swallows hard, his Adam's apple moving up and down in his throat.

The two officers look at one another. "All right," says Officer Flanigan. She indicates that they should sit down on the couches where they sat with Page the day before. After a moment of uncertainty, Caro sits on a couch with Spencer and Ash sits on a chair by herself. Officers Clark and Flanigan take the other couch.

When everyone is seated, Officer Flanigan nods at Spencer. "I'm very sorry to tell you that we've found Anthony Jameson's body. We reached out to his family for formal identification, which took place not long ago."

Spencer closes his eyes. "Okay." His face has gone very pale. Caro stands up, startling the others. "I'm going to get him some food." Her voice brooks no argument, and she walks toward the staff fridge. Spencer's phone begins vibrating on the table in front of him, and he opens his eyes. Kevin's face comes up on the screen. "That's Tony's brother," he says. "Kevin. My friend. The one who was with us in the Underground. Does he know?"

"Yes," Officer Flanigan says. "He's been at the police station. We just came from there."

"Where was he?" Spencer asks. "Tony, I mean?" Caro sits back down. In the staff kitchenette she found a fluorescent-colored sports drink and a pack of peanuts. She sets them on the battered coffee table in front of Spencer. He grabs the bottle but doesn't open it or take a drink.

"Mr. Jameson's body surfaced near a farm lower in the canyon," Officer Flanigan says. "We have a few pictures." She holds up her phone but doesn't offer it to Spencer. "I should warn you that they're distressing for the obvious reason that he is deceased, and because his body was naked when they found it."

Spencer's expression is shocked. "What does *that* mean?"

"We think it was likely the force of the water," Officer Clark says. "The SAR team has seen it happen before. He was wearing clothing when you last saw him, I assume?"

"Yes," Spencer says. Now he does twist the top from the bottle and takes a drink, swallowing once, twice, three times. Caro nods encouragingly. "We were all sleeping, so he wasn't in full hiking gear or anything. Shorts, underwear, probably." Spencer pauses. "He threw on his shoes before we left the tent. We all did."

"Remind us what time that was," Officer Clark says.

"In the middle of the night," Spencer says. "I looked at my watch when we first woke up and it was around eleven thirty. So not long after that." He puts down his drink. "We tried to cross the river, but it was too high, so we went back and were trying to climb up the canyon walls. At one point I turned around and he was . . . gone."

"Did anyone in your group see Kevin trying to climb out of the canyon?" Officer Clark asks the women.

"I didn't." Caro tips her head, thinking. "I only saw him when we were all running around by the river. We"—she gestures to Ash—"crossed to the other side. Our campsites were in different spots, so we were all doing what made the most sense in the moment. It was every person for themself."

"Was that before or after *your* friend went missing?"

"Before," Caro says.

"What was the connection between your groups?" Officer Flanigan asks. "Did you plan to hike in and camp out together?"

"There was no connection," Caro says.

"But you know each other," Officer Flanigan says, looking back and forth between Caro and Spencer.

"That was random luck." Caro glances at Spencer. "We ran into each other when we were already in the Underground. We hadn't seen each other in years."

"What are the odds?" Officer Clark raises his eyebrows.

"Decent, actually," Spencer says. "Hundreds of local kids grow up hiking these canyons and then come back again as adults." He sounds exhausted, not defensive.

"You're from St. John, correct?" Officer Clark asks.

"Yes," Spencer says.

"And you still live there now?"

"That's right."

"Remind me of your occupation?"

"I'm an accountant," Spencer says.

"And you're from St. John, too?" Officer Clark asks Caro.

"I grew up there," Caro says. "Now I live in Salt Lake City. But I visit a lot. I still have family here."

"Full name?"

"Carolina Maria Stewart."

Ash gives her name as well. "We were hoping to talk to you," she says. "Caro and I were just about to come down to the police station."

"And we were hoping to speak with you while we were up here." Officer

Flanigan sits forward on the sofa right as a staff member opens the door and then, seeing the officers, mutters apologies and backs out.

"Again, we're very sorry to have had to give you the news about Anthony Jameson," Officer Clark says to Spencer. "You're free to go." He turns his gaze to Ash and Caro.

Caro studies Ash's face, trying to read her, trying to figure out what she wants. *Should they let Spencer stay?* It might seem odd if they didn't, given the news he's allowed them to hear. Caro's not sure what the officers want to talk to them about. She doesn't think it's that Hope is dead—wouldn't they have indicated that the reason they wanted to talk to the women might be as serious as the one they needed to discuss with Spencer?—but still.

Since Ash doesn't protest, Caro says, "We'd like Spencer to stay." And then she tells the police what she and Ash decided they had to share.

"Our friend who is missing is Hope Hanover," she says. Spencer blinks, but the officers don't flinch. Caro doesn't have any kind of detective background, but she would guess that Spencer didn't know Hope was Hope and that the officers have already made the connection. How? Did Hope use her real name when she signed them in at the trailhead? Caro didn't think to check. She hands Officer Flanigan her phone. "We want to know if she texted us last night. Both Ash and I got a message from an unknown number. Is there a way for you to find out who it was?"

It's requiring a conscious effort on Caro's part to make eye contact with the police officers. The last time she was interviewed was at the hospital. *Dr. Stewart, when did* you *first notice the patient was exhibiting signs of distress?*

"Yes." Officer Flanigan's mouth is pursed, as if she's not completely pleased about how this is going down, the way the officers are being asked questions instead of the other way around. "Can we take your phones with us?"

"Is that necessary?" Ash asks. "We have families and friends we need to stay in touch with."

Officer Clark clears his throat. "We can discuss that in a moment," he says. "Right now, we want to ask you if you know anything about a LikeMe account that went live within the last few hours called @findhopehanover?"

"I'm sorry?" Ash sounds both pissed and puzzled. "You're asking us about a *LikeMe* account?"

"It has only one post, but it's gone viral," Officer Flanigan says, holding out her phone to them. "It has a picture of the three of you."

Caro takes the phone first. It's a picture of her, Hope, and Ash at Sonnet. Caro's chest knots painfully. *Hope.* She's sitting by the fire in her orange Sonnet hoodie, holding a skewer with a marshmallow on it, leaning forward to say something to Ash and Caro.

Who took this? Caro wonders with a shiver. This was the night before the hike. *Who was watching* then?

In the photo, Hope looks beautiful and intense, her mouth slightly open. And yes, she is the focus of the picture, but the other women are clearly Caro and Ash. The three of them in their hoodies, faces lit from the fire. There's a slightly vintage feel to the photo, as if whoever took it used a filter to make it look like it had been taken on film.

Caro wishes with every fiber of her being that they had never come here. She would spend the rest of her life just seeing Hope's gorgeous face on a screen, big or small, a movie screen or a computer or a phone, if it would mean that Hope were alive and safe and sound.

"Yes, this is us." Caro hands the phone across the coffee table to Ash. "We're in the photo, but we didn't take it. Obviously."

"We didn't even know it was being taken." Ash sounds shaken. "Who would have done this?"

"So neither of you began this account or have any knowledge of it?" Officer Flanigan says, taking back the phone.

"Let me head this off at the pass." Ash's tone has sharpened. "We did not make this account. We did not ask someone to take this picture and then post it. We also did not hurt our friend. We love Hope Hanover, and we will do anything and everything we can to help and find and protect her."

"You sound defensive," Officer Flanigan says.

"We're not," Ash says. She hands her phone to Officer Flanigan. "Here. You can see from this that I didn't start the account or access it. And Caro and I have been getting anonymous texts and calls. Can you find out a way to track *those*?" She takes a deep breath. "I'm sorry. I know I'm getting fired up. But we want to help."

"The way you can best help Hope is by answering our questions," Officer Clark says. He's adapted a tone of gentle mildness.

"And we're wondering why you didn't tell the police that it was Hope Hanover who was missing," Officer Flanigan says.

"We gave you—or one of your colleagues, I guess—all the details," Ash says. "The name she was using for this trip, her phone number, her address, everything we knew."

"The name you gave wasn't Hope Hanover," Officer Flanigan says.

"Holy crap." Spencer looks as if he's coming back to life, as if everything they've said over the past few minutes has finally sunk in. Some color has returned to his face, and he no longer looks like he's on the verge of passing out. "Tony was right." Spencer shakes his head. "He kept telling us that she was famous. Kevin and I kept telling him he was seeing things. And we didn't have reception in the canyon, so he couldn't look her up on his phone to prove it."

"So Tony knew," Ash says. She and Caro exchange glances. Hanging out and playing poker with the guys—it had been dangerous. They'd known that. But Hope had insisted on accepting the invitation.

And now both Hope and Tony are missing.

Tony is dead, Caro amends. They have found his body. They have not found Hope's.

A thought darts across Caro's mind, quick as a sparrow. *What happened in the canyon when the rest of us weren't there?* And then another, one that surprises her so much that she takes a step backward, her legs hitting the table behind her. *Could one of them have killed the other?*

We were supposed to disappear, Caro thinks. *But not for good.*

"You didn't recognize Hope?" Ash asks Spencer, sounding suspicious.

"No," he says. "I feel so stupid. I mean, something about her did seem familiar. But she looked, like, older than Hope Hanover. More real."

Yeah, dumbass, Ash's facial expression seems to say, and as she and Caro catch each other's eye, they both have to look away quickly so they don't laugh. It's wildly inappropriate. None of this is funny. They are on the edge.

"She was so…normal," Spencer is saying. "I mean, she was obviously gorgeous. But she didn't have an entourage."

"She *is* obviously gorgeous," Ash says. "Not *was*. And *we're* her entourage." Caro puts a hand on her back.

"Now everyone knows it's Hope who's missing." Ash draws a shuddery breath. "This is going to be a trainwreck."

35

IF THERE ARE ANGELS, *is this how they feel?*

Do they want to weep with frustration because they can see everything but touch nothing?

Someone once told me that bearing witness counts. That being present when something happens, even if it is something hard or terrible that you can't stop, still matters. Because then no one was alone.

Now that I am watching, I don't know if I believe that. What good is bearing witness if you can't bear any of the burden?

And as for angels:

I haven't seen a single one.

36

PAGE

PEOPLE WHO COME TO visit Eden treat it like their playground—it exists for their entertainment, their convenient and sporadic awe. They think it disappears when they're not here and comes into Technicolor existence when they are. And summers are the worst.

Astronomical numbers of YouTube and LikeMe influencers clog the restaurants and sidewalks of Spring Creek. They take pictures at the trailheads and pose next to the sign marking the entrance to Eden National Park. They park illegally and talk loudly. They're outraged when they can't get into the park because of the overcrowding and livestream their displeasure at the very crowds they're part of. With the disaster, it's even busier than usual. And Sonnet is at the heart of the drama now that everyone knows Hope Hanover was staying here.

Only resort guests, staff, and the police are allowed on private property, but influencers and tourists have begun to camp out next to the reporters and other media near our main entrance. The phones have been going crazy all morning with people trying to arrange a last-minute stay or book a meal at Bristlecone.

The crowd was large when I left Sonnet earlier this morning. When the police bring me back several hours later, the masses are still perched in their camp chairs under shade tents or sitting in their cars, air conditioners running. Their heads turn when they hear us coming. I duck down before we get close enough for them to see who I am.

"We're very sorry," the kinder of the two officers says as the tires crunch on Sonnet's gravel drive. He has salt-and-pepper hair and the kind of weathered skin people get from living a life outdoors. His name is Officer Joad, which makes me think of my mom's favorite Springsteen album and the book we read in English about the people during the Depression who tried to change their lives and died. "Thank you again for your assistance."

"Of course," I say, like it's no problem, like I do this kind of thing all the time. I know my voice is too falsely cheerful. I know I'm overdoing it, that my tone is off. We all know that this wasn't my last trip to the police station. Everything is just beginning. Everything has already ended.

"Are you sure we can't take you anywhere else?" Officer Joad asks. "Can you take the day off?"

"No," I say. "I'm needed here." *And I need to be here.* After all of this, after everything—I can't give up now.

As soon as the officers are gone, I walk briskly around to the back of the staff tent and throw up in one of the trash cans there. I let myself stay like that for a minute, bent over. It feels like even when I stand up straight I'm folded in half, like my organs are collapsing in on themselves and there's a heaviness always on my back. I can't ever shrug it off.

I take a deep breath. As I feel my pockets for gum, a mint, anything, my eye catches on Ty standing in the doorway of the staff tent.

"Whoa, there." Ty looks surprised. I don't drink, I don't get hungover, and I don't party, so I'm not one of staff who usually get caught using the trash cans for this purpose. "You okay?"

"Fine," I say. "I didn't sleep great the last couple of nights. I got kind of dizzy a minute ago, and I guess that made me nauseous."

"It's been wild for sure." Ty's expression is sympathetic. "You want anything to eat?"

"I'm good," I say. "Thanks, though."

I'm relieved he's not Carmel, who would definitely press the issue, would try to mother me and make me take a break or drink some Sprite or something. Still, Ty hesitates, as if he doesn't totally believe me.

"I'm fine," I say. This time my voice hits the right note. I sound like myself. I sound like I've got this. "Better get back to work." I open the door to the staff tent. "See you, Ty."

—

EDEN NATIONAL PARK TRAGEDY: WHAT WE KNOW

For once, no guests are lined up at the reception desk. Skye's sitting there alone, looking at her phone, of course, though that's against the rules while we're working. "Look." She holds it out toward me so I can see the headline she's reading. "We're everywhere. This is *People*."

"Have you seen Gareth yet this morning?" I'm not going to engage. Not going to tell her that the article is already outdated, that I have more information than she could dream of.

"No." Skye turns the phone back toward herself. "You should keep up on this," she admonishes me. "It's only going to get bigger." She's not literally licking her chops at the possibilities, but she has her lip gloss out and is applying it liberally. I wouldn't put it past her to go talk to the reporters at the end of her shift.

I need to keep an eye on Skye.

I pull up her LikeMe account on my own phone to see what she's been posting about the disaster. She's already uploaded a reel today. It's her, sitting in a yoga pose out on the plateau, dressed in a matching sage-green workout set. Her back's to the camera, and the morning light's perfect and pink. Some kind of gentle music is probably playing in the background—I don't turn up the volume to find out—and a caption in a wistful, curlicue font appears. *A moment of silence for those who are missing*, it says, with a prayer hands emoji. At end of the reel Skye turns to look at the camera, her expression somber and beatific.

Scrolling down, I see that there's no mention of Hope Hanover being one of the lost hikers in the Underground. It's good that Skye hasn't gotten wind of it yet. It's also, frankly, shocking.

She's watching a video now. My ears perk up when I hear the words *Eden National Park* and *fatalities*. Plural?

What do they know?

"Hey," Skye says. "Have you seen this yet?" She holds out the phone so I can look, too. She hits the Replay button. It's a clip of a police officer speaking to a crowd of reporters on LikeMe, posted to an account that uses the handle @unofficialedenpark.

A thirtysomething man and woman are standing in the parking lot where the SAR team and the police have been staging the rescue. Across the bottom, the caption reads *Children of Ed and Jean Harrow, couple confirmed dead in flash flood.*

Out of the corner of my eye, I see guests coming in the main entrance of the tent, but I can't tear my gaze away from the families and friends, the loved ones, of the missing. The gone.

The daughter is tearful. "We're heartbroken," she says. "But if they could have chosen how they went, it would be like this. They were together doing what they loved most."

A movement catches my eye. I look up to see Ash and Caro standing at the desk.

"They loved drowning in fear together?" Ash mutters, and I catch my breath. That was *dark*.

But I get it, and even though it's wildly inappropriate to do so, I want to laugh.

"Oh my gosh," Caro says to Ash, but you can hear a note of almost-laughter in her voice, too. They're both on the edge, a feeling and place I recognize. "Let them believe what they need to believe."

"Sorry," Ash says. "But when you know how it actually was—"

"We don't know how it actually was," Caro says. "We weren't them."

"That's true," Ash says.

Skye is looking from one woman to another as they speak.

"Sorry," Ash says to Skye. "Would you mind if we took a look at that clip again? We were in the canyon with the people who died."

"Oh, of *course*." Skye hands them her phone. "I'm so sorry about what you guys have been through." I can see her perking up. Is she going to try to get in good with them? Is she going to film them for content?

And she doesn't even know that Hope Hanover is their friend who is missing. She will soon, and she's going to lose her damn mind when she finds out.

"It *is* them," Ash says sadly as the video plays again and the faces of the couple who died come up on the screen. *Couple celebrating their fortieth wedding anniversary dies in flood*, the caption says.

"Damn it." Caro's voice is exhausted and sad.

They hand the phone back to Skye.

"If there's anything I can do to help," Skye says, dropping her voice in sympathy, "please let me know."

The women nod.

Skye gives a satisfied smile. She's probably picturing herself posting about the inside scoop she has on the tragedy, how she's BFFs with the women who lost their friend. The selfie potential! The increase in followers! Another guest comes up to the desk with a question about checkout time, and as Skye speaks with him her eyes track Ash and Caro. She thinks she's in.

Oh, Skye, I think, *you don't have any idea how far off you are.*

37

ASH

"IS THIS HOW HOPE feels all the time?" Ash mutters as she and Caro run the gauntlet into the police station. Spencer took them to retrieve Caro's car from the trailhead parking lot earlier, and they're driving it now, but they had to park several blocks away, thanks to the crowds.

The town of Spring Creek is charming: ice cream and sandwich shops, outdoor equipment rentals, Mexican restaurants, pizza parlors, art galleries, rock shops, electric bike rentals, hotels—all tucked in pioneer-esque buildings or newer, tasteful, modern ones against the base of towering red-rock cliffs. And it's *busy*. To Ash, Spring Creek feels like the opposite of Story, the dead little town on the other side of the Devil's Backbone.

The police station is also charming—a red sandstone exterior with wooden beams and xeriscaping. It looks fairly new. A small army of reporters, paparazzi, and hangers-on are milling about, and when they got wind that Ash and Caro are Hope Hanover's friends, they moved as one in their direction, like a school of fish or a flock of birds. It's unsettling.

"Where's Hope?"

"Have you heard from Hope?"

"Are you here because the police found her?"

"Or her body?"

"Ghouls," Caro mutters.

"Have you heard from her agent?" asks a person holding a microphone (a reporter? a podcaster? it could be anyone, in this day and age). "She's supposedly trying to get in touch with you."

"Do you think that's true?" Caro asks Ash.

They've only met Hope's agent once—briefly, online—but she seems like someone you'd want to have on your side. Hope never gave either Ash or Caro contact info for Raye, though. And Hope didn't tell Raye where she'd be. Is there a reason for that?

Before Ash can answer, someone shoves into her from the side. "Hey!" Caro says, immediately pulling Ash closer to protect her. "Give us space."

Don't engage, Ash thinks, but the mistake has been made. The press of people is fully upon them, and there are so many people shouting out that she can't tell what any of them are saying.

But then a voice pierces the cacophony. "What are *you* doing to find her?" someone shouts. "You're her friends! You're in all those pictures with her!"

Pictures? Ash thinks. *There's more than one?*

The door to the police station opens and Officer Flanigan comes out. "You didn't tell us you were coming," she says to Ash and Caro, her voice tight. *"Hey!"* she shouts at the crowd. "Move back!" They obey, but barely.

"You have our phones," Ash says as Officer Flanigan ushers them in the door. She takes them past the officers and receptionist in the foyer, through a metal detector, and down a hall past cubicles teeming with people.

"Here." Officer Flanigan opens the door to a small room with two-way mirrors, a table, and four chairs. The room is cold and overly air-conditioned. "I'll be back." She closes the door behind her, and things are quiet.

"She seems pissed at us," Ash says, rubbing her arms.

"She does," Caro agrees. "But maybe she found something out about the anonymous numbers." She pulls out one of the chairs and sits down, stretching her long legs in front of her. The gesture is one of trying to ease discomfort, not of nonchalance. "Did you talk to Wade this morning before we let them take our phones?"

"Yeah," Ash says. "Did you talk to Dan?"

"Yeah. It was good to hear his voice." Caro sounds wistful, and Ash feels a tinge of jealousy. Caro and Dan seem so evenly, perfectly matched, in sync in every way. They don't have kids, and Ash wonders if that's because they don't feel like they need anyone else. They even look a bit alike—tall and lanky, skin that easily tans, warm brown eyes. In fact, Ash thinks, Dan and Spencer look alike, too, except for the fact that Spencer's bald and Dan has that thick shock of dark brown hair. Caro definitely has a type. Does *Ash* have a type? Wade used to have (more) blond hair; he still has blue eyes. Does Ash usually crush on people who look like that?

She doesn't know if she has a type. She's had Wade for so long.

"I called my dad's care facility, too," Caro's saying. "He was resting and couldn't come to the phone, but they said he's been doing well the last couple of days."

"That's great." But Ash isn't ready to move away from Dan and Caro and what Dan knows. "Did you tell Dan anything about where we are?"

"Not yet," Caro says. "But when we get our phones back, we'd better let them know. If our photos are all over social media, someone's going to see that and send them any second now. It's better that it comes from us."

Ash is grateful that Caro didn't ask if she's said anything to Wade. Ash didn't tell him where they were this morning, but he didn't ask. Maybe because he already knows. She gave him plenty of hints during that phone call the first night. "Do you think you could really have gone the whole time without talking to Dan?" she asks Caro now.

"I was planning on it." Caro turns to look at Ash, and Ash wonders what she's thinking. Does Caro know that Ash broke the rule the very first night?

"Do you think *you* could have?" Caro asks Ash.

"I guess we'll never know," Ash says.

Caro rotates her neck, as if it's giving her discomfort, too. "How *is* your family? I'm sorry I didn't ask yet."

"They're fine," Ash says. "Wade actually ended up going on a trip. His mom is watching the girls."

"Really?" Caro says. "Does he do that kind of thing a lot?"

"No," Ash says. "Especially not on his own, like a guys trip. I'm glad he's doing it. Usually I'm the one who's traveling." She sits down next to Caro and lowers her voice in case there's someone behind the one-way window. "To be honest," she says, and she's not sure why she's telling Caro this, she's never told anyone, "I never know what I'm going to find when I get back from a trip these days." She exhales. "The last time I went out of town, for a buying trip, I came home and found out that he'd bought a new car."

"Oh?" Caro says.

Ash knows it doesn't sound that bad. None of the things that happen are things like *He cheated* or *He hit me* or *He doesn't do anything with the kids* or *He can't hold down a job* or *He's an addict.* The things Wade does are really, truly, not that bad, on the surface. But they hurt.

How do you describe it? The way he undercuts her, taking the wind out of her sails, wearing her down?

"He did it without talking to me about it," Ash says at last. "We'd always discussed big purchases before."

"Oh, of course," Caro says, and the matter-of-fact way she says it feels so validating that tears start to Ash's eyes. "That's the kind of thing couples should talk about. I'd be livid if Dan did that without our having a conversation first."

"Right?" Ash says. "When I said that, Wade got mad. He said it was his money and he could do whatever he wanted with it, and he didn't have to run it past me first."

"Hold on." Caro sits upright. "What does that mean, it's *his* money?"

"I mean, it *was* his money," Ash says. "The money he makes from his dental practice."

Caro looks Ash straight in the eyes. "Yeah, but do you talk about any big purchases you make with *your* money?" she asks Ash. "Money from Three Sisters? If *you* went ahead and bought a car without talking to *him* first, would he be mad?"

"Well, yeah, but that's both of our money," Ash says.

"And the dental practice isn't?"

"Well, he helped me so much with getting the business off the ground…"

"And you didn't do the same for him?" Caro asks. She pushes the chair back, and it screeches across the concrete floor, making them both wince. "Plus bear his children?"

"Our children," Ash says.

"Still," Caro says. Then they're both quiet. Ash hears the air-conditioning kick on again, and she rubs at her goose-bumped arms.

"What else has he done while you've been gone?" Caro asks.

Ash sighs. "The trip before, he cleaned out our closet."

"And what was the catch?" Caro prompts, and Ash feels that wash of relief again. Caro understood that there would be a catch, that it wasn't purely a kind, helpful action on Wade's part.

"He only cleaned out my part of the closet," Ash says. "He took all my clothes, shoes, everything out of the closet, and it was all on my side of the bed when I got back. He said I was taking up more than my half of the space."

"I don't understand why he would do that," Caro says. "Did he need more space?"

"Not really," Ash says. "He hadn't ever complained about it before."

"Don't all women take up more than half of the closet?" Caro asks. "I do."

Ash shrugs. "I could see his point. Like, sometimes you want the space even if you're not going to use it. It was—"

"The *way* he did it," Caro finishes.

"Yeah." Ash's throat tightens. "Exactly." She tries to laugh. It doesn't work.

"That was childish," Caro says. "Both of those things are extremely childish."

Wade is *so* supportive, people are always telling Ash. As if her venture is cute and sweet and—*hobbyish*. Not the main source of their income. Wade has a great job, yes. But she's making more money than he is these days. So why does she have to fit her work in around his instead of the other way around?

"Where'd he go on his boys trip?" Caro asks, and Ash feels that contrary, protective surge of emotion again. Why does *boys trip* sound so dismissive? And Wade *is* a great dad, and he *does* works hard . . .

"He didn't tell me," Ash says, and she sees Caro's mouth twist, but before she can say anything the door to the room opens and they both straighten up. It's Officer Clark this time.

Did you find anything out about the calls? Ash is about to ask. But before she can say anything, Officer Clark speaks. His tone is gentle, and his words are directed at Caro. "We've had a phone call from Lookout Pointe."

At first, the name means nothing to Ash—is he talking about a hike? Is it somewhere they could have found Hope?—but Caro blanches visibly, and then Ash remembers that that's the name of Caro's father's care facility.

"What happened?" Caro asks, standing.

Officer Clark doesn't gesture for her to sit down. Behind him, in the mirror, Ash can see his straight back, Caro's wide-open eyes. "Your father is missing."

38

PAGE

—

BEFORE

Hi!

Its Page.

You probubly guessed that. ☺

Does anyone else rite you letters?

I know everyone else probubly texts.

I wish I had a phone.

We went on a feild trip today to a ghost town. They showed us picktures of it before we went. There were old houses and old trees with yellow leaves and nobody alive lives there anymore. Everyone was saying oooh and that maybe it was hunted and I was excited. It looked scary but not too scary. I was hoping we would walk into the ghost houses and the ghosts would come and talk to us like Night at the Musuem.

None of that happened. We ate our lunches sitting in the cemetery and Brad Wilton thot it would be funny to pee on a grave and Mrs. Chavez got mad at him.

Maybe it was because of Brad peeing or because it wasn't dark enough or because everyone was being really loud.

But anyway I didn't see any ghosts.

Did YOU see any when you came on your feild trip here?

Do you think ghosts are real? Do you think they come and hunt you?

Miss you love you,
Page

39

CARO

THESE ARE THE FACTS.

According to the director of Lookout Pointe, with whom Caro has finished speaking, Caro's father, Henry, went missing this morning after she called to check in on him.

Since Henry usually wakes up around 6 a.m., eats breakfast, goes on a walk with the staff, and then takes a long morning nap, preferring to eat lunch at the later 1:00 p.m. seating, they didn't realize that he was gone until 12:45 p.m., when a staff member went to pick him up and he wasn't in his room.

They conducted an extensive search of the premises of Lookout Pointe, surrounding areas, and places that Henry has been known to frequent during his time at Lookout Pointe, such as the Wendy's where he likes to go for Frostys and locations where the staff have taken the residents on field trips.

They also conducted an extensive search of landmarks from his earlier life, including the home where he raised Caro and the building that once housed his medical practice.

Then they notified the police in St. John, who issued a Silver Alert. They were unable to get in touch with Caro, but the Lookout Pointe staff later remembered that she had given them a number in addition to her cell phone number. That number was for Sonnet.

The staff are devastated, apologetic, and cooperative. They have never experienced this before. Their memory care unit is secure and state-of-the-art.

No, they say when she asks them, no, he hasn't escaped before, ever. He has *tried* to wander off, but never successfully.

Yes, they did take a field trip last week to Story and to Cooper's Rock Shop. It was at Henry's suggestion, in fact. Many of the residents expressed how much they enjoyed the day. Yes, the owner and Henry did seem to know each other. They had a brief conversation, which Henry had seemed to enjoy.

He never told Caro. Why? Did he simply forget, or is it more than that?

She lifts up her phone to call Dan, her automatic response when anything happens in her life, good or bad or boring or bright.

And she puts it down.

Caro's led Ash to believe that she's been talking to Dan since they got out of the canyon. But she hasn't. Lately, she's been feeling like she's wearing Dan out. There's been all the stuff with her dad, of course. And then the hospital case on top of that.

And the other, bigger loss. The one so big she hasn't told Dan about it.

Which is so absolutely wrong of her.

Caro remembers the time when she and Dan were dating and she brought him home for the weekend. She'd known her dad would be gone, taking a youth group down the Underground. She had her own key, and she knew Henry wouldn't mind (he'd met Dan and liked him), but it felt somehow naughty to bring Dan home without her dad being there, to be totally unchaperoned. After existing in tiny shared college spaces, having a house to themselves felt like utter and total luxury. She and Dan had gotten a pizza—from the Pizza House, she remembered, delightfully oily and cheesy and covered in pepperoni and olives, her weird family favorite that Dan had cheerfully come to love, too—and they'd been watching sports. They had joked about how they should brush their teeth before they started making out but ultimately had been far too lazy, and things had been getting very interesting when they heard the door, which they hadn't bothered to lock, swing open.

A man stood in the doorway.

Caro had clutched the throw blanket to her. Dan, to his credit, had sprung to his feet, ready to face the attacker. Neither of them had even considered—and neither of them even recognized, for a few minutes—that it was her father.

"Caro?" he asked.

"Oh my gosh, *Dad*," she said, and her fear was replaced with a wave of annoyance and frustration. "I thought you were going to be out of town. Weren't you hiking the Underground?"

It was then that she saw he was filthy, streaked with the red-sand mud so typical of southern Utah. "Caro," he said. "You're alright."

"Of course I'm alright," she said. "What are you talking about?" and then Dan must have made some motion behind her and she said, "Dad, this is Dan, remember?"

Her father lifted a hand to Dan, but he was still looking at Caro. "There was a tragedy," he said. "In the Underground." His voice was shaky, raw. "A girl fell. Not with our group, but I tried to help her." Henry sat down on the armchair abruptly, as if his legs had given out underneath him. "But there was nothing I could do. She was gone by the time I got to her."

Later it became apparent that of course he never thought *Caro* was in the Underground; he'd just driven home in shock and horror at what had happened, and then his mind had begun racing over all the terrible things that could happen to a college-age girl. When he'd seen an unfamiliar car in his driveway, and then walked in and seen her with an unfamiliar man—he hadn't recognized Dan immediately in the dim light—

The accident in the Underground. It had haunted her father. He saw death in his profession, but of course it made sense why someone dying in Eden would break his heart in a different way.

Wait, Caro thinks. *The body we found. Could that be—*

But no, of course it isn't. People were with her. They saw her die. Her father had stayed with the girl who fell until a team came to retrieve her body. So this *other* body—

Caro closes her eyes.

40

ASH

"WHAT THE HELL ARE we watching?" Ash asks.

She and Caro are sitting in a cherry-red Thunderbird at the drive-in theater. It is the most incongruous thing they could possibly be doing, given the situation, but they've washed up here like two exhausted shipmates on a desert island. They didn't know where else to go.

"You've never seen *Planet of the Apes*?" Caro asks.

"I have," Ash says. "With Mark Wahlberg."

"That's the remake," Caro says. "This is the original."

"It's disturbing." On-screen, one of the plastic-faced apes has shot a hairy-chested Charlton Heston.

"It is." Caro sounds weary. Ash knows that they're both talking about the movie even though there are so many other, deeper things they could be talking about because they are *worn out*.

They've been looking and looking and looking, running around all over, and they aren't any closer to finding Hope.

Or Caro's dad, for that matter.

Caro drove over to St. John to speak with the director at the residential center and to look for Henry herself. She just got back, and she looks exhausted. Ash spent the afternoon talking with Raye, Hope's agent, who she's decided she likes very much. But she has a very strong sense that Raye doesn't have all of the information, either.

None of them do.

At least Hope's not dead, Ash thinks. But then her traitorous mind follows up with *You don't know that*.

Someone's walking toward their car, backlit against the movie screen. Ash's heart skips in fear. She lifts her phone to shine a light in the face of whoever it is.

"Oh," Caro says. "It's Spencer."

"Right." Ash lowers her phone. She didn't recognize him, but why would she? She barely knows him.

"Hey," Spencer says, bending down to talk to Caro through their window. "Have you guys heard anything?"

"Shhh!" someone from another car whispers. Everyone has their windows rolled down to let in the cooling evening breeze.

"Hop in," Caro says to Spencer. She climbs out and folds the front seat so that he can climb into the tiny back seat behind them. He's so tall. His knees jut up high when he sits down. He looks better, like he's rested and had a chance to shave.

"Have you heard anything more?" he asks them.

"No," Ash says. "You?"

He shakes his head. "Nothing."

"How's Kevin doing?"

"Not great."

"Why are you still here?" Ash asks. "At the resort?"

"Ash," Caro says, but Ash wants to know. Shouldn't he be back in St. John comforting Kevin? Helping with Tony's funeral plans?

"Well." Spencer sounds embarrassed. "I did think about it. But Kevin's super busy with his family, and I didn't know Tony all that well. And I thought maybe I could help out here." Ash glances over her shoulder into the back seat. Spencer's looking at Caro as he says this. "Since you have two people missing."

"There's got to be more to it than that." Ash feels Caro staring daggers at her, but she's not trying to be rude. There are so many unknowns right now that she's going to ask about the things that it might be possible *to* know.

"Okay," Spencer says, after a second. "There is."

"Yeah?" Caro says. "What is it?"

"I actually can't stand Tony," Spencer says. "Couldn't. I came on this hike as a favor to Kevin, because he's married to my sister. Monica."

"Can you also not stand Kevin?" Caro asks.

"Kevin's fine," Spencer says. "But he needed me to come along because I've been down the Underground before and he wanted some backup. This trip was supposed to be an intervention for Tony. He's been drinking too much, and it's gotten out of hand. Kevin didn't want to do it alone. He felt like since Tony and I didn't know each other very well, Tony wouldn't see it as people ganging up on him. But I'd be an extra body if Kevin needed one."

"Yikes," Caro says. "That seems pretty fraught."

Okay, Ash thinks. *No wonder he doesn't really want or need to be around Tony's family right now.*

"Yeah," Spencer agrees. "But we never had the intervention. The first night, you guys showed up. And then the second night Kevin chickened out. Tony was in a bad mood all day. So Kevin decided he'd talk to him when we were hiking out on the last day."

"Too bad for Tony," Ash says. "He died before he could be intervened." She snorts with laughter before she can stop herself. "I'm sorry," she says, horrified. This keeps happening. "I'm apparently coping with all of this by making inappropriate jokes."

"There's no better way," Spencer says.

Ash cranes her neck around to look at him again, the way he's folded into the back seat. "You look like a toy," she says.

"What?"

"You're so squished." The back seat is infinitesimal, and Spencer is tall and lanky. "You know how toy cars are barely big enough to contain the figurines? You look like that."

"You're right," Spencer says. "Toys never have any headspace in their motor vehicles."

"They don't," Ash agrees. "Think about Little People. Barbies. Lego figures."

"Unless the vehicles in question are convertibles," Spencer says.

"Which this is not," Caro says. "Spencer, seriously, come sit up here. I'll go in the back."

"You're as tall as I am," Spencer says.

"I'm sorry we didn't get here in time for the '57 Chevy," Ash says. "That's my favorite car, and it's much bigger." She checks out the people who *are* sitting in the Chevy, a young couple snuggled up together in the front seat. "Maybe another night," she says, which is ridiculous, because how often are they going to sit around and watch movies with their best friend still missing?

The couple making out in the '57 Chevy accidentally hits the horn.

"You'd think the staff would have deactivated that." Ash glances around at the other vehicles. "Hey. There's a Buick Century up there that's empty. Those have decent back seats."

"I didn't know you knew so much about cars," Caro says.

"I'm full of surprises." Ash opens her door.

"I really am fine," Spencer says, but Ash is already out of the car. She feels antsy, itchy, cannot sit still. Maybe more space will help. Caro follows suit, and Spencer has no choice but to come with them.

They scuttle across the lot, hunched low so as not to block the view of the other guests. "Caro," Ash hisses, low so Spencer can't hear.

"What?"

"I think he likes you," Ash says.

"What?" Caro asks. "Who?"

"*Spencer,*" Ash says.

He's only a few feet ahead of them. He slows, his lanky form pausing near a car. It's not the one Ash had in mind. She gestures for him to go to the end of the row.

"Why?"

"He said he was staying here to see if he could help us out," Ash says. "He could be with his sister and her husband."

"He already explained all of that," Caro says. "And it doesn't mean anything."

"I think it does," Ash says. "And he's cute."

"Hope's missing," Caro says. She sounds weary. "And I'm with Dan."

"I know," Ash says. "I'm pointing it out because it's interesting." *And might be relevant*, she wants to say, but doesn't.

They're arrived at the car Ash had in mind, the sturdy Buick Century with its nose turned toward the screen. Caro heads for the passenger side, but when she gets there she pulls up short.

"Someone's inside," she says.

"So we sit somewhere else," Ash says, but then the way the figure is seated, their posture, gives her pause. She joins Caro on the driver's side of the car, where the person is sitting, and leans in closer.

"Oh my gosh," Ash says. "Are they dead?" Her mind has jumped to the worst. It makes sense that she has, given that worst-case scenarios keep cropping up, but the figure inside moves and Ash exhales in relief. "Okay. This one's taken. We'll go back to our car, no big deal."

But Caro is frozen. *"Dad?"* she says.

41

CARO

"DAD." CARO TRIES TO keep her voice even so she doesn't startle him. "Are you okay?"

But it's clear he doesn't recognize her. This breaks her heart, though it's happened before. He has placed his hands at ten and two on the steering wheel, perfect driving position.

She tries his first name. It always feels so strange coming from her lips. "Henry," she says.

This time, he looks at her.

"Hi," she says. "Can I help you, Henry? Should we get you home?" Wait. What, exactly, does she mean by *home*? She can't take him back to where they used to live, and she's not going to take him back to Lookout Pointe after they *lost* him, is she? Her head is swimming. What *is* her plan, exactly?

But oh, is she glad to see him. Careful not to alarm him or get too close, she stands by the car door and looks him over with a doctor's eye, noting what she can in the light from the movie screen. His hands are scraped but the cuts look superficial. The knees of his khakis both seem dirty, one of them torn. There are no visible facial or head injuries.

"Something is wrong." Now Henry *is* looking at her, really looking at her. He has a very worried expression on his face, one that tears her up every time she sees it. She thinks again about how her dad's life used to be so big—hiking up and down the canyons and trails he loved, teaching, working at the hospital, going on trips, and always, always making new friends. Now it's so limited.

Maybe that's why he tried to come to Eden. Maybe a part of him remembers how much he loved it.

But then why did he end up at Sonnet? The resort itself is not a place he's ever been before. It's much newer. She's not even sure he'd heard about Sonnet before his mind started to slip.

I'm thinking about him in the past tense, she realizes. *And he's right here in front of me.*

"What is it?" Caro asks him.

"This car." Henry taps the steering wheel with his fingers. "It won't go anywhere." His eyes are sad, focused again on the steering wheel. "Why?"

Caro's phone vibrates in her hand, and she glances down at it automatically. When she sees who it's from, a complicated mixture of relief and shame and love washes over her. *Dan.*

She's worried she's wearing him down, and she's keeping a secret, and if he knows Hope is missing, if he knows exactly what's going on, he'll want to call or come see her, and she can't handle that. Caro absolutely cannot take his kindness, his Dan-ness, right now.

She reads the text.

> Hey, I know you won't get this yet. I don't want to ruin your vacation. But when you do check your phone, you're going to get some news that worries you and I want you to know I'm on it.
>
> Your dad's gone missing, and it seems kind of serious. I've driven down to St. John to see what I can do. Got a hotel as close to Lookout Pointe as I could. I'll keep you posted.

Hopefully by the time you get this we've found him and everything's good.

Dan's here. Or nearby, anyway. He came down from Salt Lake City. He's only an hour away. She will have to deal with this. But for now, she can't leave him worrying.

I've found him, she texts back. He seems okay. I've actually been in Utah. More in a minute.

Thank heavens. Dan's immediate response. Okay. I'll sit tight until I hear more. So glad he's okay. Love you.

He always knows the right thing to say. So it should be so easy to tell him everything.

And he's always been such a nice guy. But she knows—she's seen it firsthand with her dad—that even the nicest guys can break.

"What can we do?" Ash asks Caro gently.

"I want to take him to the hospital in St. John," Caro says. "He'll hate it, but we have to make sure he's okay. I want him looked over by a doctor other than me. And then—I don't know what."

"I can help you take him into St. John, if you want me to," Spencer offers.

"That would be great, actually," Caro says. It would be good to have help if Henry decides to run again. This will be twice as fast as having Dan come out and help her take Henry into St. John. Caro glances at Ash. She feels torn. Can she abandon Ash when they're still missing Hope? Ash is alone here. She doesn't have friends or family in the area. "I think one of us should stay here, too. In case anything happens with Hope."

"Okay," Ash says. "Take your time. Please. I'll keep calling the police station to find out if there's anything new."

Caro reaches out and squeezes Ash's hand. It feels odd—dangerous even?—to leave Ash on her own. "I'll have Dan look after him so I can come back to Sonnet as soon as possible. Can you stay—I don't know where—somewhere near other people?"

"I'll finish the movie," Ash says. "Then I'll hang out in the common area by the food truck. And *then* I'll lock myself up nice and tight in the Airstream if you're still not back."

"I'll hurry." Caro turns to her dad.

"Henry," she says, as gently as possible. "We have a car that *does* work. Let's have you come with us. We can get you something to eat if you're hungry. Maybe Wendy's? Maybe a Frosty?"

For a second she thinks he won't let go of the steering wheel, that he won't come with her. But then:

"Yes," he says, and opens the car door.

42

ASH

ASH IS ALONE.

She texts Wade again. Could you please tell me where you are?

Minutes pass. Nothing. On-screen, the apes are preparing to make their last stand.

Ash knows it's unfair to ask her husband for information that she's been withholding. Still, there's a pit in her stomach. *Why did she have to call him that first night?* In spite of recent events, she still doesn't know much about how hard it is to track a cell phone. She assumed that calling Wade would be fine, that he would never do such a thing, but could anyone really blame him if he had? His wife leaves on a trip and won't tell him where she's going?

She imagines him explaining it to his mom or to Derek. Lois, his mom, prides herself on being a wonderful mother-in-law, a class act in all circumstances. So Lois won't say anything outright, but her face will take on a meaningful expression and she'll say something like, "Ash is an amazing woman and you are a *wonderful* husband, Wade. I'm sure she wouldn't ask for this if she didn't need it, and I think you're doing the right thing by giving it to her." Then Wade and his brother would trade smirks at the way Lois had phrased *giving it to her,* but they wouldn't laugh outright because then they'd have to explain the joke to Lois and she wouldn't like it.

Ash is so sick of golden boys.

She texts her daughters, aiming for a light and breezy tone.

> Hey girls! How is today going? How's Grandma? Remind me again where Dad and Uncle Derek went on their trip?

She doesn't love the way she's asking the girls the question. It feels like she's using them to find out about Wade. Putting them in the middle.

Instead of feeling like she's on the inside of something special—which is how it's felt to Ash ever since the group came together that first night online—she feels like she's standing on the outside of a place where she used to live, craning her neck for a glimpse through a window. It's a feeling she's had the last year or two in her family, in her marriage. *You're everything to me! Am I even a minor character in your life?*

Ash puts her hands on the steering wheel the way Henry had his. She presses her foot against the gas pedal and imagines speeding, Thelma and Louise style, right through the screen and out among the red plateaus to find her friend. Maybe instead of Brad Pitt in a tank top she'll find Hope.

Ash glances at her phone again. Nothing more from the anonymous number. The police said they couldn't track the calls or messages, but how hard did they really try? And are the police telling Ash and Caro the truth about everything, or do they consider them to be suspects in Hope's disappearance?

We told them everything. Even what we swore to Hope we wouldn't. And it might not even matter.

Ash realizes that the movie has ended. Other people are slamming their car doors, and the screen is dark. The pathway lights glow, lighting the way, and she hears people walking on the gravel as they make their way through the juniper trees. The smells of popcorn and sagebrush still hang in the air.

It's blue-black dark now, pinprints of stars above.

Something is nagging at Ash—and it's new, besides Hope being gone and things with Wade feeling off and Tony and Ed and Jean being dead and this whole nightmarish mess—

But what is it?

As Ash goes to leave, something in the footwell sticks to the sole of her shoe and she reaches down to pick it up. A postcard. She turns on her phone's flashlight. The handwriting is familiar, one she's seen on birthday and Christmas cards over the past two years:

Hey Dad,

I was thinking about the Devil's Backbone Drive and how you and I used to go eat at the grill in Story after. I remembered how they served everything on mismatched china and had fresh rainbow trout on the menu. Do you? Should we try to go there again?
I love you.

Caro

Ash flips the card over. A photo of the drive-in theater and a familiar logo look back up at her. It's one of the Sonnet postcards. They all took them to send to people, and they all promised Hope they wouldn't mail the cards until the end of the trip. Of course Caro would write one to her dad.

But this postcard *had* been sent. From the post office in Spring Creek. To his address. Henry Stewart, Suite 34, Lookout Pointe, St. John, Utah.

Ash is cold. What does this mean?

They promised Hope they wouldn't send these. They promised Hope they wouldn't tell anyone where they were.

Other guests are gathering at the picnic tables and firepits to hang out and talk. They are silhouettes and shadows. They are not people Ash knows. She finds herself veering away from the common areas, though she promised Caro that's where she'd stay. She wants to get in her Airstream and lock the door. Anyone could be out there.

Hope had stalkers. They knew that. They should have been more careful. But Hope kept telling them she was like the rest of them, that everyone had weird things in their lives and being famous happened to be her weird thing.

And then they'd found out that someone had been watching them. And then, they made their plan to disappear—

That was Hope's gift and her curse (*please don't let it also be what got her caught and killed*): She never thought that she was better than anyone else. She never saw herself as more than the others. But she *was*. She was in more danger than the rest of them the entire time.

Ash is almost to her trailer when her phone vibrates. She looks down and there it is, another message.

Surprise!

It's me again.

There's one more thing I need you to do.

43

BEFORE

"I CAN'T BELIEVE THIS, Hope," Ash says as their faces come up on the screens of their new phones.

"Right?" Hope says grimly. She glances over her shoulder, a gesture that causes the other two to do the same.

"Are we sure this is safe?" Caro asks.

"It should be," Hope says. "But we'll have to keep it that way. We can only talk about this on these phones, when we can't be overheard by anyone, and when we're not in our houses or our cars." She's in a grassy meadow. Caro is in a park, and Ash is at the elementary school Claire attends near their home.

"Ash, are you at your kids' school?" Hope asks. She sneezes. Her allergies are terrible at this time of year, but she wanted to be able to see in all directions.

"Yeah," Ash says. "I don't think anyone can overhear me, though. I'm standing in the athletic field." She's near an industrial-strength metal garbage can. It smells awful, and there's a popped kickball on top.

"Is someone you know going to drive past and wonder why you're standing outside of your car in the athletic field, though?" Caro asks.

"I don't think so," Ash says. "I'm by a trash can, and I'm acting like I'm going through it."

"Is it possible that might raise *more* questions?" Caro says diplomatically.

"No, I'm going to say I think I threw away my kid's retainer in here if anyone asks," Ash says. "Plus there's a parents' meeting in the school in an hour I have to go to. I didn't know how long this would take, so I wanted to be able to talk for every possible minute."

"I love you, Ash," Hope says, laughing. And then, on a dime, she bursts into tears. "I love you both so much, and I'm so sorry this is happening."

"Oh, Hope," Ash says, alarmed. This is the first time they've seen Hope cry outside of her movies. "It's okay. It isn't your fault."

"Occam's razor," Hope says.

"What?" Ash is confused.

"The simplest explanation is the most likely one," Caro says.

"Oh, right." Ash has heard of this.

Hope sneezes again. "I'm the most likely person to get stalked because of my stupid job, and so I'm the most likely person to have brought this on us."

"No," Ash says fiercely. "Whoever is *doing* this brought this on us. No one else. Not you or me or Caro."

Hope wipes her eyes. "Thanks, Ash."

"How did you figure out this was happening?" Ash asks. "Do you have a background in hacking? Cybersecurity? Are you a tech expert?" Then she snorts with laughter. "Sorry," she says. "I know they aren't called tech experts. And I know this isn't funny."

"It's fine," Caro says. "We have to laugh or we're going to scream. This is creepy as hell."

Ash cocks her head. "And, Hope, you kind of *are* a tech expert. Look at *SpyFi*." She's referencing a popular high-tech heist movie that Hope filmed several years ago, the one where both her black leather catsuit and sarcastic one-liners went viral in all the best ways. "You had to know what *some* of that jargon meant."

"Actually," Hope says, "I didn't. But we *did* have this brilliant hacker as a consultant on that film. And she's the one who's helping me figure this out." Her voice is steady. She's back in control.

"Thank goodness," Ash says. "What's her name?"

"Actually, I'm not sure she *is* a girl," Hope says. "None of us ever met her in person. We were only allowed to talk to her a few times, at night, and she—or he, or they—always used voice-changing software. But she does go by the code name Jane Marple. So that's why I keep saying *she*."

"Well, *that* feels a little on the nose," Ash says. A brown paper lunch bag blows past behind her.

"She told me she uses a different name for each job," Hope says. "We got this one for obvious reasons."

"I also hope it means she's, like, eighty-five," Ash says. "I hope she knits like Jane Marple, too."

"And you trust her?" Caro asks.

"More than I trust anyone else for this," Hope says.

"How does she think it happened?"

"Someone logged on to the initial meeting without anyone else knowing," Hope says. "They didn't reveal they were there, and none of us noticed it."

"The bookstore person," Ash says. "The liaison. And all the people who work at the bookstore. That has to be where the breach happened, right? That makes the most sense."

"Well," Hope says, "that did seem likely. But I paid Jane to go to San Francisco, and she checked out a few things, like which employee physically set up the call that night and which computer they used. She also hacked into their system. She doesn't think that's where it came in."

"Hacking into their system is for sure not legal," Caro says.

"It for sure isn't," Hope agrees. "Anyway, she also managed to hack the employees' personal computers, and there's nothing there, though she admits she'd have to burglarize their individual apartments to be sure, and that's not her specialty."

"Right," Caro said. "And *also* illegal."

"So when we find who's been watching us, what are we going to do to them?" Ash asks. The others stare at her. A wind ruffles her long, loose hair, but her expression is steel. "What?" she says. "These are our lives that are being spied on. Our friendship. Our *families*."

"You're turning out to be kind of a hardass," Hope says, admiration in her tone. "Now I kind of feel like I *should* hire someone to break into their apartments. How much do you think that would cost?"

"Hope," Caro says. "How much money have you spent on this already?"

"An unholy amount," Hope says.

"I'm sorry," Caro says. "And thank you."

"Me too," Ash says. "When did you realize that someone was watching us?"

"About two weeks ago," Hope says.

"Why did you wait so long to tell us?"

"I wanted to be sure, and I wanted to figure out the best way for us to talk," Hope says. "We still need to communicate on our regular phones and keep having our meetings on our regular computers, unless we want them to know that we're on to them."

"Which we don't want to do until we know who they are, right?" Ash asks.

"That's my thought," Hope says. "But, of course, we all need to make the decision."

"It would probably be a hard thing to get the police or the FBI to investigate because they haven't made any threats, right?" Caro asks. "They're just lurking?"

"Exactly," Hope says. "Though we can try. But again, then whoever it is will know."

"How could you tell it was happening?"

"Like I said, it was about two weeks ago," Hope says. "It was the call where we talked about the murder mystery where the husband takes his new wife to Palm Springs." The others nod. "I was the last to leave. When you all exited, there was still a user on for a split second. It had a jargony, made-up name—*LikeMe Host*—and I thought, wait a minute, that's not right."

"You *must* have a stalker again," Ash says. "Who else would do this?"

"And we trust Jane?" Caro asks again.

"I mean, as much as I can," Hope says. "But she doesn't know about these phones. If you want, I can also send her out to have a look at your stuff."

"No, thank you," Ash says immediately.

"Why not?" Caro asks. "Maybe we could also figure out who *she* is somehow."

"We don't have to make that call right now," Hope says. "I wanted to get you thinking about all of this. Put you in the loop. We can talk and text as much as we want on these phones. But you've *got* to keep them secure." She stands up, the view of the trees behind her shifting. "I want both of you to go and open a post office box. Don't tell anyone about it. Text me the PO numbers, and I'll send you each a new phone every week."

"Hope, that's too much," Ash says. "How will we ever pay you back?"

"We'll figure it out," Hope says. "Don't worry about that part for now." She's walking, and a bird flits by in the background behind her. "Right now, I need you both to think—hard—about the people in your lives who might want to stalk you or spy on you or hurt you."

"Done," Ash says. "There is literally no one in my life who would want to do those things."

"Me either," says Caro.

"I hate to say this," Hope says, "but don't be so sure."

Sunday

On the chalkboard outside the Sonnet resort main office

In honor of Hope Hanover, we will be showing her films today, beginning at noon and running until midnight. Our thoughts are with Hope, her family, and her friends.

<h1 style="text-align:center">44</h1>

PAGE

HOW MANY DAYS CAN you survive without food? I think it's like a week. But that's if you have a clean source of water, and if you don't get hypothermia or heatstroke or sick or injured.

Better take more.

I'm stuffing my backpack full of snacks in the staff tent when Skye, Gareth, Mal, and Addie come inside.

I zip up the bag quickly, even though I'm not stealing. I don't want them noticing how much I've taken or wondering why I'd need it all. "We're one of the top three stories on CNN today," Addie says. She reads from her phone. "'Body Count Rises in Eden National Park After Tragic Flash Flood.'"

"'That's nothing," Skye says. "Did you see TMZ? The *Daily Mail*? *People* again?"

I have what I came for. I should go. But I want to know how much— and what—information is out there.

"Did you know that *Hope Hanover* was staying here?" Gareth asks me. He sounds accusatory.

"Yeah, Page," Skye says. "*Did* you?"

I don't answer. I wonder why Gareth is so grumpy. And why Skye is in such a bad mood if all her dreams of media attention are coming true.

Have her LikeMe numbers plateaued? Have people started turning to other sources of information, like the @findhopehanover account? Has she found herself threatened by the force of Hope Hanover's presence, even in her absence?

Because Hope *is* a force to be reckoned with. I knew that the very first time I met her.

"I looked at the log, and you're the one who checked her in when she got here," Skye says.

"Hope Hanover used her real name?" Addie sounds skeptical.

"No," Skye says. "She used a weird one. Chastity Bentley. But Page was the one working when she checked in. And even Page would recognize Hope Hanover. Right?" She takes a couple of steps closer. I keep my mouth shut and don't move.

"Come on," Addie says. "Why are you being so weird about this, Skye?"

"*I'm* not the one who's being weird," Skye says airily.

I'm so tired. I haven't slept well in days—or maybe it's been weeks, or years. I haven't been eating great, either, grabbing what I can find on my way from one problem to the next.

"Did you creep around her tent spying on her like you did Colby?" Skye asks.

The shot hits home. *She knows about* that?

"She was staying in an Airstream," I say, and I immediately want to bite my own tongue off. *What the hell, Page?* I want to ask myself. *You know better than to respond. You've gone all summer without letting Skye get to you. Why are you allowing it to happen now?*

"For all we know, Page murdered Colby," Skye says. "No one's seen him in days."

I have to hand it to Skye. I didn't think she'd come to *that* conclusion. But maybe I should have. I shoulder my bag in one quick motion, trying not to give any indication of how heavy it is and how much food I've stashed inside. *Don't give them what they want. Don't respond.* That's the advice. It doesn't work.

There are some people who will always hound and hunt out the weak. You can't stop them. It's how they feed.

But sometimes they make mistakes. I'm bone-weary, but I'm not weak at all.

"Skye, come on," Mal says. "Shut up." He catches my eye. "Skye's talking out of her ass," he says. "None of us think that you murdered Colby. We know he's out of town and you're covering for him."

Skye's pissed now because Mal is taking my side. "*I do,*" she says. "I think that. Why'd he leave all of a sudden? Why isn't he answering any of our texts?"

"You're being a jerk, Skye," Addie says. "Stop."

I stand there, for one more moment, looking at them. I think, *I don't want to be here anymore.*

And that makes me sad, because, for a while, Sonnet was the closest thing to home that I've had in years.

I open the door and slip through. But as it's closing behind me, I pause to hear a little more of what they say.

"I still think it's weird that Colby disappeared and one of our guests disappeared and Page was one of the last people to see them both," Skye says.

"If anything, Colby would be the one to kill Page," Addie says, and my heart almost stops. "They were so close. And he's so much older than she is. Didn't it feel kind of, like, inappropriate? Like he was grooming her?" I hear her slam the fridge door shut.

I feel like throwing up. I like Addie. We've been friendly. Is this what she thinks was going on?

"What about these?" I hear Skye rustling around, and I move closer to listen better. "These freaky pictures that someone keeps taking and putting up on the photo board with the other normal ones?"

A chill runs through me. *I thought I was the only one.*

"What's creepy about these?" Addie says. "They're just, like, candid photos of you around the resort and on hikes."

"They're like *stalker* photos of me," Skye says. "I don't know who's taking them."

"Before you say anything, Addie, it's not me," Mal says. "I didn't take any of these."

Addie must be looking at the photos. "Huh," she says after a second. "I can see what you mean. They *are* only of you. None of the rest of us are in these pictures. And why do they look weirdly old?"

"Because they're using a disposable camera and developing them from film," Skye says with confidence. "I know photos and filters and cameras pretty damn well, thank you very much."

"Okay," Addie says. "I agree, this is kind of creepy."

"It's been going on all summer," Skye says. "Normal staff photos go up of us doing stuff together, printed from the office computer or whatever, and then pretty soon after a couple of these show up on the board. Me at the campfire. Me eating my lunch by the food truck. Me walking across the resort. Me swimming in the pool."

"Why would they put them on the board?"

"To get my attention," Skye says. "To freak me out."

"Have you told Colby?" Addie asks. "Or the police?'

"I told Colby, and he said he'd look into it, but then nothing happened," Skye says. "And then he left. And put Page in charge. There were a couple of people I thought might be stalking me, but now I know who it is."

"Who?" Addie asks.

"Page," Sky says.

My heart hits pause. I can't breathe. *All of this is* so *bad.*

"Come on," Addie says. "Not Page again. Why would it be her?"

"Maybe she has a crush on me," Skye says. "Maybe she's jealous of me. I don't know. But she definitely hates me—"

"Because you've been rude to her all summer—" Addie interjects.

"—and why else wouldn't Colby do anything about it?" Skye says. "Something is definitely off there. You're right. Maybe it's grooming, maybe they have some weird arrangement where they cover for each other's deviant behavior. I don't know."

"Skye," Mal says.

"Why don't the rest of us know where Colby is?" Skye asks. "How come it's only Page who's in the loop?"

"We don't even know that she *is* in the loop," Mal says.

"Well, she's acting like he died and left her in charge," Skye says.

"I believe that someone's creeping on you," Addie says. "But I don't think it's Page."

"Ugh." Skye groans in frustration. "She's not as innocent as you all believe she is."

I close my eyes. Skye's wrong about so many things, but she's right about this. I'm not innocent. I haven't been for a long time.

"And Colby's not grooming her," Mal says flatly. "Colby's gay."

"*What?*" Skye asks. "Are you sure? Why didn't you say that before?"

"I didn't want to out the guy when he hadn't been specific about it with us," Mal says. "His personal life isn't our business."

"And she *wasn't* one of the last people to see Hope Hanover," Addie says. "Hope's friends were the ones in the Underground with her when she disappeared."

"I still don't believe that about Colby." Skye is hung up on the latest revelation, which wouldn't be that much of a revelation if she'd been paying attention.

Colby never tried to hide anything, but he's also discreet. "I don't know that it's fully safe to be out in southern Utah," he'd told me.

"You're probably not wrong," I'd said, thinking of some of the people I'd gone to high school with.

"Although it's probably not fully safe anywhere in this country right now," he'd said.

But I can't fault Skye for missing that, when I've missed so many other things. *Okay. How does knowing all of this change what I need to do next?* I don't know yet.

"And did you see the way she looked at me a minute ago?" Skye asks. She looked like she wanted to kill me."

I do, I think. *I really do.*

Ty's walking from the parking lot, his arms full of boxes. Probably food for the food truck. He's like me; he comes to work sometimes even when it's supposed to be his day off. He lifts his chin at me in greeting. Before he can ask me what I'm doing or offer to get me some food again, I head down the gravel road toward the drive.

I've done the best I can for Colby. He was due back today. The situation was supposed to be handled by now. I haven't heard from him yet, but I'm out of time. I have to go.

Everything is hell. But I'm laughing to myself as I cross the staff parking lot to find my Blazer because I'm so, so tired, and because Skye is so right about some things and so wrong about others. And the staff, the people I spend the most time with, don't know me the way they think they do.

What would they do if I told them that I've seen Hope Hanover?

What if I told them I'd identified the body?

Would they believe me?

45

CARO

"YOU LOOK LIKE HELL," Ash says as Caro walks up to her. A hiker going past looks over at them in surprise. They're at the trailhead at Seraph's Perch, one of the most famous hikes in Eden—deep in the park, miles away from the Underground and less affected by the flash flooding.

"Thanks a lot," Caro says, but she and Ash both crack up. "You do, too."

"I know." Ash takes a deep breath, and Caro feels like she can read her mind. *Enough small talk.* "So," Ash says. "Do you think it's her?"

They're here at this trailhead—weary, stressed out, missing Hope, worried about their families, everything unraveling all around them—because of the mystery text last night.

Caro had been with her dad and Dan, finishing up at the hospital and deciding whether she should take Henry back to Lookout Pointe or stay with Dan in his hotel room for the night, when the text came through.

Surprise!

It's me again.

There's one more thing I need you to do.

Caro had almost dropped her phone.

> Great news—I got you guys a permit for Seraph's Perch!!
> The catch is that the permits are timed. You have to arrive
> at Scout Lookout, the point right before the final ascent, at
> the right time. Or they'll turn you back and you won't get
> to hike all the way to the viewpoint at the top. TRUST ME,
> YOU WANT TO SEE THAT VIEW! That means you'll need
> to arrive at the trailhead at around 6:30 a.m. and LEAVE ON
> TIME. Don't wait for me if I'm not there on the dot.

"I don't know," Caro says. "But if it's not—"

"I know," Ash says. "I don't know what else to do."

Between Hope vanishing and her dad going missing and seeing Dan at the hospital last night (he was wonderful, of course he was wonderful, and she *still* didn't tell him what he deserves to know), Caro is worn out. She closes her eyes. "Everything's falling apart." When she opens them, she sees that Ash is looking at her with a worried expression. "I feel horrible when I'm with my dad because I'm not with you trying to figure out how to find Hope," Caro says. "And I feel horrible when I'm here because I'm not with him."

"Disappointing everyone," Ash says, and Caro nods. They've talked about this before with Hope—how if you're a friend or a parent or a wife or a sister or an employee or a boss or a caregiver or, really, a woman in the world at all, you feel like you're constantly failing everyone all the time.

Another hiker walking past looks over at them in concern, and Caro sees recognition dawn on their face. *They know who we are. Damn it.* They don't need anyone knowing that Hope Hanover's friends are on this hike.

Caro checks her watch. It's 6:35. They need to get going. They should have left by now. They're both in good shape, but this is a steep climb—they'll gain roughly two thousand feet in elevation over a couple of miles, and then they'll need to hike back.

She glances down at the text.

> The park rangers WILL ASK to see your hard copy of the permit. They can ask for it at any time during the hike and they'll for sure ask to see it at Scout Lookout. I left your permit at the Sonnet front desk. Ask for it there. The permit is in Ash's name in case I can't make it. I hope you don't mind, Ash. Make sure you bring your ID. You'll need that too.
>
> PLEASE do this for me! xx

"Are you okay?" Ash wraps an arm around Caro. "Are you sure about this?"

Caro shrugs, fiercely blinking back tears. "We have to follow the texts," she says. "What if it helps us find Hope? What if it helps us find out—" Her voice breaks.

"What if it's dangerous?" Ash asks. "I didn't call the police. Did you?"

"No. They haven't been very helpful so far." Caro exhales in frustration. "They can't seem to find *anyone* who's missing."

"I'll give them a call right now," Ash says. "I'll say we got another message and that we can't tell if it's from her." She lifts her phone and furrows her brow. "Never mind. No coverage. Should we drive back into range and call? Sorry. I should have thought of this sooner. My brain is mush."

"No," Caro says. "We're out of time. We have to go." They start along the trail together, moving quickly. They pass one cluster of hikers, then another. "Did Hope tell you she was doing this?" Caro asks Ash. "Putting the permit in your name and all of that?"

Ash shakes her head. "Maybe she got a permit for herself, too," she says hopefully. "Maybe she's planning on meeting us at the top."

"These permits are famously impossible to get." Caro feels a rare twinge of optimism. "That's what makes me think it *might* be her," she says. "Hope Hanover magic."

Below them, the park shuttle winding its way along the road snaking through the canyon gives out a sigh of exhaust. Under the sound of the footsteps and the noise of fellow hikers in front of and behind them, there are quiet sounds, of birds calling and things moving in the early morning. The sun hasn't yet crested over the massive monoliths reaching up around them, so the sky is palest blue, deepest pink, and the colors of the sandstone are rich and ancient.

It's different from the Underground. Here, they begin on a valley floor, choosing to climb up to the tops of the enormous formations. They aren't descending *into*. They are rising above. But there is risk either way. The park's official website has plenty of warnings about how strenuous and dangerous Seraph's Perch is. Especially when you reach the saddle and then head up a slippery sandstone path along the thin ridgeline to the viewpoint. There, the park service has even affixed chains into the sandstone so that hikers can hold on along some of the more precarious parts.

"What if Hope didn't send this text?" Ash asks softly. "What if it's our lurker?"

"I don't know *what* to think." Caro scrubs the heels of her hands against her eyes in exhaustion. "I don't know if this is a good idea."

"I've been reading about Seraph's Perch online," Ash says. "People die every year hiking it."

"Do you think our lurker would bring us here to try to kill us?" Caro asks, stunned.

"I don't know," Ash says. "Maybe. Why would Hope send us on a hike without her? Why wouldn't she just show up and tell us she's okay?"

"Maybe these are pre-prepared texts," Caro says. "Like emails you can have automatically sent at certain times?"

"Can you do that with texts?" Ash asks.

"I don't know," Caro admits.

They pass a couple holding hands and a group of college-age boys who have stopped to take a drink and look out at the increasingly broadened view. The parking lot already looks small, the cars like toys.

"Hey," Ash says. She's as fast as Caro, but her legs are shorter, and every now and then she has to do a few jog-steps to catch up. "I wanted to ask you about this." She pulls a paper from the back pocket of her shorts and hands it to Caro.

They both keep up the pace as Caro glances down at the postcard Ash has handed her.

Hey Dad,

I was thinking about the Devil's Backbone Drive and how you and I used to go eat at the grill in Story after. I remembered how they served everything on mismatched china and had fresh rainbow trout on the menu. Do you? Should we try to go there again?

I love you.

Caro

"I found it in the Buick after you left," Ash says.

There's a chill to her tone, and at first Caro can't figure out why—or why Ash has the postcard in the first place. Caro glances down at it again, puzzled, and then she sees.

It's postmarked. It's been sent.

Oh. That explains Ash's coolness. They promised Hope they wouldn't mail the cards until the trip was over. But how much does that matter now? Caro can't keep up with anything anymore, with what might be important and what might not. "I didn't mail it," Caro says. "I swear. Someone else must have sent it."

"It reveals our location," Ash says.

"I *know*," Caro says. Is this really that big a deal? Everyone knows where they are now, thanks to the pictures posted all over LikeMe and online—but then she realizes. For Henry to have received the postcard in the mail—to have had it in the Buick to leave it behind—it would have had to be sent while they were *in* the Underground, wouldn't it? She looks closely at the image. There's the Sonnet logo in the corner of the photo, superimposed over a picture of the bluffs near the resort.

Yes. It's certainly her handwriting, and it's definitely from Sonnet.

Which means *that's* how Henry knew where Caro was. It's *her* fault he left Lookout Pointe. But how on earth did he get all the way from St. John to Sonnet?

And Caro has another realization.

Oh no.

Did someone send *all* of her postcards?

Caro stops, fixing her gaze on Ash. "Do you think I'm lying? I swear I didn't send it."

Don't doubt me, she wants to say to Ash. *We have to keep on trusting each other for any of this to turn out okay.*

Instead, what comes out of Caro's mouth is, "Do you know where all of *your* postcards are? When was the last time you saw them?"

"I've been thinking about that." Ash starts walking again, and now it's Caro's turn to jog a few steps to catch up. "I think mine were on my desk in the tent. I'm pretty sure I haven't seen them since I've been in the Airstream." She exhales. "Does this mean someone was sneaking into our tents?"

Oh no. Even though that's the obvious connection, Caro's scrambled brain hadn't yet made it. "But why *would* anyone send them?" she asks Ash. "What's the point? Freaking us out because then we'd know someone was in our rooms? We already knew there was a lurker. Do you think they knew that we knew? What we were doing?" She can't seem to stop asking questions. "How many postcards did you write? What did yours say?"

Ash doesn't answer the questions. She just keeps hiking, one foot in front of the other on the steep path. Caro can't believe this. *Everything is going so wrong.*

"Who do you think sent them?" she asks Ash.

Finally, Ash answers. "You know who it could be," she says.

46

BEFORE

Hey Page,

Thanks for the letter. You're right, you are the only person who sends me real letters instead of texts or emails. I love your letters. I put them all up on the corkboard in my dorm room. I'm sorry I don't always write back every time you write to me. School is so busy! But it's fun, too. I bought you a T-shirt at the campus store, and I'll bring it to you when I visit next time. I think you should come to college here, too. You'll love it.

I do remember going to the ghost town on the field trip when I was in third grade! I didn't see any ghosts, either, but I did think the place had a feeling. Not haunted. But not NOT haunted. Does that make sense? You probably would have felt it more if Brad hadn't been there being disgusting. Come on, dude.

You asked if I had A BOYFRIEND yet, and I don't. (I did meet one guy who I think is extra cute.) But I have boys that are friends. And girls who are friends. And best of all I have you.

Love you miss you,
Eve

47

ASH

CARO IS STRIDING AWAY down the trail quickly and talking even faster. "People love this hike," she says. "Did you know it's become one of the most LikeMe'd spots in America? Which is a pain, because everyone knows about it now. But it *is* one of the most beautiful places in the world. I'm glad you'll get to see it."

There's something almost manic in the way she's speaking and moving, and even though Ash knows it's because of the newly strained feeling between them, she finds it disconcerting. She knows from looking at the hike online last night that the path is going to get steeper and steeper, including a section of switchbacks right before the saddle that other hikers have described as "brutal."

"Aidan Stone did a stunt here for one of the Special Forces movies," Caro says. "You probably already knew that. It was for *End Days*, and he rode his motorcycle off a cliff."

"I did hear about that." They split up to go around a couple hiking up the path. *We are* moving, Ash thinks. *What if we get to the top too soon?*

"Okay," Caro says when they're back together. "Catch me up on your conversation with Hope's agent. With Raye. And how did she find you in the first place?"

"She called when I was in my trailer last night," Ash says. They've already texted about this, but she gets the need to talk it out. She'd want to do the same. "She's arriving at Sonnet this morning, and she wants to meet us at the food truck as soon as we get back from this hike."

They've seen Raye only once before, and it hadn't even been in person. "Say hello!" Hope had told them when she was on location in France a year or so ago, and Raye had briefly appeared on-screen for a few moments while they all exchanged *So good to meet you*s. At that time Ash had had only a quick impression of dark hair, bright eyes, a warm smile.

"What was your takeaway from the conversation last night?" Caro asks.

"Raye's super smart, she cares about Hope, and she's relentless," Ash says. "She will not let up on the police or the park rangers."

"That's great," Caro says. "Right?"

"Yes," Ash says, "but she's also not going to let up on us."

"So she thinks we might have had something to do with what happened to Hope?" Caro keeps her voice down. They're coming up on other hikers.

"Yes," Ash says. "Which makes sense. I mean, I'd think the same."

"What did you tell her?"

"That we didn't," Ash says. "Of course."

They go quiet for a minute, passing a group of teenagers who have a speaker with them playing music. This, Ash knows, is one of Caro's pet peeves, but Caro doesn't even glare at them. She keeps storming up the trail.

"Are we suspicious of Raye?" Caro asks a moment later, when they've gotten some distance. "We probably should be."

"True," Ash says. "Maybe we'll be able to get a better read on her at lunch." The warmth of the sun feels good now, but Ash knows it can get too hot very fast. They should slow down and have a drink. She doesn't suggest it.

"Do you think Hope scheduled these texts?" Caro asks. "Maybe she knew she wouldn't be here."

Ash tries to catch Caro's eye, but she's looking dead ahead. "Why would she do that?"

"I don't know." A few more strides. There's something on the trail ahead that looks like a giant burr, but then it skitters, and Ash pulls up short. "It's a tarantula," Caro says. "It can't hurt you." The spider disappears into a hole at the side of the trail.

A few yards on, and Caro clears her throat. "Okay," she says. "I'm going to ask this because neither of us have said it out loud." She draws in her breath. "Did it look to you like Hope . . . *let* herself fall?"

What? Ash stops in her tracks. "She would *never* do that," she says fiercely. "How could you think that? You were the one she was saving when she went over the edge!"

They hike in silence. The incline steepens and the path leads them into a kind of crevasse, where the air cools and pines grow green. They start up the switchbacks, zigging and zagging, and for once Ash is the one pushing the pace, Caro the one jogging a few steps now and then to keep up.

Ash is outraged. Hope would never do such a thing.

Would she?

⁓

When they reach the lookout at the saddle, they pause, sweating. It's a large flat area, a kind of plateau, with a restroom and another trail map mounted on a large wooden signboard. Slabs of sandstone make natural seats and stopping points. The trail continues up the ragged spine to the viewpoint, tiny trees lining it in green along the way. Ash feels like she's in another country. Other hikers mill around taking pictures and using the restrooms. For those who don't have permits, this is the end of the road, and they're looking wistfully up at the next part of the hike—the narrow clifftop, the chains, the views beyond.

A park ranger stationed at the side of the path waves at them. "Hello," she says. "Are you planning to hike all the way to the top of Seraph's Perch today?"

"We are," Caro says.

"Could I see your permit?" the ranger asks pleasantly. She's a slim woman with a wide-brimmed hat and a cheery expression. Ash unzips the pocket of her shorts and pulls out the permit and her ID. As the ranger checks them over, Ash has an impulse. Before she can overthink it or run it past Caro, she's pulled up a photo of Hope on her phone and is showing it to the ranger. "We're wondering if our friend might be meeting us on the hike," she says. "Have you seen her today?" She ignores Caro's startled glance.

The ranger's face lights up in recognition, and Ash's heart leaps. But— "I'm sorry," the ranger says. "I haven't. This must be so difficult."

Of course. The ranger recognized Hope because at this point, who *wouldn't* recognize Hope Hanover, the famous missing actress? And even if they hadn't come across her on social media or in the news, surely the park personnel are among those who've been given her information and told to keep an eye out.

"It is," Ash says. "You haven't seen her on the trail?"

The ranger shakes her head.

"If you do," Ash says, around the sudden, immovable lump in her throat, "could you tell her we're here?"

"Of course," the ranger says. It's a lie, for sure—if she spots a missing person, she'll call the police and the ambulance; she certainly won't be letting Hope hike her way to the top without reporting it in some way—but it's the lie Ash wanted to hear. The ranger hands back the permit.

It's then Ash notices that Caro has gone a few steps away. She sinks down to a sitting position, breathing heavily.

"Caro?" Ash crouches down next to her. "What's happening?"

"I think," Caro says, between gasps, "that I'm having a panic attack."

"Okay," Ash says. "I'll talk you through it." She reaches into Caro's bag for her water. "Close your eyes," she says. "Put your hand on your heart. Focus on the sound of my voice."

The ranger glances over at them. "Everything okay?" she asks. "I have water."

"We're fine," Ash calls over, because they do not want more attention and Caro is a doctor and this will all be fine. This will all be fine, right? Ash will not be the last friend left standing, will she? Ash shifts her body to block Caro as much as possible from the view of the ranger and the other hikers.

"My mom died here," Caro says shortly. "On this hike."

"What?" Ash rocks back on her heels, stunned. "You never told us that. I thought she died in a car accident."

"I say *accident* and then people assume that's what it is. And I don't bother to correct them." Caro's face is carved out in pain.

Did she fall? Ash wants to ask. *Why are you even doing this hike? You don't have to push yourself so hard all the time!* she wants to say. But she stays quiet, her hand on Caro's back, and Caro keeps her hand over her heart, and her breathing becomes deeper, steadies. Around them the world carries on.

"She didn't fall," Caro says softly. "She had an aneurysm."

"Oh, Caro," Ash says. "I'm so sorry." She swears she can feel Caro's heart beating through her body.

No wonder she wants to get this over with.

"Why didn't you tell us?" Ash asks. "Back when Hope first mentioned coming to Eden? Or hiking to Seraph's Perch?"

"Because." Caro gestures at the view. "It's one of the most beautiful places in the world. I wouldn't want to keep you guys from seeing it."

"Have you been up here since it happened?" Ash asks gently.

"I've never done this hike before," Caro says.

"Never?"

"No," Caro says. "My dad never brought me. He was with her the day it happened, and he never hiked it again. And I never wanted to."

"Did Hope know?" Ash asks, because she cannot imagine that Hope would have them revisit the site of such a family tragedy. If Caro *did* tell Hope, then this morning's message is definitely *not* from Hope.

Caro shrugs. "I didn't tell her," she says. "But I'm realizing that I don't know what Hope knew and didn't know."

And then, in what feels like one of those heroic moments, where a mom lifts a car off her child or someone leaps from a burning building with a puppy in their arms, Caro stands up.

"Caro," Ash says. *"Wait."*

"No," Caro says. "I'm fine. Let's get this done."

"I really—" Ash says, but Caro is heading for the next part of the hike—the ridge, the sheer drops on either side, the chains.

The chains.

Ash's stomach sinks.

The formations ahead look otherworldly, like the pictures she has seen of places in China, scrappy trees clinging to jagged cliffs. But these cliffs are Technicolor orange and red in the morning light, and they're sandstone. So easy to slip. So easy to fall.

"Caro," Ash says. "Are you sure?"

"I'm sure," Caro says. "I'm steady again." She stands on one leg, arms outstretched, as if to prove it. She holds fast, she doesn't wobble.

"Okay," Ash says. They fall into line a few feet behind yet another group of college-aged kids, who are wearing good hiking boots and moving at what she feels is an appropriate pace.

Hands on the chains, feet on the stone, they make their way along. The ridge is only wide enough for them to walk single file, and so when they get to a slightly wider spot, they step aside and squeeze against the cliff to let the people coming down pass them by.

Ash feels out of body.

The men coming toward them seem familiar. The way they're moving, their strides, their shoulders and arms. Pressed up against the side of the cliff, Ash realizes the absolute trust you have to have in your fellow hikers, in complete strangers.

But the man coming down toward her along the cliff—close enough to touch, close enough to *push*—isn't a stranger.

It's her husband.

48

ASH

"WHAT ARE THE ODDS?" Wade says cheerfully. He moves aside so that he's standing next to Ash against the cliff. He's *so close*. "I wonder if you left something up on the computer when you were planning your trip and I subliminally absorbed it." Derek, standing behind him, waves over Wade's shoulder at Ash. He's wearing sunglasses, and she can't see his eyes. Or Wade's, for that matter.

Ash is shaking. She glances at Caro, who looks as shocked as Ash feels. "Did you and the girls get my postcards?" Ash asks. *Maybe that's how he found her. The postcards. Someone else's fault, not hers.*

Ash does not like anything about this conversation. Not the setting—*why is he here?*—not the timing of it, not the way Wade is giving her that smile that doesn't reach his eyes. It reminds her of when he cleaned out the closet, when he bought the car. He's daring her to call him on what he's done so he can act like she's unreasonable, crazy.

Daring her to cry.

"Postcards?" Wade shakes his head. "I don't think so. You'd have to ask the girls, though." He takes off his hat and runs his hand through his hair, a gesture that was more effective back when he had a full head of it. Now it serves only to make the strands stick together, the overall effect one of scarcity. She wonders what Caro thinks, seeing him in person. Perversely, impossibly, Ash hopes that Caro's impressed, that she likes him.

When Wade puts his hat back on, he doesn't pull it down as far as it must have been before, because now she sees a strip of red on his forehead. He's always sunburned easily. These are the things that, when you love someone, can bring out the deepest tenderness: these signs of their mortality showing through, the way you can lose them when they are so precious to you. And when you don't love them, or they look at you with no light in their eyes, the tenderness gives way to what is actually in front of you. Wade's burned face and scalp, his changed eyes, bring to mind a condor, a vulture, a bird of prey. "But it wouldn't matter if we got them or not, right?" He glances over her shoulder at Caro. "I mean, you called the first night and told me where you were."

Caro inhales sharply. Ash feels as if she's been punched in the gut. She stares at Wade. "I didn't tell you," she says.

"You may as well have." Wade laughs. "You told me you were glamping and staying in a tent. And maybe you *did* leave something up on the computer, or your phone, and I saw it." They're causing a traffic jam. People are building up behind Derek, impatient, craning their necks around him to see what's going on.

Someone's going to slip, Ash thinks. *Someone's going to fall.*

"Okay," Ash says. They need to get moving. "Do you want me to come back with you? Do you want to come stay with me?" There's an eagerness in her voice, a hopeful note, that she can't seem to keep out. "I've got a whole Airstream to myself; it's so pretty there…" Her voice trails off.

"I wouldn't want to interrupt your girls trip," Wade says, and he's still not quite looking into her eyes. *If I had to describe him right now*, Ash thinks, *I'd say he looks like a mean bird.* He's not ugly, exactly, but he does not look like the young dad in the family photo Ash keeps as the screensaver on her phone. His shoulders are hunched; there's a curling-in of posture even though he's not that old, a coldness in his eyes that she can see even when he's looking past her.

"I'll see you when we get home," Wade says. And it's not a threat, so much, but Ash is still chilled. It's dismissiveness, and disdain, and she takes a step backward. Now Caro is there to put her hand on Ash's back, to steady her.

"Oh," Ash says. "Okay."

And then he and Derek are gone, past them, down the trail. She and Wade were close enough to touch, but they didn't. Others come down after the men, annoyed at having had to wait, and it takes a moment before Ash and Caro are climbing again, their hands on the chains.

"Ash," Caro says from behind her. "Why did you do that? Why did you call him?"

"I wanted him not to be mad at me." Ash keeps her eyes on her feet and where to place them so she doesn't fall. *Don't cry*, she tells herself. *That's not how you survive.*

"I have to ask," Caro says. "Do you think he sent the text? The one to get us up here?"

"No," Ash says. "No, why would he?"

"Because he's *here*," Caro says.

They climb in silence.

They get to the top.

There is no Hope.

Deep down, they knew there wouldn't be.

49

I'M STILL ALONE, AND *watching.*
  Perhaps the reason that there are no angels here is
  that I am the only one.
  That thought picks me up in its mouth like a dog and shakes me.
  It blows through me like the wind in a canyon.
  I'm no angel, but
  it is the loneliest thought of all.

50

PAGE

THE POLICE STATION IS the last place I should be right now. But they called as I was leaving Sonnet, and I couldn't resist. I want to see what they have. To know what they know.

Officer Flanigan leads me to a small room. Three chairs, a table, no windows.

A stack of photos on the table.

"These are the pictures that we were able to salvage once we had the film developed." Officer Flanigan shakes her head. "I didn't know anyone used disposable cameras post-1998. Unless they're at a wedding or something."

It's because they didn't want to take their phones. I don't say it out loud. *Too poor to risk losing them.*

"Take your time," Officer Flanigan says. "Go as slowly as you want." She leaves the room, and I wonder if she is watching me for my reactions behind the one-way glass.

My hands tremble as I go through the pictures. It's what I expected. The Underground, its scenery.

Her.

A text comes through on my phone. I glance down at it. Mal. Are you okay? I'm sorry about what Skye said.

I don't respond. I have nothing to say.
Back to the pictures.
There she is, again.
But wait.
My mouth has gone dry.
There's someone with her.
And I know who it is.

51

CARO

CARO IS FINALLY AT the top of the hike, looking out at the one view her dad wouldn't take her to see. The one her mom loved so much that she died trying to get to it.

And she feels nothing.

Other people, other groups, are taking pictures, exclaiming, throwing their hands into the air and spreading their arms wide to take it all in. Caro's hang at her sides. The small daypack she brought on the hike weighs on her shoulders. She doesn't know what Ash is doing, how she's feeling, what she thinks about being at the top or if she likes the view. Caro doesn't care. Her phone vibrates in her pocket—receiving texts, she supposes. Normally that would bother her—*Cell phone reception, up here? In the middle of this beautiful natural spot where you should be able to get away?*—but she doesn't care about that, either.

"Should we split up and look for her here at the top?" Ash, always focused on Hope. Even after seeing Wade here where he shouldn't be.

"Sure," Caro says, because that's easier than arguing with Ash. "You look around. I'll stay in this spot in case she shows up." But she knows, they both know, that Hope's not here. The viewpoint isn't tiny, but there are only so many places you can be, and if Hope wanted them to come here—or, if someone wanted to find them, or to bring Hope here and make some kind of threat (that's so stupid, why would anyone do anything like that in such a public place?)—they'd make themselves known.

Ash is back within a few moments. "Nothing?" they ask each other at the same time, and they both answer, "No." Caro is interested by her tone, which is flat and pleasant, and she can tell by Ash's expression that it sounds strange to her, too. "Well," Caro says. "I guess that's it. We tried. Should we go down?" New hikers have arrived and are now taking their turns exclaiming and posing for photos. "Should we take a picture for Hope?" she asks. "So we can prove to her that we came?" Will that placate Ash and let them get off this mountain?

But Ash is now staring at her phone.

That seems to indicate that Caro should probably look at hers, too, so she does.

She has a notification. The @findhopehanover LikeMe page has been updated.

It's a photo—a screenshot—of the three of them meeting online a few months ago. Caro is smiling, big, right at the camera, at something that someone—probably Hope, whose mouth is open, whose hands are caught mid-gesture on the screen—is saying. Ash has turned her head, distracted, and her office door is opening behind her, but you can see from her profile that she's smiling, too.

There's a lump in Caro's throat. There they are. When they thought no one was watching.

But someone was.

And now this picture is out in the open. A moment they thought was private is there for everyone to see.

"I hate this," Ash says.

"Me too." Caro's hand holding the phone has begun to tremble. "Something is messed up here."

"I know," Ash says. "But we need to find Hope and—"

"Something is messed up here," Caro says again, raising her voice, "and I think it might actually be Hope." She looks at Ash. "How long have you been her puppet?" she asks. "You've been the one sending these texts, haven't you? Or, wait. Are you so obsessed with her that you're pretending to *be* her?"

"No," Ash says, looking stunned. "No, wait—"

A couple nearby has begun to pose for a photo, but they seem to have caught on that Caro and Ash are arguing and they move away.

"This screenshot." Caro holds up her phone again. "It had to be one of us who took it."

"*Or* our lurker," Ash says.

"Right," Caro says. "I think all of us—myself included—need to ask, *Who lives in our houses? Who has access to our computers, even when we're gone?*"

"Fine," Ash says. "I'll go first. Wade, obviously. And my girls live in the house, but I can't imagine any of them—"

"So you *can* imagine Wade," Caro says.

"That's not what I said."

"It is weird that he's here," Caro says.

"It's weird that *Dan* is here," Ash counters.

"He's here to help with my dad," Caro says. "He lives in the state. And he told me he was coming. *And* I didn't call and tell him where we were the very first night."

"I didn't *tell* him," Ash says. Caro leaves that there, hanging.

"*Your postcard* told your dad," Ash says. "Who is out of his mind."

Caro feels a flash of anger knife through her. How *dare* Ash say that about Henry?

"And what about Spencer?" Ash asks. "Pretty weird and convenient that he happened to show up here and have booked the campsite right next to us."

"I didn't even know he was coming!" Caro hisses.

"Are you sure?"

"*Of course!*" Caro spits.

It's not going to work out. Caro knows this now. She's standing up here on top of the world, and she can see it so clearly. Her mom is dead. Her dad is as good as gone. She saw a woman die. She lied to her husband. She's had these friends. She won't anymore. "What are you saying?" Caro asks. "You think Spencer has been spying on us? Somehow, even though I haven't had contact with him since college? Or wait. Do you think I brought Hope here to offer her as—what—some kind of sacrificial *lamb* to Spencer's friends?"

"No," Ash says. "I—"

"Don't you think *Wade* showing up here is creepy?" Caro asks. "Don't you think he's probably the one who's been watching us?"

Ash doesn't answer.

The corners of Caro's mouth twitch.

"What?" Ash asks. "Go ahead. Say it. Whatever it is."

"It's what I said before." Caro takes a deep breath. "I've been wondering if Hope is behind all of this, somehow."

"You think she stalked *herself*?"

"Not that, exactly."

"Why do you keep doubting Hope?" Ash's voice is shrill with disbelief. "She might be *dead*, Caro! Why are you so hard on her? She's your *friend*. Why do you keep asking me these things?"

Caro looks Ash right in the eyes. "I want to know if you've been in touch with Hope since she left."

"*No!*" Ash says. "No, of course I haven't!"

Their phones vibrate again in their hands. They both look down.

It's another picture, but this one is texted to the two of them, not posted to the @findhopehanover LikeMe account. It's of Caro and Ash, here. At the top of Seraph's Perch. Arguing.

Caro spins around. Who is taking their picture? She tries to see behind the sunglasses, under the ball caps and sun hats, past the scrawny trees clinging for life to the rocks—

"Oh no," Ash says. "They're *here*."

Caro's throat has gone dry. "We know it isn't one of us, then," she says.

"We know that neither of us could have taken this picture. We've been talking. This is from seconds ago." Her hands are trembling.

Their phones vibrate again, but this time Caro sees the text is just for her. Her heart skips a beat. She looks at Ash. She seems to have gotten one, too. But she doesn't ask what Ash's text says. She can't trust her anymore.

They came here with a plan. They were so close.

But they've failed.

52

BEFORE

IT IS THEIR FOURTH book club meeting, before Hope has revealed who she really is. They've finished reading *The Grapes of Wrath* (Hope's choice, because she'd never read it and there might be a remake of it coming up that will be absolute Oscar bait). The others don't know that she has an ulterior motive. They think she's the kind of person who reads classics for fun, apparently. Their lovely faces are up on the screen, and hers still shows the photo of her on a hike with her back to the camera.

Can she trust them?

She *wants* to trust them.

"I have to say," Hope says, "I know I'm the one who picked this book, but I hated it."

"You did?" Caro asks. "Why?"

"They made Rose of Sharon nurse a total stranger at the end," Hope says. "Only a dude would write that."

"She wanted to, though," Ash says. "Or, like, Grandma wanted her to. And Grandma's a woman. And Rose of Sharon did it because she wanted to save his life. I think it's beautiful. It represents sacrifice." She tilts her head. "But yeah, you're right, Steinbeck *was* a guy, obviously."

"It's gratuitous." Hope doesn't know why she's so furious about this, but she is. Maybe because Rose of Sharon was the only decent female part, and now Hope doesn't want to read for it because she's not going to nurse an old man on camera, even if it might win her an Oscar. "They could have, like, put it in a bottle," Hope says. "Or a cup."

"Oh my gosh," Ash says. She is laughing so hard that Hope can see literal tears streaming down her face.

"I think what the book shows is true," Caro says. "The women are what holds the center."

She's right. They're both so wonderful that Hope decides she's going to go ahead and do it. This is getting ridiculous, and if her being who she is ends up being a dealbreaker, better to find that out sooner rather than later before she gets too attached. (It's too late. She's already too attached.) The pandemic has been far, far easier on rich people and famous people (and Hope is both) than it has on about anyone and everyone else, but she is lonely as hell.

"Guys!" she says. "I think my camera is finally working."

"Oh, wow!" Ash says. "Are we going to get to see you?"

Hope clicks the camera button so that her face now shows up on-screen. They've only known her as Grace—that's the name she used the first time they met and she's logged in under that name every time since. "Hey," she says. There's a quaver in her voice. "I didn't give you my real name to start with. I'm Hope."

The response is gratifying. Ash gasps, covering her mouth, recognition immediate. Caro takes a couple of seconds longer, as if she knows who Hope is but can't quite believe it. "Oh," she says, finally, "it's *you*."

And even though Hope has heard this before, even though she knows the *"It's you"* only means that they know who she is, somehow it sounds different this time. Somehow she feels like they really do recognize her, that they've known her and been waiting for her, all along.

53

NOW

—

TEXTS

To Ash, from Wade:

Ash, I changed my mind. I'm waiting for you in the parking
lot of Seraph's Perch.

You've spent the past two years in a relationship with these
women instead of where you should be, with me.

What has it really gotten you? Are you happy?

Come with me.

Let's go home.

———

To Ash, from Maggie:

Mom what is going on?

Why are you and Dad being so weird?

He's in Utah doing some hike with Uncle Derek.

Where are *you*?

————

To Caro:

Hello. My name is Owen Nelson.

My wife Esther died during a c-section where you were the anesthesiologist. You and I have run into each other from time to time in the neighborhood over the past few years.

I need to talk to you.

————

To Caro:

I received your postcard.

I think we should talk in person as soon as possible.

When would work for you?

54

CARO

WE BROKE, CARO THINKS, *our friendship broke*, and she wants to cry.

Ash left her after they descended from the viewpoint of Seraph's Perch. "I'm going the rest of the way down on my own," she told Caro. "I didn't want to leave you up there in case you had another panic attack. Are you okay now?" Ash looked at Caro, but she clearly wanted to be away, gone. And even though Caro felt it too, it hurt. "Do you think you're going to have another attack?"

"No," Caro said. *"Ash."*

"What?" Ash asked.

But then Caro didn't know what to say.

Caro came the rest of the way down the trail without hurrying. She returned to Sonnet without knowing if it's where she wants to be. She tries not to think about the texts she got at the top of Seraph's Perch, or about Hope, but she can't think of anything else.

What the hell happens next?

She stands in front of the main tent of Sonnet, uncertain. It's past lunchtime. She should eat. She should sleep. She should look for Hope. She should text Owen Nelson back. She should call Dan. She should check on her dad.

In the midst of her indecision, she hears sounds that take her a moment to place. Then she realizes they're coming from the direction of the drive-in theater. It's people talking, music playing. A movie? Right now? But it's afternoon, not even close to evening.

Caro walks toward the theater. The soundtrack to the movie isn't only coming from the cars. It's also coming from the speakers that have been set up throughout the viewing area so that people sitting on the bleachers or on blankets under the trees can hear, too.

And there on the screen, larger than life, is Hope Hanover. In *Undeniable*, her most recent movie. She'd walked the red carpet for that one in a rose-gold dress they'd given their opinions on over an emergency group call. It had been between the rose-gold dress and a blue one. Caro had secretly preferred the blue. "Next time I have a premiere," Hope had said, "I'll fly the two of you out to walk the red carpet with me."

Now, Caro stares, heart thudding, mouth dry, at the movie screen. "What the hell?" she says out loud.

"I know," someone says behind her.

Caro spins around. It takes her brain a few seconds to place the tiny, dark-haired woman. *Hope's agent. Raye.*

"Caro, isn't it?" Raye says, holding out her hand. "Can I buy you a late lunch?"

—

The food truck is closed, and they end up in the restaurant. Caro hasn't been inside it before, and she doesn't want anything to eat, but she doesn't have anything or anyplace else to suggest.

"Was showing Hope's films your idea?" she asks Raye as they take their seats. The place is almost empty, but Caro keeps her voice low. The waitstaff are casting interested glances at them. Of course they know who Caro and Raye are. Caro lifts up her napkin and sets it in her lap. Her hands are still shaky and it slides to the floor. She doesn't bother picking it up.

"Absolutely not." Raye pushes her utensils aside. Her mouth is set in a firm line, and her eyes are bright but weary. "I'd never let them do this without paying us a pile of money."

"Do you have *any* idea where Hope is?" Caro asks.

"No." Raye's sunglasses are perched on top of her head, and she's dressed all in black. Somehow even in the heat, even in the desert, she doesn't seem out of place. She owns every room she walks into. *What would that be like?* Caro wonders. She used to be so confident in who she was—a doctor, Dan's wife, Henry's daughter, and, most of all, *herself.*

"Do *you*?" Raye asks.

"No."

"Well, we've gotten that out of the way," Raye says. "Something is wrong. Hope doesn't disappear like this."

"Do you think it's one of us?" Caro asks. "Me or Ash?"

"I think one of you might be the link," Raye says. "I don't know that I suspect either of you personally. Do you suspect me?"

"I don't know," Caro says honestly. She doesn't, not really. But Raye is so absolutely competent that it's hard to rule out her doing . . . well, anything.

"I'm the executor of Hope's will," Raye says. "And, the last I heard, I do get some money if she dies. But she's worth a lot more to me alive." The server arrives, bearing a small carved wooden bowl full of chips and a little ceramic saucer full of salsa for them to start with. "Do we need more time, ladies?" he asks, and they both nod without looking at him.

Are we really *going to eat?* Caro can't imagine being hungry ever again. "I don't know if that makes you trust me more or less." Raye looks Caro dead in the eyes. "Please understand that this is not information I would share in other circumstances. But Hope has been gone for three days now, and I am very, *very* worried. I want to find her." She takes a chip, dips it in the salsa. "I'm sorry," she says. "For whatever reason, I'm very hungry."

"It's fine."

"She loves the two of you, you know," Raye says. "Hope does. I've been her agent since she was twenty-three years old, and you are the best friends she's had."

"She loves you, too," Caro says.

"I know." Raye leans forward, her elbows on the table. Caro does, too, feeling drawn in in spite of herself. "She's left each of you two hundred and fifty thousand dollars in her will," Raye says. "Did you know that?"

Caro sits back, shocked. "No," she says. "I had no idea."

"I'll have to trust you on that," Raye says. "Do you think Ash knows about the will?"

"I don't think so." Caro feels like that would have changed things among them, that there would have been some kind of shift in the relationship if they knew Hope was leaving them that much money—any money, really—in her will. But who is Caro to say there hasn't been a change, one she didn't catch until now? They let Hope talk them into this crazy plan, they thought it would work, and *now* look at what's happened—

"If Hope didn't tell us," Caro says, "are *you* supposed to be saying this now?"

"She trusted me to handle her affairs," Raye says. "I'm hoping you can trust me, too." She holds up a hand. "I know," she says before Caro can speak. "That's not very likely." She gives Caro a long look, and Caro feels horribly, terribly stripped down under that gaze. "You don't even trust each other," she says.

She's right, Caro knows. *We did, but it's gone.*

It vanished with Hope.

55

ASH

"YOU READY?" WADE ASKS. He's sitting on the small couch in Ash's Airstream, scrolling through his phone. Checking on work, he told her. She hears a faint chime. Something on the screen makes him smile.

"Almost." Ash doesn't know what she was hoping would happen. That she'd get to the bottom of the hike and see Wade and they'd throw their arms around each other and...what? Make out in the parking lot of Seraph's Perch like teenagers? Say how much they missed each other and that they were sorry and that things were going to be different? It had felt epic, standing up on Seraph's Perch and making the choice she did. It had felt important and symbolic, leaving Caro behind and hurrying down on her own.

But both Wade and his brother Derek had been waiting for her in the parking lot. "I hate leaving when we don't know where Hope is," she'd told Wade, and he'd said, "You can't do anything from here. You should be home with me and the girls." Then they drove back to Sonnet, and Derek went to get food while Wade came back with Ash to the Airstream.

So here she is disappointed again, and again, what was she thinking? That Wade was secretly hoping to ravish her before they left? He did give her a quick kiss when they got inside the trailer, but then he sat down on the sofa and began scrolling through his phone while he waited for her to pack.

"How much longer do you need?" he asks now. Ash is standing at the Airstream's tiny sink and making sure the lids on all her toiletries are screwed on tight so that they won't leak. The impatience in Wade's voice and the words themselves remind her of a night this past December.

Ash had been feeling accomplished. She'd gotten through a long day of holiday orders at work, and everything was still on track for her to make it to the annual party that Wade and his partner held for their dental practice. They'd have enough time for Wade to change, and then they'd turn around and head back into Portland. She found a sitter (Emily, the girls' favorite) weeks ago for Kit and Claire (Maggie had her own events and life that didn't always line up with babysitting the others). Ash had made dinner (yes, it was in the slow cooker, but it was chicken taco soup; the girls always ate that) around work, running back to the house from the shed at the point when she needed to shred the chicken and return it to the slow cooker and when she needed to bake the rolls that had been rising all morning. She set the table and made a salad before she went to her room to change and get ready.

Ash was wearing a black leather pencil skirt and a black sweater (her goal for those kinds of occasions was to look classy and not farm-y, nice but not flashy) and her favorite earrings. Her hair actually looked—well, kind of fantastic. She'd blow-dried it straight instead of letting it do its natural waves, and for once in its life Portland wasn't humid enough to make her hair curl immediately.

"You ready?" Wade had called out to her the minute he'd come in the door.

"Yes!" she'd said, hurrying out to the kitchen to meet him. "Emily's on her way. We can leave whenever you're ready. The girls know they might have to look out for themselves for a few minutes." She grinned at Wade, who was looking very handsome. She'd done it. She'd gotten everything finished in time. They were going to have a night out.

"Come on, Ash," Wade said. "Give me five seconds before you start bossing me around." He threw his coat over a kitchen chair, loosened his tie, and strode toward their bedroom.

Ash was taken aback. Did she sound bossy? She probably did. She certainly hadn't hurried over and open-mouthed kissed him the way she used to do, even two kids into their marriage.

Although, maybe later…after they'd had dinner and a chance to be out for a while, and if they got home late enough that the younger girls were in bed…

She wandered back to their room to hang out with Wade while he changed clothes. "How was work today?"

"Fine." He was looking through their newly organized closet, trying to figure out which shoes to wear. She had a suggestion but bit her tongue. *Maybe she really* was *bossy.* He chose a pair, put them on, reached for a jacket. He looked up and caught her eye. She was sitting on the edge of the bed, waiting for him, smiling. She stood up right when he said, "How was work for you?"

"Good!" she said. "Actually, great! Someone sent a bouquet to Samantha Saunders, and she found me on LikeMe and messaged me saying how much she loved them." Hope's endorsement had been another game-changer, ricocheting through the celebrity community and adding to Ash's client list even more. And Wade was a sports fiend—they both were, actually, that's part of what they had in common. They both *loved* Samantha Saunders, the former Olympic swimmer—she'd been Wade's high school crush—and Ash had been dying to tell him all day. "Isn't that wild?"

"Wow," he said. "Sounds like that Hope Hanover magic you're always talking about happened again. Can you believe how lucky you've been?"

Hope had actually given Ash words to use in a situation like this, to reframe the way she thought of her business. Whenever Ash said, "Oh my gosh, I'm so lucky to be your friend, thank you so much for recommending Three Sisters," Hope would say, "Ash, remember. You did the work. Luck doesn't happen if the work isn't being done in the first place."

Hope told Ash this was true for her—Hope—too. Yes, luck happened in that she was born with the kinds of looks that get attention, yes, luck happened in that she finally got noticed being an extra in a really crappy movie, but if she hadn't been out there trying, the lightning couldn't have found her.

"Plus," Hope reminded Ash, "you were doing pretty damn well before we even met."

Ash decided to try out this new response on Wade before she said it to anyone at the party (it would inevitably come up and be said in ways that somehow made her feel smaller).

"That's true," Ash said. "But luck doesn't happen if you're not doing the work in the first place."

"Right," Wade said noncommittally. Ash pulled out her phone to show him the photo of Samantha Saunders with her flowers. "See?" she said. "Fun, right?"

"Right," he said. He gave the photo the most cursory of glances.

"She looks so good," Ash said. "I swear she hasn't aged."

Wade had finished tying his tie and headed out of the bedroom toward the kitchen. Ash put the phone in her bag and hurried after him. She wished he'd had more of a reaction.

"Okay," Ash said as he picked up his keys from the counter. "We'll be back by ten or eleven, right? That's what I told Emily."

"We're not going," Wade said. He didn't turn to look at her.

"Wait," Ash said. "Why not?" The obvious answer. "Shoot. Did Emily cancel?" Although, she realized as she asked it—did Wade even have Emily's number?

"No," Wade said. "But I realized I'm exhausted. You're on me nonstop. You've taken all of the enjoyment out of this."

Ash was stunned. She tried to think back over the last few minutes. She could see how she'd been too much. Too talkative and overexcited. "I'm sorry. I was trying—you're right. I'm so sorry. Can we still go?" She *was* annoying. She *was* bossy. She could feel it. She felt it all the time, how she had become *wrong*.

"But what about Emily?" Ash said, picking exactly the wrong thing to focus on. Who cared about Emily? The problem was that Ash kept screwing up.

"Text her," Wade said. "Cancel."

"But she's on her way," Ash said, again focusing on the thing that didn't matter. Having to cancel Emily was nothing. The thing that mattered was the way Wade was looking at her with those eyes that she knew so well. He wasn't looking at her the way he had for years. When they had sex for the first time (they'd both been each other's first, delighted and enchanted by the other). When he got into dental school, when their kids were born, when they both found something funny at the same time that no one else in the room seemed to catch.

Wade was looking at her as if he hated her.

Ash stopped talking.

"I'll go on my own," Wade said.

And he did.

Ash looks up at the Airstream's mirror. She has been bringing Wade bits of her day like a cat with a mouse, a dog with a bone, for *years*. "Look at what I did!" she can practically hear herself saying.

It wasn't always like this.

She wasn't always like this.

He wasn't always like this.

Her phone chimes. She looks down to see a notification from Kelly, the secretary of the nonprofit charity she runs, Second Bloom. **Can you call me when you get a chance?** the message says. **We have a problem.**

Ash glances at Wade. He's still on his phone, but she doesn't want to make him mad by calling Kelly back.

Can text but not talk, Ash says. Can you tell me what happened? I'm worried now.

Okay, but call when you can, Kelly says. Really sorry to drop this on you on your vacation. But I went to pay the fees to reserve the caterer for the Second Bloom Gala and the funds aren't there.

Wait, Ash texts. What do you mean the funds aren't there?

The account only has $500 in it, Kelly texts. I don't see any withdrawals I don't recognize, but nothing has come in in months.

Only three people have access to the nonprofit's account. Ash, Kelly, and Wade. Wade is the treasurer for the charity. He has been since the beginning, when Ash came up with the idea as a way to spend more time together.

Ash pulls up the bank account info on her phone. She hasn't looked at the account for Second Bloom for ages, because Wade and Kelly are in charge. The finances for the gala have always run very smoothly. Wade submits the invoices to the companies, who agree to have part of their purchase earmarked for the charity, they send him the money and he deposits it, and when Kelly needs it for the annual gala, she withdraws it. The gala helps get word out, both about Second Bloom and the facilities they serve. Second Bloom is a shoestring operation, and they keep their costs very, very low. But they need the gala. And there should be enough money for it.

Kelly's right. The money's not there. Nothing's been withdrawn, nothing shady, but there have been no deposits in the first place.

"Hey, Wade." Ash turns to look at him. "Kelly texted. She can't make the payment for the Second Bloom Gala."

Wade doesn't look up. "Huh," he says. "We'll have to look into that when we get back."

"She needs to make the deposit for the caterer today," Ash says. "I think we have to look into it now." She has a horrible sick feeling in her stomach. She doesn't want to push him. But she has to know what happened.

And now Wade does look up. "Are you serious?" His eyes are very blue above his blue T-shirt. She loves him. She hates the way he looks at her now. He didn't used to treat her like she was stupid. He used to think she was his equal. "Is this really what you want to do right this second?"

"I'm wondering if you remembered to invoice the businesses this year." There is a tiny tremor in Ash's voice. She hopes he didn't hear it. She loves Second Bloom so much. Even more than the Three Sisters business at this point, she realizes. And yes, maybe she loves the charity because it makes her feel like a good person (Wade has accused her of this before), but she also loves it because she loves the *people*. She loves the nurses and the patients and the women.

"I'm not going to do this right now," Wade says.

Her heart sinks. He didn't remember. Or—and she feels horribly disloyal even thinking this—did he not invoice *on purpose*? A sin of omission, not commission, but devastating nonetheless in its results? Because will they even be able to recoup the money, after so much time has passed? And what will the businesses think? Will they still trust the charity?

She thought he still supported Second Bloom. She thought they still had *that*, at least.

"Wade—" she begins, but he holds up his hand.

"No," he says. "We're not going to talk about this, Ash. Not when you still haven't apologized."

"Wait." She's missed something. "Apologized for what?"

Wade's full attention is on her. "You're kidding me."

"I'm not," Ash says.

"You're really going to pretend like you don't know?"

"I *don't* know," Ash says. For the trip? Is she supposed to apologize for the trip? But he said she should go. She tries that anyway. "I'm sorry about coming on this trip," she says. "I know the timing wasn't ideal, and that I've been traveling a lot for work lately." She's holding her breath. Did she get it right?

But Wade sighs, like he's disappointed. He folds his arms. She focuses on them. He's tan from hiking and strong from the gym—he's been going more lately, now that he's pushing forty. "The trip is the tip of the iceberg, Ash."

"I don't know what I've done." Ash hears tears in her voice, and she knows that's only going to make things worse. Wade hates it when she cries. He says it's manipulative. "Can you just tell me?"

"You're missing the whole point," Wade says. "I shouldn't *have* to tell you."

"But I've tried." Ash is so tired, so exhausted. "I've tried so many things." Couples counseling (she'd found the counselor; she'd begged him to go). Finally losing the ten pounds she gained with the kids (getting up at 4 a.m. to work out before the workday started and the kids needed help getting ready for school). Offering to give up the flower farm (but he likes the extra money it brings in, likes the lifestyle it helps provide even though he won't say those words out loud). She's doing her best to turn herself into a person that he will love again.

"They haven't been the right things," Wade says.

"Then what *are* the right things?" Ash asks.

Wade exhales in frustration. "You really don't get it. If I have to tell you, Ash, then it doesn't *mean* anything."

Ash's tears threaten to overflow. And standing here with her husband in the tiny, tight quarters of the Airstream, she realizes.

She isn't sure where the knowledge comes from. Revelation or experience, her body, her heart, her soul, her mind, everywhere, nowhere. But as she looks at Wade, she realizes, *Nothing I do will ever work.*

And the reason it will never work is this:

He doesn't want it to.

Oh, Ash realizes. *Oh, I'm going to have to do this, too. Like I've had to do everything else.* A deep, weary grief comes over her. *Just once,* she wants to ask him, *just once could you take action? Accountability? Do the heavy emotional lifting?* She's not being fair. She knows that. There were times he did. But that Wade no longer exists.

Ash's heart is broken. She doesn't know what else to do. So she picks up her bags and the key to Hope's rental car.

"Okay," she says. "I'll see you at home, then."

"Excuse me?" Wade says.

"I'm going to stay here until we find Hope."

"It could be years until they find her," Wade says. "They might never find her."

"What makes you say that?" Ash asks, briefly livid. "You don't know."

"You'd leave me and the girls to stay here and wait around for a friend?" He clenches his jaw, and she hates how cold his eyes are. "I've known you care about your friends more than us for a long time, but this is bullshit, Ash."

"That's not true." Ash tries to keep her voice even. "If we don't find her soon"—her throat aches at saying this—"then I'll go home to Portland and get the updates from there. But I can't give up on her yet."

"Ash." Wade's walked over to the door. Will he block her if she tries to leave? His voice is tight. "Why are you changing your mind? You said you were coming home now. This doesn't make any sense."

No, she wants to say. *It doesn't. None of it does. Where did you go, Wade?*

He steps aside from the door and his eyes are hard. So is his voice. "I'm not going to come get you again," he says.

She knows.

56

CARO

"HOW COULD THIS HAPPEN?" Caro is at the Spring Creek Police Station, her head in her hands. She doesn't know why she's asking this. It's not the police's fault.

"I'm so sorry," Dan says next to her. It's not his fault, either. She knows this, even though she's furious at him. He was bringing Henry to see her, and he lost him.

She can't look at Dan. She knows he's there—his steady presence, his brown eyes and hair, his hand on her knee. She knows there is more comfort there if she would turn and fold into his arms, but she can't.

She is so angry with him, with the staff at Lookout Pointe, with everyone, but she knows it's only her brain trying to create a distraction from where the blame really lies.

It's her fault. Hers alone. She is his daughter. She is the one responsible for him.

Dad, where did you go?

"What about his tracking device?" Caro asks Dan, lifting her head. They'd picked one up yesterday, and the bracelet is supposed to be impossible to remove. "Was he wearing it when you went inside the grocery store?" The last time the device updated it said that he was at the hotel.

Now it says it's "inactive," which means it's either not working or he's turned it off. But he's not supposed to be able to do that.

"Yes," Dan says. He had taken Henry into the Spring Creek Grocery on their way to Sonnet, to get some snacks Henry wanted, and he'd given Dan the slip somehow. Her dad is still fast when he wants to be. "I don't know why it's not updating and saying we were there. He had the bracelet. I saw it on him." His voice is deep and sad. "Caro, I'm so sorry. All I did was look down and pick up a box of granola bars and he was *gone.*"

"We have a Silver Alert out on him," Officer Clark says. "We usually find people quickly once we've done that. I'm sure he'll turn up. The waiting is the hardest part." He slides a phone and a wallet across the table to Caro. "Someone did find these in the Wendy's at the edge of Spring Creek, about half a mile away from the grocery store."

"He loves Frostys," Caro says. *Okay. This is good. He's been seen since he disappeared. He's going to places he likes.*

"That's good to know," Officer Clark says. "Are there any other spots he likes to go? Or places from his past that he might want to revisit?"

"Yes, but they're mostly in St. John," Caro says.

"We'll call the police there and have them start looking, too," Officer Clark says.

"All the Wendy's, the diner on Main Street, the independent bookstore, gas stations." Caro lists them out. "The library. His old house. Do you need the addresses?"

The officer takes them down.

"And the university," she says. "He used to teach a class there."

"Wait," Officer Clark says. "Dr. *Stewart.*" His face lights up. "I actually took medical anatomy from him as an undergrad, years ago. I hadn't connected the dots. He's a wonderful person."

"He is," Caro says around the lump in her throat. Dan's hand grips her knee, gently. She still can't bring herself to look at him head-on. In spite of knowing it's not his fault, she's so damn *angry* with him. And, of course, even more so with herself.

The receptionist comes over with two bottles of water. "He helped us out here once, too," she says. She looks about Caro's father's age, but her eyes are sharp and lucid. "That awful case with that girl, years ago."

"He did?" Caro asks. That must have been the girl who fell in the Underground, the one he couldn't save. Right? Or had there been another?

Officer Clark gestures to Henry's phone. "Do you mind checking that out, seeing if everything looks normal?" he asks. "I assume you might have had some hand in setting it up for him, given it's a very new model?"

"Yes," Caro says. "He likes having a good camera on his phone. He loves taking pictures."

She gives the phone a once-over while the others make small talk in the background. For the most part everything looks fine: There are the apps she has installed. Libby, for the audiobooks she checks out for him from the library online. Weather, messaging, email, of course. Spotify, for his music. He's on her account, and it's bittersweet to look it over each day, seeing what songs he's listening to, getting the tiniest glimpse into his brain. She can sometimes tell it's been a bad day by what he's listened to— the same song, over and over and over, likely to comfort himself, or perhaps because on those hard days he can't remember how to select another song. Either option breaks her heart.

She has always felt torn since she moved away, but these last few years have been excruciating. Her job and Dan's are in Salt Lake City. That is their home. Henry needs to be in St. John, because that's his. And so she has two homes and no home; her heart is in two places and she rarely feels whole. The ache and measure of what she can and can't do, of how badly she is failing everyone, is breaking her.

But there's one app she didn't install for him. Uber. *What?* She clicks on it, sees that there have been a few rides to and from the library and Lookout Pointe. That place did *not* keep close enough tabs on him. None of them are suspicious—the library is fine; he does like to go there—but that's not the point. She had no idea he could use Uber. And he's been going to the library a *lot*. She hopes, hopes, hopes that none of these drivers took advantage of him in any way. Financially, emotionally—she can't even bear to think about the other possibilities—

She opens the notes app on a whim, in case he's somehow managed to learn that, too, but there's nothing there. His email looks normal—she's heartened to see that he has been keeping in touch with a few more friends than she realized, talking with them about old memories they share and current political events. There might be something there, but a cursory read of a few of them doesn't result in anything immediately jumping out at her. Some of his emails are more lucid than others, which is par for the course with all his communications these days.

Then she opens the photos on his phone. They seem boring at first—he has taken a picture of every Frosty he's ever had, every time he eats dinner, all the books he's reading. It takes her only a few seconds to realize what he's doing. He's trying to keep track of his day. He's trying to remember what he does. Her heart is sick. She is about to close out of the photos when she sees a screenshot of something that looks familiar.

An article about Hope.

That's not all that strange. She's mentioned her friendship with Hope to him. She assumed he wouldn't recognize or remember the name. But as she goes back she sees that he did. There are many screenshots on his phone of articles about Hope over the past two years. About her movies, who she's dating, what she wore to different events. And a couple of the old articles about how she had a stalker who the police didn't take seriously, who ended up making it all the way into her house before they took him down.

It's no big deal that Dad has these articles, she tells herself. *That's part of what he was doing, trying to keep track of things and people and learn about and remember my life.* Yet it's vaguely unsettling, seeing her friend's face so many times on her father's phone.

And she still feels guilty about telling her father who Hope really was when she didn't tell Dan.

"There's nothing obvious," Caro says. "Can I hold on to it? Keep looking?"

"Yes, of course," Officer Clark says. "We may ask for your permission to sign off on our accessing his data at some point, but we're not there yet. I assume you have power of attorney?"

"I do."

He pushes back his chair. "Then I think what might be best for you to do is to go back to Sonnet, where he went the last time he was missing, and stay there. Would that work? He was in the drive-in movie theater, correct?"

"Yes," she says.

"Do you remember which car he turned up in?"

"I think so." Caro pushes back her chair, too, the phone in her shaking hand. "Have you heard *anything* about Hope?" She should have asked that the minute she got here. The twin worries, the twin losses, of Henry and Hope, are eating her alive one at a time, consuming everything in her so there's no space for the other.

"No," Officer Clark says. "I'm sorry. We'll let you know as soon as we do."

He sees them to the door, and as they step out into the afternoon heat and bright of southern Utah in summer, Caro blinks and reaches for her sunglasses.

"I'll come to Sonnet with you," Dan says.

"No." Caro says it sharply, and he flinches. "I'm sorry. I don't blame you. I'm not mad at you." She is, but Henry is her responsibility. She shouldn't have handed it off. "It seems to make more sense for you to go somewhere else to look for him, since he knows you. What if you go back to St. John, maybe, to our old house, and wait there? He might get freaked out if he goes back and sees police officers."

"Of course," Dan says. She doesn't mean to look at him full-on, but he won't let her glance away this time. And *oh*. There he is. Her Dan, with his kind eyes and his floppy brown hair. His mouth with its Harrison Ford quirk at the side when he's worried or amused. He's the former now.

"Caro." He puts his hands, very gently, on either side of her face. "I'm so sorry."

"It could have happened with me," she says, and she feels that same flash of recognition—the feeling she described to the other women earlier on this very trip. Even though she's upset with Dan for losing her dad, he's the kind of person you could ask to keep an eye on your dad in the first place. He's so good. He's the best person she's ever known, and she's been lying to him.

"Is anything going on?" he asks. His voice is very gentle. He knows there is.

"Besides my father being missing and my friend getting swept away in a flash flood?" She lets all of the anger she's feeling at herself out in her voice. She lets him think it's for him.

I am a terrible person.

"Okay," Dan says, after a moment. "I'll be in touch."

"Same." She turns away before she can see the hurt in his eyes.

⌣

It's late afternoon now, but the cars at the drive-in theater are still unbearably hot inside, even with the windows rolled down. The chalkboard says that they're showing Hope Hanover movies all day, but this one is a sci-fi alien western movie called *The Last Portal*. It's so bad it might actually be classified as a B movie. Caro can't imagine that Hope's ever been in one of those. Almost no one else is watching, and those who are brought camp chairs and quilts to sit under the patchy shade provided by the trees Sonnet has planted—cottonwood, because they grow fast. As Caro watches, the movie rings more and more of a bell. It was filmed near here when she was in college. Everyone made a big deal about how low-budget it was at the time, but everyone wanted to be an extra on the set anyway.

She remembers the weekend two years ago when she and Dan came down to St. John to check out residential care facilities for Henry. They'd arrived at Lookout Pointe, and Dan had been unable to get over the incongruous lighthouse built in front of it, painted red and white and emblazoned with the name of the facility.

"What's up with the lighthouse?" Dan had asked when they started the tour. "We're landlocked by a few states in each direction."

The director had clearly been asked this question before.

"It goes with the name," she said, sounding defensive. "Lookout Pointe. We're keeping watch over your loved ones."

"I like it," Dan said. "It also feels kind of like the eye of Sauron."

"Excuse me?"

Caro had punched his arm.

Dan had begun referring to the facility as *"Lookout Pointy,"* because of the extraneous *e*, which had cracked Caro up. She'd needed that.

It wasn't as funny when she brought her dad to check it out the next day. He was having one of his affable, gentle days, clearly unsure as to what on earth they were doing but determined to be a good sport about it nonetheless. He gamely walked around with her, expressed appreciation for all the things she pointed out. ("Look, Dad, they have a soft-serve ice cream maker! You love soft-serve ice cream!") But at the end of the tour, when she'd said, "So what do you think about living here?" as gently as possible, he'd been baffled.

"*Who* would live here?" he asked.

"Well, you," she'd said.

"Me?" He sounded genuinely astonished. She supposed it made sense. He'd spent so much time taking care of other people, being the expert, that his being the one who might need to live here did not compute.

Her phone begins to ring.

Wait, not her phone. Her dad's phone. Henry's phone. It's a number she doesn't recognize. She almost drops it in her haste to answer. "Hello?"

Tears instantly flood her eyes when she hears Henry's voice. "Hello?" he says. "Who is this?"

"It's Caro." *Oh, thank you, thank you, thank you,* she thinks, to whatever higher power has done this. "Dad, where are you?"

"Why do you have my phone?" he asks. "I've been looking for it everywhere."

"You left it at Wendy's." She's trying to level and calm her voice. She doesn't want to frighten him. "The police found it. Where are you now? Whose phone are you calling from?"

"I lost her," Henry says.

"Okay," Caro says, trying to understand. "You lost her?" Is he talking about her mom? It's a common way of describing someone who has died, but his tone sounds so urgent, like this is happening right now, like there's still a chance that this person, *this* her, could be found.

"That's what I'm saying," he says, his tone now entirely unlike him. It's angry, unkind. "Do you need me to repeat myself?"

"*Dad,*" she says, shocked.

"I don't have time for this," he says, and hangs up.

Caro stares at the phone. Her father has hung up on her. This has never happened to her before. As far as she knows, he has never hung up on anyone, *ever.*

Something is so wrong.

Hands shaking, Caro calls the number Officer Clark gave her and puts the phone on speaker so she can text. "I heard from my father," she says. "I'm texting you the number."

"Got it." Officer Clark's voice is energized, which Caro is going to take as a good sign. "We actually have a call in from that number right now," he says. "Hold on."

Sweat trickles down Caro's back as she waits, but the sun is lowering. She doesn't want her dad to still be lost when it gets dark. *Come on come on,* she thinks. More people are bringing chairs over to the lengthening shade of the trees. The alien movie has ended. The popcorn machine is still going. A few kids run past, and Caro's heart aches. *There is so much I can't have.*

"Okay." Officer Clark is back. "A woman just called us from that number. She said she picked up your dad because he was hitchhiking and something looked off. He asked her to drive him to Eden, but she didn't want to take him all that way. She asked if there was anyone he could call, and he said yes, and then apparently he called his own phone."

"Yes," Caro says. "He's had the same number for years. It might be the only one he can remember off the top of his head."

"Okay," Officer Clark says. "After the call with you, he ran away. She called 911 and now she's trying to follow him in her car. We have officers on our way to her."

Caro's on her feet. "Okay, great. Where should I meet you?"

"Stay put for now," Officer Clark says. "I'll be in touch shortly."

"Okay," Caro says. "Thank you—"

But he's already ended the call.

This is good, Caro tells herself. *We have a lead, and Dad was physically okay, at least, minutes ago.*

But what does *I lost her* mean?

Who, exactly, is he looking for?

She opens the photo app back up on his phone.

And why, Caro wonders, *does he have so many screenshots of Hope Hanover?*

57

PAGE

Dear Eve,

Graduation was a pretty good day overall. I'd been dreading not having any family there now that Grandma can't go out much, but it was fine. At first I wasn't going to walk, but the school counselors and everyone made it into such a big deal that it felt like less work to just do it, so I got the cap and gown and went to the ceremony.

I remembered your graduation and how everyone talked about how you were going to college and how you were going to become a doctor someday and Grandma was so happy.

The ceremony was in the morning. When it was over, I went home and showed Grandma my diploma. After she fell asleep for her nap, I went and drove the Devil's Backbone like we used to do. I stopped at the rock shop and bought you a rose quartz, your favorite. I put it with the rest of your rock collection. I don't think anyone else can tell that it's there. I don't know that anyone else would ever look.

I miss you all the time.

Love,
Page

58

ASH IS IN THE Airstream and Caro is in the parking lot when the text comes through.

Hi. It's me.

Could you come to the drive-in?

There's something I want you to see.

                                    59

                                   # ASH

"WHAT THE HELL IS going on?" Every nerve in Ash's body is tin-
gling. *Can this be real?*

It's Hope. On the screen, in full color, larger than life. But this isn't a
movie Ash has ever seen before. It's not a movie that should even be *out*
yet. The release date isn't until September. They were all going to go to the
premiere together. Hope had promised them she'd help them choose their
dresses.

Hope walks across the screen, her head thrown back, wearing a trailing
green gown. She is in a forest. There is a crown on her head.

"*Oh,*" Caro says, the sound like a sigh, because Hope is so beautiful and
alive right there in front of them. "Isn't this—"

"*The End of Camelot,*" someone says, and they turn to see that Raye is
standing there as well. "Hope's newest movie."

A crowd is gathering. Ash overhears someone near them checking their
phone, saying, "See? It says right here that the release date is September
29." But most of them are standing there, transfixed by Hope. The sun is
still out but the light is lowering, and even in less-than-ideal viewing con-
ditions, it is impossible to take your eyes off her.

Another text comes through.

I thought it would be nice, it says, if my last movie was shown where my first movie was filmed.

"Her *last* movie?" Caro says. "I don't like the way that sounds."

"And *Echo Chamber* wasn't filmed here," Ash says. Hope's first role was a bit part in a movie about a murder that was filmed entirely on a studio lot in Hollywood.

"*Echo Chamber* wasn't her first movie," Raye says. "*The Last Portal* was. She was an uncredited extra."

"Wait," Caro says. "*Hope* was in *The Last Portal*?"

"What's *The Last Portal*?" Ash asks. How is it possible that she hasn't heard of one of Hope's films? But something is nagging at her. *Hope told me that she got noticed playing an extra in a film. Why didn't I ask her which one it was?*

"It's a terrible movie with aliens that they just finished playing." Caro looks at Raye. "Did *you* tell them to show it?"

Raye shakes her head. "No," she says. "I have nothing to do with any of this." For the first time, she looks truly worried. "I'm going to go call the studio," she says. "If we figure out who did this, maybe it will help us find Hope." Raye spins on her heel and heads for the main tent, already pulling her phone from her pocket.

"Maybe it *is* Hope," Ash says, after Raye is out of earshot. There's a buoyancy sparkling up in her now, like bubbles in champagne. *What if. What if?!? What if this is all going to be okay?* "What do you think?"

"What?" Caro's distracted now, looking at her phone. *Of course she has to keep checking it,* Ash realizes. Henry is still missing. Ash can't imagine. She's stressed, too, given that she walked away from Wade to be here and her life is in shambles, but at least she knows that everyone she loves is accounted for and safe.

Except for Hope.

"Okay, interesting," Caro says, still scrolling. "It says that some of *The Last Portal* was filmed in a slot canyon near the Underground. I knew it had been filmed in the area—it was kind of a big deal at the time—but

I didn't know they went *into* a slot canyon." She stops, looks up at Ash. "And they used some long shots of Seraph's Perch from outside the park."

They both let that sit for a moment. Hope kept that from them. What else was she hiding?

"Do you think Hope is sending us *clues*?" Ash asks. "If everywhere in the movie is somewhere we've been or we're going? Where else was the movie filmed?"

Their phones both ping. It's a text.

One stop left.

A town of ghosts.

60

This is the last stop. I promise.

The road you're going to drive on will say Closed to Tourists, but don't worry about that. I've made arrangements (I always do, don't I?) ☺ When you get to the chain and the ROAD CLOSED sign, park to the side of the road. You can walk the rest of the way into Afton, the ghost town. It's not far.

You'll see.

And I'll see *you*, soon.

I'll explain everything.

61

PAGE

SO FAR, THEY'VE DELIVERED. But according to our deal, they owe me one more thing.

I'm finished. I've done everything they asked of me.

And now I'm waiting for my reward.

I sit cross-legged on the floor with my back against the mud-plastered bricks and scroll through the photos on my phone. The backpack of food sits next to me. If they don't need it, I can take it with me when I go. I'm not going back to Sonnet. I'm finished there.

I can see the spot where they slept last night. It's a clean place on the dusty floor, near where the altar used to be.

Dusky light comes through the old windows of the ghost town church, the wavy panes making it watery.

They should be back soon.

Go home and rest, their most recent text said. You've earned it. I'll be in touch tomorrow.

No, I wrote back. Let's finish it tonight.

Officer Flanigan let me take pictures of the photos they showed me at the police station, the ones they developed from the disposable camera in the yellow plastic dry bag they found with Eve's body. Even though I've been through them before, even though they've told me so much already, I go through them again now one by one. Scrutinizing. Zooming in. Making sure that I haven't missed anything.

Here's one of my sister and my grandma at the events center where they used to work. Their arms are around each other and they are laughing. They're wearing their uniforms: black blouses, black slacks, white aprons, hair pulled back. Eve's is in a high ponytail; Gram's is in a chignon. I was ten years younger than Eve, and so on nights when they both worked, I'd stay home alone, falling asleep on the couch waiting for them.

There are several other photos of them with the rest of the staff, the college students and older people like Gram who needed money and could work evenings and weekends. Gram got the job because it supplemented her income as an elementary school teacher, and once we moved in with her (I was four, Eve was fourteen), she needed the extra cash. These photos must have been taken after a wedding, because the tablecloths are white and the flowers cream-colored.

I remember how Eve and Gram would come home with leftovers from weddings that the parties didn't want. We often had bouquets of flowers and miniature cups of butter mints and pastel-covered almonds and crab salad for puff pastries in our fridge or on our countertops. The guests left disposable cameras behind, too, sometimes with only one or two shots taken on the roll, and the staff brought those home as well if no one ended up claiming them. No point in wasting the film.

Officer Flanigan didn't understand why you'd take disposable cameras into the Underground or on a hike. There are a few reasons. If you don't want to take your phone or you can't afford it getting ruined. Hope and her friends took them because of the former; Eve and I because of the latter. We didn't have money to replace our phones if they got dropped or ruined or broken or lost.

Sometimes we didn't have the money to develop the film. After Eve vanished, I developed them all, hoping I'd see something that clued me in to her disappearance, but I found nothing.

The pictures from *this* roll, though, are different. She must have brought this camera to college with her, had fun taking pictures. I can't believe they've lasted all this time, that they weren't ruined in the canyon. There are pictures of her in her dorm room, making faces with her roommate, Meg, who she loved. I wonder where Meg is now.

Eve loved everything about going to college. She loved living in the dorms; she loved making friends; she loved the classes. She thought maybe she wanted to be a doctor. "The professor thinks I can," she told me. "He said I'm smart enough and that he thinks I could get a scholarship and some funding. Medical school is *expensive*."

"You want to be a *doctor*?" I'd been impressed but also surprised, because Eve and I were so much alike (at least, I wanted to believe that), and I hated the sight of blood.

And there he is, on the film from the camera in her dry bag. Right after the shots with her roommate and right before the pictures of the Underground—her last hike—begin. Eve, standing in a classroom, with a smiling, glasses-wearing professor. Dr. Stewart. Caro's dad.

Pay attention to the details, Eve would tell me when we were doing our homework. When she was in high school or home for the weekend, I would pretend to do mine long after I was finished. That way, I could sit by her at the kitchen table and watch her brow furrow and clear, furrow and clear, as she figured things out. I have never seen anyone as beautiful as Eve in real life, except maybe Hope Hanover. *The details are how we get into college*, Eve would tell me, as she checked over one of her assignments for a third or fourth time, revised a paper she was writing until it was perfect. *They're how we get out of here.* Eve and I loved where we lived. We were fiercely proud of where we came from, and we wanted to return to Spring Creek, to Eden. But we also wanted to *go*. We didn't want to be drunks who never had enough money and died on I-15 heading to Vegas like our parents. We didn't want to be sad all the time like our grandma, even though we loved her with all our hearts.

The key, we decided, was that you had to *choose* this place. Not in the way the tourists or the move-ins chose it, with their LikeMe accounts and the photos they took for their followers and their demand for organic groceries and their second homes with heated flooring. But year-round, on the ground, because you grew up here and you couldn't get it out of your bones. And to choose it, you had to leave it first. You had to have other options and see other things and *then* come back.

I have questions for him. I'm going to make him answer.

I couldn't leave before now because I didn't know where Eve was. But now I do. I'm paying attention to the details. I will take care of the last things. And then I'm going to go.

No one's here yet. They should be soon. Then I can tell them what *I* know, and we can figure out what to do next. Go to the police?

I flip through the photos one more time. Yes, there he is, Dr. Stewart. It's definitely him.

But wait. As I keep flipping through the photos, my eyes catch. How did I miss this before? In another photo, something else.

My jaw drops. "Oh *no*," I whisper. *Did I make a mistake?* Do I have the wrong idea about . . . *everything?*

Footsteps. I left the padlock on the front door of the chapel unlocked for them. It creaks open, but my eyes are glued to the photo. "Hey," I say. "You won't believe what I found."

"Try me," a voice says.

My heart ricochets off my ribs. My stomach drops and I look up.

No.

It's not who I was expecting.

It's not Hope Hanover.

It's *him.*

The person from the photo.

The person who killed Eve.

62

HOPE

HOPE IS NOT DEAD, but she is going to die. He gave her something that knocked her out, and now she is awake and it is very clear, from the way that her hands are tied and her mouth is gagged, from the way that he dragged her here and left her behind the chapel, that he doesn't plan on her being able to tell anyone about any of this later.

A thin line of birds hangs in the sky.

They are moving, but not, to her eye, forward. They seem to be hanging there, undulating, but waiting. Why?

Are they waiting for her?

A whisper of a breeze crosses her face, and she closes her eyes.

Who else is here?

63

CARO

"DID YOU CALL THE police?" Caro asks. The gravel crunches under the tires of the car, and a dust cloud rises around them. She's going too fast. *Slow down*, she thinks. *Anyone near Afton is bound to see and hear us coming.* But isn't that what she wants?

She doesn't know, she doesn't know. She doesn't know a damn thing in this world.

Why does her dad have so many pictures of Hope Hanover on his phone?

And why did he have an old newspaper clipping in his wallet about a young woman named Eve Herriman who went missing twelve years ago? The year they made *The Last Portal*? She remembers the case. Everyone wondered if someone from the film had been involved because *bad things don't happen around here*. Even though they did, they do. It was the same year her dad couldn't save that girl who fell in the canyon.

"I'm waiting until we get there, and then I'm going to send Officer Flanigan a pin," Ash says. "I've got her cell number."

"Okay." Caro doesn't push for Ash to message sooner or offer to do it herself. Because does she really want the police there? Her dad's tracker began working again.

And it shows that he is—or at least that he was—*here*.

In the ghost town.

Dad, what are you doing?

It's the dimming time, the "ether hour," Henry used to call it, because it feels magical, golden, and yet it signals that darkness is on its way. The road snakes along the flank of the bluff, miles away from the highway and Spring Creek, contouring itself around a base of sandstone buttresses. The few isolated houses along the road are set back, a stark contrast to the glass-windowed, modern buildings dotting the bluffs nearer the town, the second homes of rich people. These are first homes, Caro thinks, with their metal whirligigs standing still out front in the absence of wind, parched gardens, American flags, KEEP EDEN WILD signs. *Do they hate us, the visitors?* Caro wonders. *Do we stand out like a sore thumb, or are we nothing to them?*

If we scream, will they hear us?

If they do, will they come?

"Caro?" Ash's voice is steady, but Caro hears something in it that she doesn't like. They are fractured, the two of them. Are they broken?

"What?" They must be getting close. Caro thinks she came here once before, as a kid on a field trip. She has a vague memory of old buildings out in the middle of nowhere, hidden from the main road by the undulations of the bluffs. She remembers the teachers and the ghost town docent talking about how the pioneers settled this land. Revisionist history. The land was settled long before that, thousands of years. *We have been the worst of caretakers*, Caro thinks, considering the glass houses, the new roads, the resort where she herself is staying.

"What's really going on with your dad?" Ash asks.

"What are you saying?" Caro thinks she sees a sign ahead, maybe the one mentioned in the text. She slows the car. She can't bear to think about what Ash might mean. She can't bear to think about the track on which her own mind is racing, spinning. "Isn't Alzheimer's and going missing all the time enough?"

"It feels like there's more," Ash says. "I feel like you're keeping something from me."

There's a chain hanging across the road, and sure enough, a sign is affixed to it. ROAD CLOSED. Yes. This is it.

"Here we are." Caro turns off the car. She climbs out and slams the door harder than necessary. The sound echoes, ricochets against the bluffs.

Dad, are you here?

Hope?

She starts walking down the dusty road.

64

ASH

"CARO?" ASH ASKS. "YOU didn't answer my question. And I have another one for you." They are walking, almost running, down the gravel road. Ash tastes dust in her mouth.

"What's the real story about the mom who died in delivery?" Ash asks. "And why is it killing you? Because that happens. It's horrible, but it happens, and you must have seen it before. And if anyone *were* to blame, it would likely be the ob/gyn." Ash pauses. "Did something go wrong that you're not telling us about?" And then, one more question, she can't help herself even though, out of the corner of her eye, she sees unflappable Caro flinch: "Did *you* do something? Did you make a mistake?"

The moment the words are out of her mouth, she wants them back. Next to her, Caro stumbles, puts a fist to her mouth. *Who among us could bear all this scrutiny?* Ash wonders. *What person in all the world doesn't have something they want to hide, secrets they want to keep?*

"We're all hiding something." Caro takes a deep, almost-gasping breath. "Ash, you too." She looks Ash full in the eyes. "You've always been obsessed with Hope. You know more about Hope's disappearance than you're saying, don't you?"

"*What?*" Ash says, but her response is too fast, the answer too at-the-ready.

They have stopped walking, they are looking at each other, and Ash has a terrible thought.

"What if there is no lurker?" She can't believe she's wondering this, she can't believe she's saying it, but as she looks in Caro's eyes, she sees she's wondering it, too. "What if it's one of us?" *Us.* Hope, Ash, Caro. And with Hope gone, that leaves—

—the two of them.

They've arrived at the cemetery up on a knoll away from the rest of the ghost town. It feels like a proverbial tumbleweed could roll across their path. Farther down the road, the cottonwood trees lining it have ancient trunks so twisted and knotted that they look like the wrists of giants, all elevated lines and straining sinews. As the dirt road continues, it falls into ill-repair, and Ash sees the remnants of the town—a church and several houses.

But there are no trees here at the cemetery. And it is not near the church.

Both of these things feel strange to Ash. The pioneer settlers of southern Utah were big on planting trees everywhere else. So why not here? Why not for their dead? Only the dusty hill behind the burial ground offers any measure of shelter from the wind and the sun that burn their way across the land.

And there is no grass, only dirt. The graves are mounded over, as if they are recent. It chills her how they don't lie flat, how the mounds call to mind a body, something human.

"Why are they aboveground?" Ash asks. "Wouldn't it be easy enough to dig here?"

"I don't know," Caro says.

The iron gate is padlocked shut. It's flanked on either side by two plastic evergreen wreaths, which have been tied to the gates with twine. The fence comes up to Ash's waist. It would be easy enough to hop over, but it feels like a desecration.

They walk silently along the fence, looking in at the graves. Ash breaks the quiet. "It's weird. Some of these stones are the same age, but some are so much more worn than others. And who would have expected the wooden ones would last so well?" They are splintered and beaten but remarkably legible. Many of the sandstone ones have been worn down, the details and dates erased.

"You disappear eventually no matter what," Caro says quietly.

There's a newer stone at the back, some kind of shiny granite laid almost flat into the ground, but they can't get close enough to see it without climbing the fence. So they leave the graveyard behind and walk toward the town.

It's still and hot. But the desert evening drop in temperature is coming, Ash can feel it. She's afraid. It's colder, too, because of what they have said to one another, things that can't be taken back.

"We're so far away from where we last saw Hope," Caro says. "How would she even get here?" She glances at Ash. "Do *you* know?"

"The lurker wanted to drive us apart," Ash says. "We can't let them." She takes a deep breath. *Am I really going to do this?* She is. "And you're right. I've been keeping something from you." They're almost to the town. The dirt their feet kick up stings her eyes, but she'd be crying anyway even without it. "Hope intended to disappear in the Underground all along."

"*What?*" Caro pulls up short. They're in the middle of the road.

"She wanted to use herself as bait for the lurker," Ash says. "She thought that if she disappeared, they'd follow her, and we'd be safe."

"And you let her *do* that? I thought we were going to do this together!"

Now the tears are spilling down Ash's cheeks. "You think that anyone could 'let' Hope do anything?"

"What the hell was she thinking?" Caro asks. "She'd draw off someone who'd been stalking us and—what?" Her fists are clenched and the muscles in her neck are taut. "Why didn't she tell me?"

"She didn't tell *me*," Ash says. "I figured it out. She was acting weird. I could tell she was hiding something. So I asked her what was going on."

"And the two of you didn't decide to fill me in?"

"We were trying to protect you," Ash says. "And it's not like Hope told me *everything*, even when I figured part of it out."

The cliffs around them are burning orange as the sun keeps on coming down.

"Hope trusted you more," Caro says. "It's as simple as that." But her voice sounds lighter, and Ash knows what she's about to ask.

"So she's *okay*?" Caro's voice is bright with hope. "I can't believe it. We *saw* her fall."

But we didn't see her land.

"I don't know." Ash's heart aches. "I don't know when she was planning on taking off on her own, but I don't think it was right then. The flood—"

"Right." Caro's voice is grim again. "Even Hope Hanover can't predict or control the weather."

But Ash desperately wants Caro to keep hoping. She can't do it alone. "I know she had canyoneering equipment with her in her backpack. She'd been rappelling before, and she also did a lot of climbing lessons at one point for her role in *Downfall*."

"But none of this is what we agreed on," Caro says. "We were supposed to stick together to lure the lurker. We *never* planned for one of us to go off on our own."

"*We* didn't," Ash says. "Hope had other ideas. I'm so sorry I didn't tell you, Caro."

"It's too late for that now." Caro's words sound bitten off at the edges. She's angry. Ash doesn't blame her, but she's angry, too.

"Nothing went like she planned," Ash says, after a moment. They are leaving footprints in the fine sandy dust of the road. "I don't know if Hope's still alive. I've been getting the same texts you are." She laughs bitterly. "You accused me of being obsessed with her and of keeping things from you. I'm not obsessed with her, but I love her. Like I love you. And I did what she asked. That's all. You don't have to believe me, but I'd do the same for you, too." She licks her lips. Her mouth is so dry. "I'm not saying that's a good thing. I'm saying it's true."

"I do believe you," Caro says, after a pause.

And then, here they are. In the town. A sandstone church with a wooden cupola stands across the street. *Why sandstone for graves and churches?* Ash wonders. *Did they not know how fast it would erode? Did they care that they were making the monument to their faith out of the softest, slipperiest stone?*

They walk through the two-story house nearest the church. It's the fanciest dwelling in town, with gingerbread trim. It would be so much work to have anything nice out here, to keep a flower bed alive, to carve and then to protect and repaint any ornamentation you tried to have against the elements.

Nothing. The house is quiet except for their echoing footsteps on the old wooden floors.

"Do you—" Ash stops. She bites her lip. "Do you feel like we're being . . . guided?"

"By Hope?"

"No." That's not quite it.

"Like by God?" Caro asks, sounding profoundly skeptical.

"No," Ash says. Her eyes dart back and forth. She's searching for words. "Something not as . . . benevolent."

Caro waits.

"Directed," Ash says finally. "Like, without our knowledge."

They leave the house and walk down its splintered steps.

The one next to them has a barbed-wire fence around it and a PRIVATE PROPERTY sign, though it doesn't look like it's been well taken care of or visited in years. Caro walks right up to the fence.

"Don't you feel it?" Ash says, and Caro looks over her shoulder, her eyes flashing.

"Yeah," Caro says. "I do. I've been feeling it the whole time." She finds a spot in the fence without a barb, presses it down, and climbs over. Her injured leg almost catches on a barb farther down the wire, and Ash's breath hitches in her throat.

"Caro," Ash says, "be careful," and then she notices where Caro's heading.

There's a shed behind the house. Dilapidated but intact. And there's a car inside.

You'd only park inside that shed if you didn't want anyone to know you were here.

It can't be Hope who's here. Can it?

"Caro," Ash says, low. "Come back. Let's call the police."

"You do that," Caro says. "Now. Keep your voice down. Tell them we're in Afton and that we might have found Hope Hanover." She's still now, her body wired, tense. Can she hear something Ash can't? Ash is frozen in place.

And then Caro goes into the house alone.

"*Wait,*" Ash says. This is a very, very bad idea. Ash puts her hands on the fence to climb over. Can she do it? Caro's so much taller, and the fence is high.

But it's only moments before Caro is back out. "Nothing in the house," she says. "The shed—"

And then the screaming begins.

65

CARO

THE SCREAMING IS STILL coming from the church, tearing through its porous walls and howling through Caro's ears. She races up the steps three at a time and yanks open the splintered wooden door, Ash on her heels. They almost crash into one another as they stop short at the sight of what's inside. Beyond the sparse wooden pews, lying on a surprisingly well-varnished wooden floor, is a body.

It's not Hope.

It's the young woman from Sonnet. Page.

If she was the one screaming, she's not anymore. She's lying flat on her back and her hands are tied. Is she dead? Unconscious? Somewhere else in the church—below them?—a door slams.

Caro dodges between the pews, slipping on the floor. The varnish is still wet and smells so strong that Caro's head instantly begins to ache. She drops to her knees next to Page. *Alive. Thank goodness.* There's a pulse. But it looks like she's just been knocked out, a small pool of blood already forming beneath her head. There's a backpack near her, Caro notices.

"Did you get the police?" Caro asks Ash. She carefully lifts Page's head. Page stirs. The wound doesn't look terrible. Everything might be okay.

If whoever did this to Page doesn't return.

And where is Hope?

"No," Ash says. "I can't get a signal."

"Try again," Caro says. "Page?" she says. "Page, can you hear me?"

"Caro," Ash says. "The floor is covered in something. I think it's gasoline."

"*Shit*," Caro says. Ash is right. What she took for a scent of varnish is far too strong, and the floor is slippery everywhere with the petrochemical. *This is all very, very wrong.* "Okay. I don't really want to move Page, but we can't stay in here with these fumes." *And because it feels like someone might be about to light this place on fire.* She isn't seeing any obvious signs of a spinal injury in Page, but this is still a risk. She hesitates. Is she making the wrong call?

She doesn't know what else to do.

"Can you help me move her?" she asks Ash. "I'll take her head and shoulders, and you can take her feet?" The wavery window glass casts watery light on Ash as she hurries over. They will have to maneuver Page through the wooden pews, but it should work; there aren't very many of the benches left. It looks like people have torn them out over the years. As souvenirs? Kindling? Caro's mind is reeling. They have to get out of here. There is no pulpit, no stained glass, no paintings. The church is bare-bones and smells of something underneath the gasoline.

Caro coughs. She has always been sensitive to fumes. She slides her hands and forearms under Page's head and shoulders. "We want to keep her as stable as possible," she's saying, when a sudden sound makes her turn.

The door to the church has swung open and ricocheted back off the wall. Standing inside the doorway is Caro's father.

"*Dad?*" Caro says.

Page is stirring. Her eyelids flutter.

We have to get her out of here. Caro can't do it alone. "Ash?" she says. "Ash, can you help me?"

But Ash is still staring at the doorway, where, Caro realizes, Dan has appeared behind Henry. Caro looks at them both, the two men she loves most in the world. Dan, with his kind eyes and his floppy brown hair; Henry with the whole of her childhood tied up in his being.

A sound. Page, clearing her throat. Caro leans down to hear what she's saying.

"It's him," Page says, her voice raspy. "He killed my sister."

66

ASH

PAGE HAS GONE UNDER again. "We have to get her out of here," Caro tells Ash in a low voice. "We *all* have to get out of here," she says, louder. "Ash, can you help me?"

But Ash is frozen. Has Caro had some kind of mental break? Did she not hear what Page said? That Henry—or possibly Dan?!?—*killed Page's sister?*

And who *is* Page's sister? Ash stares at Page's face. The coloring—it's so similar to Hope's—and her build—it's slight but strong, like Hope's—

"I know her," Henry says, pointing at Page.

"Dad," Caro says. "*Shhh.*" She looks at Dan. "What are you doing here?"

"The police brought him in," Dan says. "None of us could get through to you, so I went and picked him up." He sounds bewildered and sincere, but is he gaslighting Caro? Ash can't tell. She doesn't know him, not in person, not for herself. "He wanted to come out here, so I brought him. He was really agitated." Dan coughs. "We should get out of here. These fumes—"

They look at Henry, who does not look agitated. He looks deadly calm and very focused, his gaze locked on Page. "Eve Herriman," he says. "That's Eve Herriman. She's one of my students."

"Dad," Caro says again. "You don't know—"

"Who's Eve Herriman?" Ash asks.

"Eve Herriman went missing twelve years ago," Caro says. "It's her body that we might have found in the canyon."

"*What?*" Ash says. *How does Caro know that? What the hell is going on here? Has Caro been sending the texts? Where is Hope?* "How do you know?"

"We *have* to get out of here," Caro says. "Dan. Help me with her?"

But Dan doesn't move either. Is *he* a killer? Or is it Henry? All Ash knows is that she's the odd one out in this grouping of Caro, Henry, Dan. They're a family unit. They're going to stick together. *Blood is thicker than water, than friendship, than anything.* But Dan isn't technically Caro and Henry's blood. Maybe *he's* the killer?

Ash's mind is swimming She should run. She would, except for Page. She can't leave Page. And at least Caro wants to get Page out of here. That's good, right?

"Did your dad kill Eve?" Ash asks. "Did he do this to Page?"

"*No,*" Caro says. "He couldn't hurt anyone. Ever. I think Eve was his student. He had lots of students." But there's a waver in her voice. Henry is coming closer to Page. "I'm sorry," he is saying, over and over. "I'm sorry." He kneels down next to Page, gasoline soaking into the knees of his pants. His eyes are unsettled. Ash doesn't know what to think. Is he the man Caro has always described—gentle, competent, beloved by all? Or is he someone else entirely?

"*Dad.*" Caro's voice cracks as she touches his arm. "Come on. Let's get out of here. We need to get Page out, too. This woman's name is *Page.* She's not Eve Herriman."

Ash looks over at Dan. He's bewildered, shocked, his puppy-dog eyes staring at Caro and Page. "Dan," Ash says. "You were standing in the doorway, too. Was Page talking about *you?* Did *you* kill Eve Herriman?" *My survival instincts,* she thinks, *are terrible.* Her need-to-know compulsion, however, is apparently alive and well.

"*No,*" Dan says. "You think *I* killed someone?" He sounds stunned, but his eyes flick to the side as if he's looking for someone to back him up. No one's there. "Why would you think that?"

"Because Page said it," Ash says. "And she was looking in your direction."

"She was also looking at Henry." Dan takes a step closer. His eyes lock on Caro. "Caro. You don't believe this, right?"

"We can talk about it later," Caro says. "We need to get Page out of here. We *all* need to get out of here."

But the doorway has darkened. Somone else is here. Two people, Ash realizes. One of them is a man wearing a ski mask, his head almost brushing against the top of the doorway. Someone smaller is silhouetted with him, and Ash's heart leaps in her chest. She knows that shape. And when the other person speaks, Ash knows that voice.

"Hi, guys," Hope says. "I'm sorry. Really sorry. As you can see, things haven't exactly gone according to plan."

67

CARO

THIS CAN'T BE REAL, Caro thinks. *It has to be staged somehow.*

She *wants* it to be staged. She wants Hope to have orchestrated this for some reason because then it won't mean that a strange man is holding a real knife to Hope's throat and that Page from the resort hasn't accused either Caro's father or Caro's husband of murdering Page's sister, whose bones they found in the Underground.

None of this can be happening. The fumes are making her sick and dizzy. Maybe she's hallucinating? But Hope is alive, and *that* is good. She looks very tired and thin, dark circles under her eyes, her skin pale under her tan. But that electricity, that *something about her* that draws people to her, is still there. Dimmed, but shining.

"Hope?" Caro says. "You're alive. You didn't die in the Underground."

"I did not." Hope's voice is very calm, her tone dry. "I think you should all get out of here," she says. "He only has a knife. Not a gun. There are five of you. Six? I'm sorry, these fumes and him cutting off my windpipe are making it hard to count."

"Just let us all go," Ash says to the man, her voice desperate. "The police are coming."

"Then I'd better be fast," the man says. His voice sounds vaguely familiar.

Who is he? "There are more of you than I expected." He nods to Caro. "There's a flare gun in the backpack next to you. Bring it to me."

"Who the hell are you?" Caro asks. "Why should I do what you say?" *Why would I let you shoot flares into the gasoline and set us all on fire?* She sees that Dan is ready to spring, to try to take down whoever this man is. *Don't,* she thinks to him. *Please don't. It's too risky.*

"Because I'll kill her if you don't," the man says.

Okay, touché. Caro will indeed bring him the flare gun. Can she shoot him with it without setting them all ablaze?

"You can let us all go." Ash's tone is level now, but her outstretched hands are shaking. "We don't even know who you are. Everything can still be fine. We won't turn you in. We won't even look for you. Will we, you guys?"

The man laughs. "You've been hunting me down ever since you knew I existed."

Because you were spying *on us, you pervert.*

"You need help," Henry says to the man, rising to his feet from where he's been kneeling near Page. Caro grabs his arm. *"Dad,"* she says. "Stop." Ash and Hope are right. There has to be a way around this. Why can't she think of it?

"The gun," the man says again. *"Now."* And he presses the knife so hard into Hope's windpipe that she gags. Caro grabs the backpack, unzips it. Packages of food—ramen, granola bars, fruit snacks—and bottles of Gatorade fall out. Some of the bottles roll their way across the uneven flooring. Caro glances up at the window nearest her. Could she smash the glass? Could someone climb out? The minute she takes the flare gun to him, they're all dead. The minute she doesn't, Hope is. It's impossible math.

There's the gun, at the bottom of the pack. Caro removes it. "Let's talk about this," Henry says, using his gentle doctor's voice, and oh no, he's walking toward the man. He's going to get himself or Hope killed.

"Dan," Caro says, not sure if this is the right choice. "Get him. Can you hold him?"

Henry tries to dodge away but now Dan's got Henry, he's holding him, and Henry is fighting back. Her eyes meet Dan's, and she sees so much pain there, but he's pulling Henry toward the door, bit by bit, making it look like it's part of the struggle so the man doesn't notice and turn on them. *Yes*, she thinks to Dan, as hard as she can. *Get out. Get the two of you out.*

"You were supposed to disappear," the man says. "But none of you could. I wouldn't let you." Hope looks tiny in his arms. She's fighting for breath, the knife still pressed to her throat.

Caro doesn't think anymore. She's across the room, the gun in her hands, slipping but not falling, bent on one thing only. Ash moves at exactly the same time.

They rush for Hope.

He draws the knife across her neck.

68

THEY DON'T EVEN KNOW I'm here. Except Page. I think she can tell.

Of course she can tell.

And Hope, because she's close to where I am. But not dead.

Not yet.

Are you a ghost? *someone might ask me. I am asking myself.*

My little sister wrote me a letter saying the ghost town was "hunted,"

and I am.

Well, not hunted

but hunting.

Him.

He will not have her.

69

CARO SLAMS INTO THE man and the knife, and it slices her hand before they both lose hold of it and it flies across the room. She has so much momentum that she hits the wall of the church behind him. It looked like stone when she first came in, but up close Caro sees that it's bricks laid over with mud, the strokes used to apply the mud visible even now, hundreds of years later. She leaves bloody handprints on the walls as she pushes away from them. Her mind flashes, thinking of the people who built this place and who lie in the cemetery, of what they might have suffered, of who they might have *made* suffer. The ones who came first. The ones they made leave. *This man will not hurt Hope.*

He's strong, but Ash hit him at the knees when Caro went for the knife, and now he's down. Before he can get up again, Caro presses the flare gun into his groin. *"If you move,"* she hisses, *"I will shoot."* There are some things all men are afraid of, and she is banking on this. He might not care if he dies, he might be the kind of person who would relish going up in flames if he can see them die, too, but she doesn't think he wants her to do *this*. She will, too. His body will absorb the impact of the flare gun, there might be sparks, but she thinks they'll still have time to run. Probably. "Get him *out*," she says to Dan, and he pulls Henry through the door. It slams shut behind them. Ash throws the bolt in the lock. Caro hears Dan hammering against it, calling her name.

Stay out. Stay safe.

Caro's hands are bleeding all over the man. There are a million reasons they have to hurry.

Hope is breathing again. Ash helps her stand. The trickle of blood across her neck is drying.

Where have you been? No one asks, but Hope knows the question.

"Here," Hope says. "I've been here in the ghost town. I climbed out of the canyon and I hid here. Page has been helping me and bringing me food and sending the texts. Then he found me. I'll tell you the rest later." She coughs. "We need to tie him up. There's rope in that backpack. Not the one on the floor. The one on the middle church pew."

But before they can do anything, the man shoves himself to his feet, pushing Caro off-center enough that she falls back onto her butt. She lifts the gun, points it at his groin again. "Stay right there," she says.

"Get Page out of here," Hope says to Caro. "No matter what happens, we keep her safe. This piece of trash killed her sister."

"Who *is* this piece of trash anyway?" Ash asks.

"Go ahead and take off the mask," Hope tells the man. "Try anything else, and she'll shoot."

The man rips off his mask. Blond hair, tan skin, a weatherbeaten, outdoorsy face. She can't make out the color of his eyes but she can feel the coldness of them right down to her bones. *Damn these fumes*, Caro thinks. *Where have I seen* him *before?*

"You don't recognize me." He's laughing. "That's funny. Because I know all of *you* so well." He drops the mask on the floor. "I've been in your meetings," he says. "In your phones. Your computers. Your houses, your rooms. Your girls are beautiful," he tells Ash, and bile rises in her throat.

"Yeah, yeah, we know," Hope says. She holds out her hand for the flare gun and Caro gives it to her. "Why do you think we're here?" She smiles at him. "We didn't come to disappear. We came here to draw *you* out." She lifts her chin. "And we sure as hell didn't come to die."

70

THEY STAND IN THE gas-drenched church, Hope holding the gun.

He terrorized them. He killed Eve Herriman. And those are only the things they know about.

They've come so far. Through the canyon, out of it again, to the top of the cliff, all the way to this town of ghosts.

Too far to walk away now.

"*Ty*," Ash says. "You're the food truck guy."

He laughs again. "Right. The food truck guy." He spits out the words.

Hope thinks, *He's going to take us with him.*

"Ty," Ash says. "*Ty.* You don't have to do any of this." She keeps saying his name. She's trying to humanize him, because she wants to go home to her girls. Can they talk to him? It was not supposed to go like this, and for a moment she is *so pissed* at Hope for going off script and disappearing in the canyon.

"I'm sorry," Hope says, as if she's reading Ash's mind. "I thought I was keeping you safe, but here we are, and I hate myself for putting you both in this much danger."

Caro has Page. She's slung the young woman over her shoulder. She is worried how long she can stay upright. Page is slender, but she is dense, wiry with muscle, and Caro is breathing fumes and bleeding steadily.

"You should," Ty says. "They're all going to die because of you."

"In my defense, I legitimately almost died in the flash flood, which I did not plan," Hope says. "But there's still no excuse." She glances at Caro, at Ash. "I'll take care of this," she says. "You *will* make it out alive."

Ty laughs. "It sounds like you're saying lines from a movie."

"You're not going to get away with this," Caro says, realizing that she *also* sounds like she's speaking lines from a movie. *This can't be real. It absolutely is.*

"I have before," Ty says, and his smile chills them all to the core.

"Eve," Ash says softly, and he nods.

"Why?" Caro asks. "Why us? Why Eve Herriman?"

"Because this is what he does," Hope says. "He terrorizes and kills. He wants women he can't have. They start out liking him, thinking he's handsome and charming and real, but almost immediately they see him for what he is. They feel the rot that's at his core and he can't have that."

"*Shut up,*" Ty snarls.

Stop, Caro and Ash think. *Why is she baiting him?*

"Even when you killed them," Hope says, "you didn't count. Their lives ended because of you but you still didn't matter to them. You can't, when there's nothing to you."

She's merciless, Caro thinks.

She's being so dangerous, Ash thinks.

"Let's each shoot once," Caro says. "Pass the gun and then we'll never know whose shot actually killed him." She can't believe she is saying this, but Page is so heavy and they have to go. She has to go. Her hands hurt so much and her body is so tired. Her knees buckle a bit, but no one seems to notice.

"Very Agatha," Hope says approvingly.

"We're out of time," Ash says.

Ty lunges.

Hope lifts the gun.

He's so fast, so strong. He catches Hope around the ankles, and she goes down hard. She drops the gun and it slides across the room. He pulls another knife from his pocket. "You forced my hand," he says to Hope. "You couldn't leave things alone. You couldn't let us be together after I found you here." He's panting, holding the blade over her. The others have frozen in place.

"We were never going to be together." Hope's voice is calm. "You might have watched our lives, but you've never been a part of them."

And in that moment Ty brings down the knife.

71

ASH GRABS THE GUN from the floor and shoots.

The flare catches Ty in the stomach, and the impact is horrible, the most terrible sound of flesh and pain. Caro remembers that her dad used to say, *Death is only easy for a lucky, lucky few*, and Ty isn't dead; this won't kill him, will it? She knows she said they should shoot but did she mean it, does she want someone to *die*? Caro remembers how her dad saved a boy who had a firework go off while he was holding it, but is this the same thing? It's not, and now they've done this, she told Ash to do this to a human being—

The screaming is awful. Even though he terrorized them, tried to kill Hope, *did* kill Eve…Ash can't bear it. She's weeping, pushing her way toward the door to help Caro with Page because they have to get Page out; no matter what, they have to do this. Hope has gotten up; she is with them. Ash fired in time.

In a sharp split second, the three women meet each other's eyes. It almost feels more merciful to do something, instead of leaving him like this, screaming on the floor.

Will we shoot the gun and light the fire? Will we cut the string? Will we end, at last, what began over a decade ago, with a girl killed in a canyon?

It is almost finished.

They could burn it all down.

72

WE ARE WITCHES.
But we don't burn.

73

"I KNOW," HOPE SAYS. "I'm the worst friend ever. Do you think I'm a narcissist?" She coughs, and Ash and Caro lean closer. They are in one ambulance with her, Page in another with Dan and Henry, Ty in a third on his own. "Give me some space," Hope says. "I'm not pulling a Beth from *Little Women*. I'm not going to die right here." She's on a gurney, and the others are sitting near her, crowding the EMTs. *We are horrible patients*, Caro thinks. *The very worst.*

Hope coughs again, but it sounds clearer, and the other two relax slightly. "Now *that's* a role I never wanted to play," Hope says. "Give me Jo every damn time."

"You're not a narcissist," Ash says. "You were looking out for us. We *all* agreed on this. We *all* wanted to lure the lurker."

"If I were really looking out for you, I never would have come up with this disaster of a plan in the first place," Hope says.

"We would never have forgiven you if you'd tried to do this all alone," Caro says. "Which you *did* actually attempt."

"Not alone," Hope says. "I had Page. Which was another horrible choice. I should never have brought her into any part of this." Her green eyes are wide, clear as sea glass in the overhead lights of the ambulance. "I wanted to fix everything because I wanted you guys to keep loving me."

"We *do* love you," Ash and Caro say at the same time.

"I know," Hope says. "But this whole time, ever since we met, I've wanted you both to *love* love me. Like, people are always coming up to me and saying, 'Oh my gosh, I love you!' because of my movies, but they don't know me. I didn't want you to like me because of that. That's why I didn't show you my face at first. And then I did, and things kept going so well! And *then* I realized someone was stalking me."

"He might have been following *me*," Caro says. "We didn't know for sure yet."

"Or me," Ash adds. "You're the one who pointed that out."

Hope shakes her head. "I know I said that, but—" The movement cracks the cut on her throat and blood seeps from it again. Caro tears into a sterile gauze pad, and the EMT gives her a murderous glare but doesn't stop her from pressing it very softly against Hope's wound to stop the bleeding. Caro's hands have been wrapped until a doctor at the hospital can stitch them up. Her white bandages are bright against Hope's face. "I know I said that," Hope says. "But the night before we went into the Underground, the expert I'd consulted—Jane—sent me a message. She'd figured out that it *was* me that he was stalking, and it's been going on for years. Ever since I came here as an extra for *The Last Portal*." She shifts, and Caro pulls away the gauze. The bleeding has stopped. Hope swallows. "We'd already made all the plans to disappear to draw out the lurker. We'd sent the messages on our regular phones, we left a trail online for him to follow. And I knew I had to see it through. I had to draw him after *me* and take care of it."

"It would have been nice if you'd kept us in the loop," Ash says.

"I *couldn't* tell you both everything, or you'd insist on coming with me, or calling the police, and that wasn't going to work." Hope presses her hand to her throat. "They never do anything in cases like this. They never do *enough*, anyway. Not in my experience."

They're quiet. The siren outside is screaming.

"But I put you in danger. I'll never forgive myself for that," Hope says. "In my mind, at the time, it made sense. I knew whoever it was would follow me. I knew it was the only way to get rid of him for good."

"Hope." Caro's eyes are wide. "Were you planning to *kill* him?"

"I don't think so," Hope says. "I was hoping to take care of it another way."

"You don't *think* so?" Ash's voice is shrill. "Were you going to make us accomplices? Were you going to *accomplice* us?"

"*No,*" Hope says. "That's another reason I didn't tell the two of you what I was doing."

"We would have still been accomplices!" Ash can't believe what she's hearing. She could have lost her girls! She could have lost everything.

"They say not to meet your heroes," Hope says.

Caro breaks out in a laugh. "I don't know that you're our hero, Hope," she says drily.

And then they're all laughing, in a slightly unhinged way not unlike some of their late nights online. They glance over at the EMTs, who have slightly horrified looks on their faces, and that makes them laugh harder. *What the hell were we thinking, with any of this?*

"Did you know it was Ty?" Caro asks when they've calmed down. "Because if you did, it would have been really great if you told us."

"No." Hope's voice has gone raspy again. "I thought it was for sure one of the guys in the canyon. Spencer or one of his friends."

"Holy crap," Ash says, horrified. "Tony's *dead*."

"I didn't kill him," Hope says, putting her hand over her heart. She holds Ash's gaze. "I swear. I never even saw him after the flooding began."

"Didn't you?" Caro's voice is steady. "Hope, I saw you coming out of their camp the morning of the flash flood."

"What?" Ash's eyes widen. "*Why?*"

"I was looking around for something that might help me link them to the lurker," Hope says. "Like I said, I thought it *had* to be one of them. But I wanted to try and find actual evidence."

"You went in their *tents?*"

"No," Hope says. "They'd left a bunch of their gear out, and I was going through it. I was so focused that I didn't even pay much attention to what was happening with the water. It came on so *fast.*"

"It's hard to believe it until you've been there," Caro says. "I've seen videos of flash floods. Actually being *in* one is completely different."

"I still can't believe it even though we *have* been through it now." Ash bites her lip. "You guys, we came so close. Especially you, Hope. The fact that you hit the water instead of the rocks, the fact that *you* didn't die and that you climbed out of that canyon and made it here is a freaking miracle."

"I won't argue with you there." Hope is somber. "I thought I was directing this whole situation. I was sure I had it all planned out, and it was an unmitigated disaster." She looks at them, her audience of two, and both Ash and Caro feel the pull of Hope, her sincerity.

"I did do my research, though," Hope says, after a moment. "Page told me about Mystery Canyon. I came a few days early, and she and I made sure I could find it and climb it. Page got my phones for me from the lockbox. Once I made it out after the flood, she picked me up and drove me to the ghost town. I stayed there while Jane and I tried to figure out who it was. That's when I started sending messages from the burner. I also brought Page the movies for the Hope Hanover Film Festival to show as another way to get to him if we needed it."

"Why send us up Seraph's Perch?" Ash asks.

"I wanted you to be away from here while I confronted Ty," Hope says. "Right when I got out of the canyon, Jane figured out the IP address belonged to someone at Sonnet. But she hadn't been able to track it further. Once I knew the lurker was there, I wanted you guys away from the resort as much as possible." She sighs. "But then nothing worked. Everything started backfiring so badly. Page wasn't ever supposed to come back to the ghost town after she dropped me off. It was too dangerous. But she got worried about me and came out to make sure I was okay. Ty followed her without her knowing. She wasn't supposed to be there." Now Hope is crying. "Do you think she'll be okay? I should never have involved her."

"Physically, yes," Caro says. "Emotionally, she's pretty tough, too."

"I *told* her not to come," Hope says. "And I sent you up to the Perch because I thought you'd stay up there. But Ty found me after I sent the text. He took the phone and drove over to Seraph's Perch. He did the hike as fast as he could and came back here where he'd left me tied up."

"So the @findhopehanover account? And the photo of us at the top?" Caro says. "And the pin, and the last message?"

"All from him," Hope says. "He used the burner and sent them. He started the @findhopehanover account to mess with us. He missed being able to watch us." She shudders, and Caro puts a hand on her shoulder to steady her. "The texts sounded like me, didn't they? He's been watching me long enough that he knows what I'll say. How I'll say it." Hope closes her eyes, opens them. "He texted Page to bring food. And she thought he was me, too. I meant to keep all of you away. I'm so sorry." She wipes her eyes furiously with the heels of both hands. "I thought I could keep everyone safe and catch him," she says. "Put an end to this. I thought I could take him down, and I couldn't."

"How, exactly, were you going to catch him?" Caro asks. "With your bare hands?"

"I had a Taser," Hope says. "And a phone to record him with."

"*Hope.*" Ash is angry. "This wasn't—isn't—none of this is a *movie*. These are our *lives*."

"I know," Hope says quietly. "It was complete hubris to think I could catch him. And I'm never, *ever*, going to forgive myself for any of this."

Ash reaches out and gently takes one of Caro's bandaged hands in hers. She threads the fingers of her other hand through Hope's. "That's where you and Ty were both wrong," she says.

"There *is* strength in numbers." Caro's voice is firm. "We did what we came here to do."

"But from now on, you tell us *everything*," Ash says.

"I will." Hope squeezes both of their hands. "I was wrong not to. It's just—I was the one who brought the lurker upon us. It was because of me that you were being watched all that time. I felt like the only way to get you to love me again was to fix it, and the only way to fix it was to go off on my own."

"We didn't stop loving you," Caro says.

"I know." Hope sounds like she can't believe it, like it's too good to be true. "I'm so sorry. I'll say that for the rest of my life. I'll *be* that for the rest of my life."

"It's okay," Ash says.

"We didn't die," Caro says practically, and they all laugh. And then they remember Eve, and they go quiet.

74

PAGE

EVE HAS BEEN GONE for twelve years. I've had plenty of time to imagine all of the scenarios.

She was scared.

She was screaming.

She was begging,

She was silent.

She fought like hell.

She never saw it coming.

Now I know more than I did, but still not everything. Ty's picture on Eve's camera from the Underground was the first clue. Now that the police have looked into things, I know that Ty met Eve at the events center, where he worked in catering. I know they dated, but she never told me or Grandma about him because it didn't last long. I know he killed her when she tried to break up with him. He talked her into hiking the Underground with him—one last day together. He killed her there and hid her in a crevice. At some point, a flood brought her out for the women to find.

I never suspected Ty. I never saw him until I came to work at Sonnet. I wonder how long he knew I was her sister. I wonder how long he was watching me. I would notice them, sometimes this year, the photos of me tacked up on the bulletin board that looked slightly different because they were taken on a disposable camera and then developed. He stalked me, he stalked Skye. Both of us took down our photos before the other saw them. I wish we had talked more. I wish we hadn't disliked each other so much. Maybe we would have figured things out.

Caro saw the last photo of me before I did and took it down before I saw it. She thought it looked like Hope. The three of us *do* look alike.

But only Eve and I are sisters.

When the police searched Ty's house, they found a darkroom for developing film. They found lots of things there. I don't like to think about it.

Eve's disappearance happened when Hope was here filming *The Last Portal*. It was constantly in the news. The story stuck with Hope. She wanted to see if she could make a movie about it, draw some attention to Eve's case. She came to me with the plan and said I could be a co-producer. That I could have half of the proceeds. *I want to help you*, she said. *And I want to find out what happened to Eve.*

No, I said. *Please.* I was sixteen then. *I don't want a movie about her. Please leave her alone.*

I couldn't believe it when Hope said, *Okay.*

And then she came back, years later. *If I wanted to disappear from the Underground*, she asked, *how would I do it?* I wasn't afraid of the Underground. Because Eve and Ty didn't sign in at the hike register, and no one saw him come out at the end, I never knew my sister died in the Underground. I never knew she was there.

You could cut over to Mystery Canyon, I told Hope. *It's hard, technical canyoneering. Not anyone can do it.*

Mystery Canyon? she said. *That's a little on the nose.*

And that made me laugh.

I need to make someone disappear, she said. When she saw the shocked look on my face, she said, *Don't worry. The person I want to make disappear is* me.

I flick my turn signal and leave St. John. There is a blue paper box holding my sister's ashes on the front seat next to me.

What, the police had asked, did I want to do with the body?

The collection of bones that used to be Eve?

Who do you recommend? I asked. I had had years and years to research this, and yet I never did.

Are you looking for a cost-effective mortuary? they asked.

I want the nicest one, I said. *The one where you would take your kid if they died.*

The officer blinked. *Okay,* she said. *Well, then, it would be the Paintbrush Mortuary.*

That one, I said. *Let's do that one.*

Would you like to cremate her or have her remains placed in a coffin? the mortician asked. He was sorry for me, but he was also in the business of death. *You're the next of kin?*

Yes.

You're the only *kin?*

Yes. There are cousins, aunts, uncles, but I didn't want to get into it. And they didn't matter, not for this.

I'll give you this sheet with the rates, he said. *But I can arrange for a discount on any of the services. You're too young to have to go into debt for something like this.*

Thank you, I said. I went out to the car and looked at the sheet. I can afford lots of things now. Hope was very generous with my payment for helping her. She added extra as an unintentionally-almost-dying bonus. All of the money makes things easier for me and for what comes next.

My grandma left me her house when she died. It's small, not fancy, bare-bones and away from town. Not in Spring City itself, where the second-home people and the move-ins have driven up the prices. Still, selling the house would give me enough money for college tuition and room and board. But I couldn't do it. When I got the job at Sonnet, I locked up the house and moved to the staff tents. I couldn't sell it, but I also couldn't live there alone. A little ghost town of my own, made of a single home.

And I couldn't decide what to do about Eve's body. I wanted to ask someone about it. I wanted to ask her.

What would you want, Eve?

Would you care?

It's easy to say, *Doesn't matter, they're dead, I'm dead, it's over,* but when you are confronted with the disposal of the bones that held your sister up, that used to be covered in flesh that held you, that used to shield a heart that beats, well.

What I wanted was to bundle them up in a blanket and hold them close. To look at them with attention, because her bones are a part of Eve that Eve herself never saw. But I knew that would be strange. I knew I might not ever be able to put them down.

So, cremation. And now, laying her to rest.

It's dusky, September evening light. Since I'm going to scatter the ashes anyway, I didn't pay for an urn. All I have is this blue cardboard box, with a number and Eve's name printed on a label on the outside.

I don't know where I'm going, but I'm not taking her to Eden. I want to take Eve someplace she has never been before. I want to take her to someplace where *I* have never been before.

I'm on this road in the desert that I've never driven, and I keep going and going. I don't even know if I'm still in Utah or in Arizona by now.

I might keep going. Colby called. He's not coming back. "Thank you for covering for me," he said. "But the situation's worse than I thought. I'm going to have to stay here and take care of her. She's going to need me when she comes out."

"I understand," I said, because even though Colby leaving changes Sonnet for me, I understand siblings. Colby's sister overdosed. She lived, and he's gotten her into rehab.

She lived.

"I can put in a good word with the owners to hire you as my replacement," Colby said. "You're young, but you can do it better than anyone else. For crying out loud, look how you've handled *this*. Page, I'm so sorry. I left at the worst possible time."

And he didn't even know the half of it. "Don't worry about it," I said. "But I think I'm going to move on from Sonnet. I might leave Utah, in fact."

"Good for you," Colby said. He sounded proud. He is the closest thing I have to a brother, and he's a good one. "Keep in touch?"

I told him I would.

It's darker now. The stars are coming out.

Eve and I always said, *You have to leave to come back.*

We are very far down this road, she and I. "Okay, Eve," I say, "let me know when," and I glance over at the box, and it's ridiculous as hell, what I'm doing, so I begin to laugh, and I'll admit there's a note of hysteria in it. I've taken my eyes off the road for a split second, but when I look back at the road, there's something huge, with animal eyes flashing in the headlights.

A deer.

I slam on my brakes, my head snapping forward on my neck. A thunk, heavy and hard. *I bit my lip when I hit the brake*, I realize, tasting blood. I look up. The road is empty and dark.

I didn't hit the deer.

The thunk was the box. Eve's ashes have gone flying out of the seat belt and into the footwell. The box has split open. In the dim light from the dashboard I can see that something is on the floor, spilling from the box, something gray and ashy.

Oh no.

I pull over to the side of the road, well onto the shoulder, and rest my head on the steering wheel. Seconds ago, I was laughing, and now I'm crying. Am I going to have to pick up my sister's ashes by hand, try to put them back into the broken box? Is Eve literally going to slip through my fingers once again?

There's nothing to be done but to do it. I unbuckle my own seat belt, walk around to the passenger side of the car, open it, and shine my phone's flashlight into the footwell.

Oh.

The ashes *did* come out of the box, but they're still sealed inside a plastic bag. The relief is absolute.

"Let's tuck you back in there," I say to Eve, and I pick up the bag and the box, ready to slide it back inside, get on my way. But as I do, I look over at the side of the road. There's a gentle incline leading up to the kind of sagebrush-y, juniper-tree landscape that is common in the desert. It's nowhere special. But even with the light pollution from my headlights, there are so many stars.

"Okay," I say. I pick up my keys and the plastic bag with Eve's ashes inside. It's heavy. I hold it close to my body as I walk.

At the top of the incline, I stand looking out at the road, up at the stars, back down at the bag in my hands. Using the pocketknife on my keychain, I slit the bag open. And then, without thinking too much or too hard, I shake the ashes out onto the ground. "I loved you," I say. "I love you." Because I do, still. Eve being gone does not change that fact. I will love my sister all my life.

I walk back down to my car, toss the empty blue cardboard box into the back seat. I start the engine, check behind me, pull onto the asphalt. I leave my sister somewhere by the side of the road. I do not make note of any landscape clues so that I'll know where I've left Eve's ashes. It's too dark, anyway.

I will never know where my sister is again.

75

THEIR FACES COME UP on each other's phone screens, one by one by one.

They're all sitting in their cars, in varying stages of light, depending on where they are in the country. It's brightest for Hope, darkest for Caro.

"So how is everyone?" Hope asks, and they all crack up, because, well. "Caro, have you gone back to work?"

"Not yet," Caro says. "My hands are still kind of a mess."

"Oh my word, of course," Hope says. "But they're going to heal completely?"

"That's what we think," Caro says.

"And I didn't mean to sound like you have to return to the hospital," Hope says. "Everyone acts like you *must climb back on the horse* or whatever. You don't. You don't have to keep going back to the place that hurt you."

"Or where I hurt someone else," Caro says.

"You didn't hurt anyone," Hope says. "It was not your fault that woman died."

"I know," Caro says, "but I made it harder for her." She's crying, the others realize. "I didn't manage her pain well. She was thrashing around. I'm not sure what I did wrong, and that's the thing that terrifies me. I keep going over and over and *over* it, and I'm not sure what I could have done

302

differently." She clears her throat. "Hope, you weren't the only one keeping a secret from the rest of us. I didn't tell either of you mine." She looks straight ahead at the screen. "Dan and I have been trying to have kids, and it's not going to work. None of my egg retrievals were successful." And now she closes her eyes. "It's made me feel and do the worst things. I lied to Dan. I told him that the retrieval had worked." Tears stream down her face. "How could I tell him that he's not going to be a dad? He was *born* to be a dad. But then how could I *lie* to him about it?"

"Oh, Caro," Ash says. No one speaks for a minute. Caro wipes her eyes furiously with the back of one hand.

"I was going to *try*," Caro said fiercely. "I started some drafts of letters on their postcards. To Dan. To our fertility specialist to tell her we were done."

"Who mailed those, anyway?" Ash asks. "It had to be Ty, right?"

"But why would he want to bring people we loved *there*?" Caro asks. "It would make what he was trying to do so much harder. To gather people who might be additional suspects, maybe, if things went wrong?"

"Page mailed them," Hope says. Caro and Ash tilt their heads in shock, mirror images. "I asked her to go into my trailer and mail one for me after I left. Apparently that gave her ideas, and she decided to mail yours, too. She didn't love that I was doing all of this—that *we* were doing all of this—on our own. She felt like the people in our lives should know where we were."

"Oh, Page," Ash says. "She's been through too much."

"She made kind of a mess with them, though," Hope says. "Do you still want to talk to her?"

"Of course," Ash says, and Caro adds, "Absolutely."

"Great," Hope says. "I'll text her and see if she can call us now."

Once she's finished sending the text, Hope looks up. Her eyes are bright, the line across her throat barely visible anymore. "So, Caro," she says. "That's all that's holding you back? The eggs?"

"*Hope,*" Ash says.

"Well, they're kind of an important part," Caro says, trying to laugh.

Hope's expression is serious now. "I'm sorry, Caro," she says. "I'm bad at this. Really bad. And I know it won't be the same as if your own retrievals had worked. But, and this is only if you and Dan want, I can help you. I froze a *ton* of eggs in my twenties, and they're apparently amazing. You're welcome to help yourself if you want any of them."

"*Hope.*" Caro looks stunned.

"I'm serious," Hope says. "Think about it." She's trying to keep her tone breezy, but they can hear the emotion behind it. "It would be nice to know I helped you guys, since having kids might not be in the cards for me."

"Don't say that," Ash says fiercely. "You never know."

Hope shrugs. "I still don't have anyone to raise a family with."

"You have us," Caro says.

Hope smiles at that. Her voice is raw when she asks, "What about you, Ash? How are things?"

"I'm okay," Ash says. "Wade moved out last week." They know this— they've been texting and sending messages on Marco Polo—but she feels like she should say it again. Because this is monumental. This is the end of an era that she thought would be her *only* era, in so many ways. "And I was keeping a secret from you guys the whole time, too. I never talked about how bad things with Wade were getting."

"Oh, honey, you didn't have to," Hope says.

"We knew," Caro agrees.

"One of my issues—and of course it's not the *main* issue—with Wade is that he's named *Wade*," Hope says. "What is this, 1960? Is he a surfer?"

Ash is laughing through her tears.

"I mean, that's more on his parents than it is on him," Caro says.

"You're right," Hope says. "It's a terrible name. And he's terrible. So they must be terrible."

"But seriously, Ash." Caro's dark eyes are warm with sympathy. "Are you doing okay?"

"I'm doing terrible." Ash squares her shoulders. Her summer freckles are out in full force from the busy season at Three Sisters. "And I'm also okay."

"And the girls?" Hope asks.

"The same," Ash says. They're quiet again for a moment, and it's comfortable. Ash feels held.

"How's Henry?" Hope asks.

"It's hard," Caro says. "Really hard." She moved Henry to a care facility in Salt Lake City to be closer to her and Dan. "He keeps saying he wants to go home." When he says it, he sounds frightened, and she feels a bottomless ache and fear for him. He has no home. She can see it in his eyes. He has been her home, but she cannot be his, no matter how desperately they both want her to be. The disease won't let him rest with her.

For a time, not knowing him now made her doubt that she had known him during all the time that came before—even made her wonder if he had killed someone, and she can't yet forgive herself for that—but she *did* know him. As well as you could ever know a parent. It's an incomplete knowledge. A knowledge at once hampered and enhanced by being their child, defined in that relationship in some ways forever, even when you are the one doing the caretaking, even when you are the one acting, largely, as parent. She will always be Henry's daughter.

Whether he remembers it or not.

"Hold on," Hope says. "Someone's joining the call."

A pause, and then, there she is.

Page.

She holds up an empty blue cardboard box.

"I did it," Page says, and then she bursts into tears.

"Oh, Page," Ash says. "Oh, sweetheart."

"We're here," Caro says.

"I might cry at you the whole time," Page says. She looks at them through the camera, her face young and open.

"Of course," Hope says. "As long as you want."

THEY HAVE HER NOW. I can rest.

I am floating. I am flying. I am looking down.

I am nothing, I am a will-o'-the wisp, I am a ghost.

I am everything, the sister you lost, the girl you can't forget, the dust in your eyes, the catch in your throat.

I am everywhere and nowhere at all.

Somewhere, bones drift on the wind. In other places, they rest in the ground. In life and then death, they carry and break and are laid to rest.

The desert can erase you quickly or keep you forever.

But you saw my bones.

And I am bearing witness: I see you.

And this is also true:

You were always coming home.

ACKNOWLEDGMENTS

This book is dedicated to my agent, Jodi Reamer. We have been working together for sixteen years (and counting!) and I do not take one day of her brilliant, hilarious, wise presence in my life for granted. We have wandered in the Alps together; she has shown me New York; I've taken her hiking in the canyons of southern Utah, and perhaps, most importantly, she was the first person with whom I ever went on the *Cars* ride at Disneyland. (Also, I made her go on the *Matterhorn* for her first time, my sole contribution to our relationship.) We're both very big fans of some of the best Baltimore athletes (but, as it is her hometown, she has greater claim). So much of my career, and my life, would not be possible without her. Thank you, Jodi, for absolutely everything.

I also feel deeply lucky to have had Karen Kosztolnyik as my editor for both this book and my previous mystery, *The Unwedding*. The team at Grand Central, past and present (including Andy Dodds, Kamrun Nesa, Danielle Thomas, Luria Rittenberg, Lori Paximadis, Carrie Andrews, Theresa DeLucci, Allison Schuster, Leena Oropez, Rachel Rodriguez, and Cordelia Calvert) has been a delight to work with every step of the way.

The Unwedding was a Reese's Book Club pick, one of the happiest surprises of my life. Reese Witherspoon brings women's voices to the forefront in a myriad of ways and I admire her very much. I've loved meeting the wonderful team at Reese's Book Club, including Jane Lee, Olga Khaminwa, Melissa Seymour, and Gretchen Schreiber. Thank you all.

And thank you to the entire team at Hello Sunshine and to my fellow Reese's Book Club authors for your support (and for making things so much fun).

Thank you also to the King's English, to Folklore Bookshop, and to Poppy Books, my local independent booksellers, for your support. Thank you to every bookseller who has ever supported my books, from picture books to middle-grade novels to young adult novels to adult novels. The work you do is much appreciated.

Fellow authors Ann Dee Ellis, Lindsey Leavitt, Shannon Hale, and Yamile Méndez have offered support and adventure along the way. Prince Edward Island forever. Jared Robinson provided expert knowledge about canyoneering in southern Utah and was patient with my many, many questions. Melissa Baumgart answered my queries about film and movies with wisdom and expertise. Any mistakes that remain are mine alone.

My parents, Robert and Arlene Braithwaite, took us to the national parks of Utah almost every weekend when we were growing up. My mother, an artist, paints their landscapes; my father protected them as a federal magistrate. I am indebted to them both for a wonderful childhood, for a love of nature, and for the belief that beauty and diversity should be cherished.

I am also indebted to our national park workers and to anyone who works to preserve and protect our land. This is the geography of my childhood, and I hope it has a place in my children's as well. It has been a pleasure to visit these places with you, Calvin, Ian, Truman, and Lainey. I love you with all my heart.

ABOUT THE AUTHOR

Ally Condie is the #1 *New York Times* bestselling author of the Matched Trilogy and of many other books (including the Edgar Award Finalist *Summerlost*). *The Unwedding* was her adult debut novel, a Reese's Book Club Pick, and a *USA Today* bestseller. A former English teacher, she enjoys hiking with her family in the mountains near their home in Utah.